N THE RAVI PI SERIES

htly Embrace

D0332717

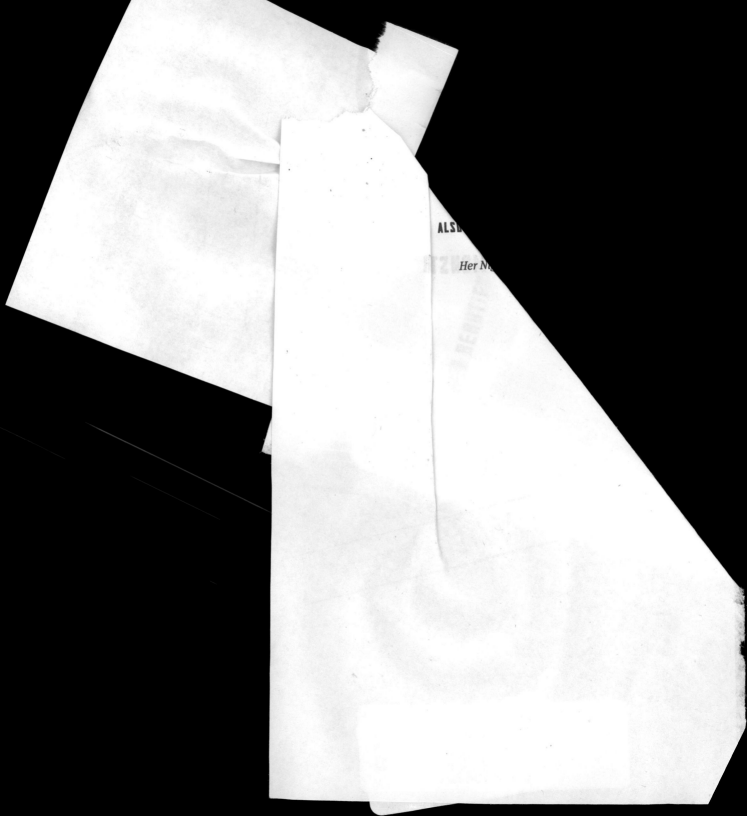

ALSD

Her Nu

HER BEAUTIFUL MONSTER

THE RAVI PI SERIES

ADI TANTIMEDH

MULHOLLAND
BOOKS
HODDER

First published in the USA in 2017 by Leopold & Co/Atria books
An imprint of Simon & Schuster

First published in Great Britain in 2017 by Mulholland Books
An imprint of Hodder & Stoughton
An Hachette UK company

1

A CIP catalogue record for this title is available from the British Library

Paperback ISBN 978 1 473 65981 0
eBook ISBN 978 1 473 65980 3

Printed and bound by CPI Group (UK) Ltd, Croydon CR0 4YY

Hodder & Stoughton policy is to use papers that are natural, renewable
and recyclable products and made from wood grown in sustainable forests.
The logging and manufacturing processes are expected to conform to the
environmental regulations of the country of origin.

Hodder & Stoughton Ltd
Carmelite House
50 Victoria Embankment
London EC4Y 0DZ

www.hodder.co.uk

To my sister, Orathai, who gets things done no matter how hard it is,
with love and respect

THE HUSTLE OF THE GODS

ONE

Pack of racists in bomber jackets called me a "fucking Paki" on the street the other day. The usual stuff about going back to where I came from. Racists never need facts or accuracy, and I wasn't going to correct them and say I was actually Hindu, of Indian ancestry, not Pakistani-Muslim, and born and raised in Parsons Green in West London. I wasn't going to break cover since I was on the job.

Buddha used to say there was no need to take revenge. If you waited long enough, the bodies of your enemies would eventually float by in the river. In my case, I had Ken and Clive to beat them up for me. Two violent, trained ex-coppers built like brick shithouses against four gangly racists in tracksuits? No contest. And did I say Clive used to be in the army before he became a copper? Soldiers were taught to kill people with their thumbs, if necessary. It had been a few weeks since Ken and Clive last fed their bloodlust.

"The fat one looks like a human version of a boil," Julia said.

"He's like everyone's cartoon of what a British racist looks like," I said. "I didn't think that look actually existed."

The blob of a man hit the ground. He wasn't getting up again for a bit. He made me think of the Millennium Dome.

Two broken noses, one fractured jaw, and at least one concussion later, Ken and Clive walked back to us, happily sated. Their grins did not make me comfortable anymore.

Ken and Clive didn't do it for me, of course. They just wanted any excuse to kick off and fuck someone up. It had been three weeks since they had gotten to quench their lust for violence, and these idiots fit the bill. The violence also reinforced their cover as my bodyguards.

Julia squeezed my arm as we continued on our way, Ken and Clive falling in line alongside us. Mark just nodded in approval.

This aggressive show of power seemed to impress our mark. Tarquin Gaskell-Bridger. I was a tycoon from Mumbai here to see his pitch for his dodgy anti-drone technology. He watched in awe at the short work my "bodyguards" made of those unfortunate dickheads. I was a prospective investor in his dodgy venture, and this was the kind of power at my command. Having Ken and Clive with me meant I was not to be fucked with.

"A perfect snapshot of the dystopian Dickensian nightmare that Britain is becoming," Mark Oldham declared cheerfully.

He would say that. Mark was our disillusioned poet at Golden Sentinels Private Investigations and Security Agency. He looked upon the world through a haze of marijuana smoke and saw it broken and sad, and he could only laugh and make jokes. We were here because of him, and he wouldn't have missed it for the world.

TWO

And so, from the street to a posh office, from street violence to boardroom jiggery-pokery in Canary Wharf. Snapshot of Britain, indeed.

Tarquin Gaskell-Bridger, the founder of Advanced Drone Defence Technologies (ADDT), laid it on thick for us. The speech he gave in his boardroom (on whose rent he was behind—we'd checked) was largely the same as the prospectus for his company, only this time the speech was presented with PowerPoint.

This particular wheeze was Mark's idea, an undercover sting to schmooze a dodgy entrepreneur and get the goods on him.

To summarize: Golden Sentinels Investigations, our agency, had been hired by the shareholders of Advanced Drone Defence Incorporated to look into dodgy dealings in the company. They suspected that their money was being misspent and that the share price of the company was being massaged. Olivia Wong, our resident forensic financial analyst, had hacked into the company's financial accounts and found that it was operating a pyramid scheme. No money was actually being earned from the shares. Gaskell-Bridger, the supposed inventor of the device, was paying himself a nice fat salary while funneling the shareholders' money back and forth to make it look like the shares were paying off.

Unfortunately, this information had been obtained through hacking, which made it illegal and thus inadmissible in court, but it gave us a result from which to work backwards. So Mark Oldham went up on the roof of our office, smoked a couple of joints, and came up with a social engineering hack with which we could get close enough to catch Tarquin Gaskell-Bridger. That was how Mark rolled.

So here I was, "Sunny Rajaratnam," a reclusive telecoms billionaire from Mumbai in town on a company-buying spree, complete with Julia posing as my personal assistant, Ken and Clive as my burly and extremely violent bodyguards, and Mark as our liaison with ADDT. Olivia had created an entire history for Rajaratnam's many deals and acquisitions in India and across Asia, from starting out as a humble seller of cheap mobile phones to handling tens of millions of pounds and euros at a time, investing in various start-ups and humanitarian ventures, building ashrams and spiritual healing centers, with an interest in charities for victims of war. That made him surely an easy target for Gaskell-Bridger's supposed drone defense technology. For Gaskell-Bridger, Rajaratnam was the ideal mark: the foreign lunatic with too much money. Mark had made sure that Gaskell-Bridger heard Rajaratnam was a bit touched. He was deeply preoccupied with his karma and claimed to have a very personal relationship with the gods.

The clients were paying full whack for this job, so we were offering the complete service. It wasn't just the odd millionaire who had bought stocks in ADDT, but pensioners as well. Gaskell-Bridger had printed up impressive brochures boasting of the drone detectors his company was producing to make it safer for civilians in war zones to avoid becoming collateral damage. With code written by expert programmers who had previously worked for the government, he had set up the company to own the lifesaving software they were writing. He claimed he was talking to drone manufacturers about collaborating with them to make his proposed AI compatible with the drones' friend or foe recognition systems—in an international cooperative bid to make drone warfare more humane so that only terrorists and not children would get blown up. He was in line for government military contracts worth tens of millions, which would shore up the company's share prices. He'd had charts printed up and everything. After the initial investments were paid in, he had videos produced of the first units of the ADDT coming off the factory: sleek black boxes the size of footballs with Bluetooth and Wi-Fi enabled. There was a very professional-looking video of a prototype of the unit being tested in an open field in Hertfordshire: a noncombat drone flew while a laptop computer was operating the anti-drone unit to communicate with the drone's recognition software. The computer displayed an interface that showed the drone sending back a signal acknowledging the unit's signal and not targeting the dummies set up on the field. There was additional footage of the units being packed into boxes and being shipped to the Middle East.

Of course, all of this was complete bollocks.

As Benjamin Lee, our resident techie, had explained back at the office, "First of all, how would they be able to communicate with a drone's operating system? Those are bloody classified, otherwise every enemy soldier and terrorist would hack them while they're airborne. Second of all, that drone in their demo video is CGI. They just put extra grain in the footage to hide that."

We did our search and found that yes, Gaskell-Bridger was selling units to Iraq, but there was no record of any anti-drone technology in the area. Marcie Holder even used her CIA contacts to confirm this for us. Yet Gaskell-Bridger had sold a hundred units to the Iraqi government at thirty grand a pop. Olivia checked with her hacker contacts and found that no one had written any code or program that had succeeded in interacting with the combat drones currently in operation anywhere. Benjamin reckoned anyone could make sleek little black boxes with some motherboards stuck in them to look like serious tech.

We were well aware of all this as we sat in Gaskell-Bridger's boardroom listening to his effusive speech about wanting to expand the company and make the ADDT more accessible to countries that really needed it. And how Sunny Rajaratnam was the perfect partner to do it.

THREE

In the corner of my eye, a goddess watched.

She was enjoying the show we were putting on, as if it was all for her. If only my colleagues could see her . . . No, thank God my colleagues couldn't see her.

O Bagalamukhi, I see you and know why you are here. My job is always a good show for you, isn't it? We deal in truth and deceit, as you do. You might as well be the patron god of our business.

The gods were looking awfully flash these days. Whenever they showed up, I could recognize them by their blue skin and the symbols of their power—the headdresses, the weapons, the scepters, the lotuses in their hands—but they wore what everyone was wearing on the streets of London. Ganesha, watching over us from on high in his infinite patience and wisdom, wore a baseball cap and bomber jacket. Shiva had taken to nice suits. Kali seemed to like to mix it up on the streets and wear a leather jacket and jeans. And Bagalamukhi—today she was wearing an expensive tracksuit, texting the other gods about what we were up to and having a laugh.

We locked eyes (something I usually avoided) and she winked, giving me the thumbs-up.

I supposed they approved. I seemed to be an endless source of entertainment for them. Such was my lot. #Myownpersonalholyfool

She was texting now. I knew what would come next. She was telling her mates the show was about to start and they should come watch. It would be a giggle.

Social engineering was all about performance, of course, and it was my turn. I was wearing an expensive silver silk suit and tie with an Armani scarf and overcoat, my eyes hidden behind a ludicrous pair of large sunglasses, all the more to make me look so incredibly rich that I could look and say whatever the hell I wanted without being told off.

I nodded sagely at everything Gaskell-Bridger said and waited for him to finish talking.

"Any questions?" he asked, eagerly, nervously.

I looked at him, his middle-aged paunch, his respectable suit far less expensive than mine, the desperate gleam in his eye, the type I used to see in my secondary school students when I knew they were lying and they were afraid I would call them on it.

"The gods are here with us," I said, trying not to oversell the thick stereotypical accent that would have made Peter Sellers cringe.

Julia and Mark nodded sagely. Ken and Clive stifled giggles. Gaskell-Bridger smiled, uncertainty creeping across his face.

"The gods are always with us," I continued. "In fact, they're standing in the room with us now!"

Gaskell-Bridger looked to the corner of the room where I pointed, a bit alarmed. He didn't see anyone there. Only I did. Bagalamukhi had texted the family to come and see the show. Sure enough, Shiva, Kali, Vishnu, even Ganesha with his sage elephant head—the lot of them that bothered with our petty dealings—were there.

"They watch in judgment, and everything we do adds to our tally. So what we do today is of great importance."

"Amen," said Mark.

Am I entertaining you, my lords and ladies of the sky? Am I showing you a good time? I hope so, since I'm here making an utter prat of myself and blowing off a bit of steam, a bit of on-the-job catharsis.

So yes, Mark was well into my bringing the gods into this op. My colleagues by now all knew I saw gods. A few months ago, Mark had noticed I was glancing off to the side of the office and reacting to Kali hanging around my desk again, then asked me about it when we were up on the roof sharing a spliff. He'd suspected for a while, ever since I bought some pills off him to try to stop the visions. I came clean there, and decided to tell both Roger and Cheryl about it, telling them they had every right to sack me if they thought I was too mentally unstable and risked compromising my work.

And they were all right with it.

My boss Roger had been perfectly happy with my work for the past year. His reasoning was that given the crazy shit we put up with in our cases, my condition, if anything, helped me do the job better, so who was he to judge?

"You're the sanest bugger in the room, in fact," he said. "So more power to the gods, I say."

Mark found it terribly exciting. He envied me seeing gods without the need for psychoactive drugs. In fact, he was appalled when I tried to get pills from him to *stop* seeing them. As far as he was concerned, I should carry on, "the more the merrier." Olivia thought it was interesting, and it wasn't unusual for her since she prayed to Chinese deities and consulted a fortune-teller in Chinatown. Marcie had always known because she'd secretly vetted me back when Roger hired me, and had seen my medical records. Benjamin just thought it was fun. Ken and Clive could take or leave the gods, as long as they got to fuck someone up along the way. Julia continued to monitor my condition, but she was my girlfriend, so she was more privy to my worries about my sanity than the rest of them. Cheryl didn't offer any opinion beyond occasionally asking me how I was doing. God knows what she really thought of it, but she made it clear she didn't have a problem with me at all.

Back to the present:

I spoke of gods to Gaskell-Bridger in the most matter-of-fact manner, as if I were just discussing the weather. That was the best way to sell madness. (I didn't speak in tongues. That would have been overcooking it. I drew the line at speaking in tongues.)

"Mr. Rajaratnam is a great man," Julia said without a trace of irony, putting her palms together in supplication. Somehow, we'd *all* decided there was no such thing as laying it on too thick here.

"A great man, indeed." Mark jumped in, following suit with his palms and bowing. "This is why your company is a good fit for his plans."

"We all do our part to create Nirvana on Earth," I said sagely. "You, Mr. Gaskell-Bridger, are securing your place in paradise."

Gaskell-Bridger nodded eagerly. I was sure he didn't give a toss about any of this, as long as he got Rajaratnam's money. Ken and Clive stood at the back of the room and settled into stone-faced stoicism. They would much rather have been dragging Gaskell-Bridger into an alley and kicking the shit out of him.

We were all wearing pin-cameras on our lapels, recording Gaskell-Bridger and every detail of his speech and his office, the footage streaming back to our servers at Golden Sentinels, where Marcie, Benjamin, and Olivia sat watching at their computers and recording every second.

"I have heard enough. My people will draw up plans," I said.

And with that, we were out of there. Gaskell-Bridger even came down to wave good-bye as we drove away in our big, black Mercedes.

The next thing to do was to lead him on with a sense of momentum. We followed up with phone calls reiterating interest in buying a controlling interest in Gaskell-Bridger's company and expanding it, opening a factory in India to manufacture more of the ADDT units. Plans were being drawn up by Rajaratnam's team, which was really Benjamin indulging in some amateur engineering and architectural design. Julia promised to send Rajaratnam's bank details, an elite private establishment that was really a dummy account created by Olivia, with the plan to open an escrow account for depositing the first payments. Mark asked Gaskell-Bridger to start transferring his company's funds to the escrow account so that Rajaratnam's money people could start properly budgeting and allocating the funds.

Contracts were duly drawn up. Gaskell-Bridger signed them. Eagerly. He did everything eagerly. But who wouldn't be eager if they were being given nearly a hundred million pounds? He didn't know that the hundred million pounds was vapor. The forty-five million he transferred into the escrow account, however, were very real. The investors' money, in fact. What was left after Gaskell-Bridger spent it on champagne parties, holidays in Monte Carlo, and expensive furs for his wife and call girls? Marcie and Mark had drawn a detailed psychological profile for Gaskell-Bridger once we started researching him. We shadowed him for weeks, noting his routines, his watering holes, his favorite shops, his sports clubs. We knew whom he played squash with, how average he was, how long he liked to stay in the sauna.

That was how we knew which buttons to push by the time Mark contacted him posing as "financial advisor to Sunny Rajaratnam."

Julia kept Gaskell-Bridger on the hook with regular phone calls where I would get on the line to talk about karma and the gods and our great work again. Sunny Rajaratnam was back in Mumbai running his telecoms company but taking time out to inspect the sites where the new ADDT factory was being built. All this to distract Gaskell-Bridger while Olivia tallied up the money and set to work.

FOUR

I haven't mentioned my friend David Okri yet. David and I were close back in university. David was the one who got me this job at Golden Sentinels. David was the agency's lawyer and had been approached by one of his other solicitor friends to see if the agency might be able to help Gaskell-Bridger's investors. David was the one who introduced the investors to Roger and Cheryl, who in turn gave it to Mark Oldham as primary since he was good with the complicated cases. Marcie Holder was probably qualified, too, but she insisted on sticking to her chosen area of expertise, which was celebrity clients' needs. David was a very good lawyer and would never suggest anything criminal. That was why he insisted on client confidentiality and usually recused himself from hearing anything that might constitute a crime.

But guess what Mark proposed to the investors?

If Gaskell-Bridger got exposed and arrested, it would take at least two years for him to go to trial and eventually be sentenced, and who knew when the investors would get their money back? Mark proposed that we could get their money back, and much sooner than the police ever could. As long as they didn't ask how we did it.

The money drained out of the accounts, back to the investors. All it took was for Olivia, who controlled the account, to do a bit of typing and hit RETURN.

Then we went radio silent.

The night before we were to be at Gaskell-Bridger's company, Benjamin snuck into the place and hid webcams in the office, the reception area, and the boardroom. This was where Benjamin was most at home, sneaking in and bugging. Hardware and surveillance were his thing. Every now and then he would get a job offer from GCHQ, but he always turned them down. Benjamin did not work well with rules and restrictions, and certainly not the Official Secrets Act. He liked to cause mischief, though he wasn't actually malicious. He wasn't a troll. He was your typical sarky Chinese lad who had grown up in Peckham and liked to fuck with people.

Once Gaskell-Bridger found the money gone, he would start to panic. First disbelief, then the dawning horror of the con man getting conned. The frantic attempts to get Rajaratnam or his people on the phone, but every number Mark and Julia had given him was out of service.

Sunny Rajaratnam was vaporware.

Sunny Rajaratnam was in the wind, his time was up and thus dispersed like a mirage. Olivia had erased all traces of him. His website was gone. His entire digital footprint was but a vague memory.

And Tarquin Gaskell-Bridger was well and truly buggered.

We'd given the investors all the evidence we'd gathered for them to do with as they pleased. That was what they'd hired us for, after all, to gather proof that Gaskell-Bridger had swindled them.

The investors voted to turn it over to the police, one of the rare occasions where our clients actually did things by the book and went to the Old Bill. Well, after we stole their money back for them. They left that bit out. The Serious Fraud Office began an investigation that didn't take very long at all since they already had our evidence.

We knew Gaskell-Bridger was a flight risk, so Olivia hacked into his personal bank account and froze it. She reported fraudulent activity on all his credit cards and had them suspended. He wasn't buying a plane ticket anywhere. He was stuck in Blighty, ripe for the Fraud Squad to come a-knocking. The day they came for him, he ran out the window and stood on the ledge of his tenth-floor office in Canary Wharf. It took them an hour to talk him off it, and it was all over the news.

"Good result," Roger grinned as we all watched the telly in the office.

Cheers all around as Gaskell-Bridger stood on that ledge, exposed for all the world to see.

"He's not gonna jump," Marcie said, chewing on popcorn. "He's too much of a narcissist. This is a cry for help. It's about getting attention."

Over a year ago, I might have felt sorry for his humiliation, but now I felt no sympathy whatsoever. I was on the side of the pensioners whose money we got back.

When we got home that night, Julia and I celebrated in our own way. Addicts didn't stop being addicts. They're either in recovery or they aren't. Julia was a recovering sex addict. Our job seemed to placate her addiction by substituting sex with the risk-taking behaviors of going undercover and pulling off feats of deceit and duplicity. She felt no urge to have one-night stands with awful blokes, staying monogamous with me. We were in for the long haul. And when Julia and I made love, the gods didn't show up to watch. They granted me that bit of privacy, at least.

As Julia lay asleep in my arms, I thought about where I was now, since I first started working as a private investigator.

This is what it's like to dance for the gods.

FIVE

Sundays were dinner with my parents.

My father seemed in good spirits since his surgery and recovery from prostate cancer, though he still didn't approve of my job. My mother seemed a bit high-strung, but at least she wasn't gambling or racking up debt. My sister and her husband, on the other hand . . .

"When are you going to give us grandchildren?" my mother would ask.

"When we're good and ready," grumbled Sanjita.

"Your father and I would like to see at least one before we drop dead."

"Arrgh!" cried my sister.

Vivek stuffed his face with naan to avoid having to say anything.

Then my mother would ask Julia when we were going to marry. Julia would charmingly deflect, as usual. In my mother's mind, it was no longer "if" but "when."

At least it wasn't as awkward as when Julia finally introduced me to her parents. We'd gone over for Sunday lunch a few months ago, and they were relieved that I was a normal, middle-class bloke instead of some sleazy nutter she might have picked up from a club. Julia told them I used to be a religious scholar, which helped.

"So you were a PhD candidate?" her father asked, impressed. "Why did you give that up to teach secondary school?"

"I decided that academia wasn't really for me," I said. "I felt I needed to be in the world, to be engaged, and teaching was a way to see how the world was evolving."

"Ravi's mother was a teacher," Julia said, filling in the colors. "He was following in her footsteps."

"She must be very proud," Julia's mum said, beaming. "So how did you two meet?"

"When I was being treated for my addiction." Julia said matter-of-factly.

"Addiction?" Both her parents froze.

"Mum, Dad, I'd been meaning to tell you," Julia said. "I have a problem with alcohol."

The Sunday roast sat cold as the mood changed.

"What kind of problem?" Her mother choked.

"Alcoholism."

"Surely that's an exaggeration," her father said. "Everyone has a tipple every now and then."

"That was what I thought," Julia said. "I did it to unwind. The course work at uni was quite intense, I had some relationship problems, and I started binging."

What Julia binged on was not booze but sex. Sex with strangers. Sex with creepy men. Sex with unsuitable men from a club. Sex with at least one of her professors.

"Did . . . did Louise know?" her mother asked.

"She did. I swore her to secrecy."

"Oh, poor Louise." Her mother wiped away a tear.

"To think she didn't even tell us about what you were going through when she was ill . . . ," her father mused.

"It was Lou who got me to seek treatment," Julia said. "I woke up one morning in a man's bed and I couldn't stop crying. I called her and she came to fetch me. She took me to the doctor and I got a referral for treatment."

"You two always looked out for each other, more than we knew how to," her father said.

"And that was how I met Ravi," Julia said, suddenly brightening up as she squeezed my hand.

"Were you in treatment as well?" her father asked, a veil of suspicion coming over his eyes.

"No," I said. "I was a volunteer sober companion. I was assigned to help her cope, to keep her focus on her recovery, to not judge but help her if she relapsed."

"Ohh." Her mother nodded in approval.

"Eventually, we found we were attracted to each other, and I had to stop being her sober companion in order to be her boyfriend. We had to follow strict ethical guidelines. Julia continues to go to group meetings, but our relationship is now personal."

"I see," her father said.

Then her mother brought out a treacle tart.

"Well," I said when we left. "That was all very English. Aside from the blatant lying."

"Oh, *including* the blatant lying," Julia said with a laugh. "Lies are as English as they come."

"You could have warned me you were going to spring that on them."

"Well, I thought I ought to confess to them I was in recovery. They'd been suspecting I had a problem and they worry about me."

"But they didn't know you were a sex addict."

"They don't know what that is. Dad certainly wouldn't. They would say I was just oversexed or a slut. They don't get it and I can't be arsed to spend the next six months trying to convince them it's a real thing."

"So alcoholism is a more acceptable problem than sex addiction. Great," I said. "And you were testing me as well, weren't you?"

"I wanted to see how you were going to play along. Given how good you are on the job, I was curious."

"You just used me to socially engineer your mum and dad."

"And you passed the test," she said, and gave me a kiss.

"You get off on this. That's how you haven't relapsed. You've traded social engineering for sex."

"Win-win," she said.

"It's still acting out," I said.

"But with more benefits."

No wonder Bagalamukhi was following us so much these days. She followed us all the way from Julia's parents' house to my folks', and lingered in my parents' dining room when we visited them later. And it turned out even here, someone other than Julia and me was hiding something.

"Mum and Dad aren't having sex," said my sister when we stepped out to the garden for her ciggie break.

"I don't generally think about our parents having sex," I said.

"No, I mean he hasn't been interested since his recovery. He just goes about his routine except for the sex. It's driving Mum spare!"

"No wonder she seemed a bit tense. Wait— How do you know this? Did Mum tell you?"

"Course she did. Women talk. It's what we do. What do you blokes talk about, just football?"

"Sanji, dads do not generally talk to their sons about how they bonk their mums."

"Well, it's becoming my problem because Mum is channeling all her pent-up sexual energy into nagging me and Vivek into getting pregnant. Bollocks to that! We've got to get more job security first! I have to deal with Mum, but you have to talk to Dad."

"What do you want me to do? Throw a box of Viagra at him and say, 'Here, Dad. Mum needs a good rogering. Have at it!'?"

"Don't be a dick. For God's sake, think of something. She's going to get the nosy relatives involved. They're going to form a whole group to gang up on me and Vivek and bully us into getting pregnant!"

I couldn't find a way to talk to Dad about, oh my God, making more of an effort to have sex with Mum, but I had at least sussed out a way to get her out of the house and feel less frustrated.

Mrs. Dhewan, Mum's friend and our local neighborhood loan shark and gang boss (under the guise of her grande dame persona), had opened a local food bank to help keep the poorest local residents and their kids from going hungry. It wasn't a big one like the Trussell Trust, and its charity registration was still pending, but it had become an essential local fixture.

Mum, as a former schoolteacher, would be good with helping organize and distribute the food. That should take up enough of her energy to not dwell on Dad's negligence and hopefully get her off Sanjita's back.

Little did I know the chaos this would unleash, but that was much later.

So life was good.

Well, as good as it could be when you're paid to do dodgy things to clean the dirty laundry of the rich and powerful, and you're hallucinating gods.

As private investigators, we are not nice people. We are not paid to be nice people. We are paid to solve problems by not being nice.

So that became our routine. Solve a big case, get paid handsomely, go out for drinks to celebrate, Julia and I, bonk each other's brains out at the end of the evening. Wash, rinse, repeat.

I didn't even think about it when we went to the wine bar near the office in Farringdon to celebrate the result for the ADDT case. As I sipped my gin and tonic, I glimpsed Kali standing in the corner of the bar, watching me intently. She wasn't sticking out her tongue. She seemed oddly subdued. That was not the smile of someone who was amused or happy. Had she just shaken her head at me?

She was walking towards me now, past the punters in suits drinking and laughing.

I tried to ignore her, but she came up to my shoulder and, as she passed, whispered in my ear.

"You're getting entirely too comfortable in your status quo, my lovely boy," she said.

And with that, she walked out of the bar, texting on her phone.

. . . *Fuck.*

THE TRUE PRICE
OF LONDON PROPERTIES

ONE

Lev Sergeyevich Mayakovsky was one of the major Russian oligarchs who had swept into London in the 1990s and come close to taking it over, buying properties in Mayfair, as well as mansions, and football teams, and setting up all sorts of organizations and charities.

Throughout the early 2000s, Mayakovsky was rarely out of the news. It was impossible to avoid him and his fellow *oligarchskis* as they seemed on the verge of taking over London the way Arab money had been flowing into the capital since the 1970s. The Russians were the shiny new rich kids on the block, and the government welcomed them with open arms, more than happy to accept their lovely money to shore up the London and UK economy.

Julia, who was still pursuing her literature degree part-time, compared Mayakovsky's story to a thick Russian novel.

"Just think," she said. "He comes to England an outsider, in some people's eyes a pariah. A man with money and resources but very little connections, which he remedies by throwing that money around to buy influence and a place on the map. He starts to step out in society with Cecily Harkingdale of the Sussex Harkingdales."

"Landed gentry gone to seed," smirked Marcie.

It was true. The Harkingdales were of that class that had lived off the rent on their land for over a hundred years, but had since fallen on hard times. Landowning wasn't all it was cracked up to be these days if you were not the Royal Family. The Harkingdales branched off into The City and, what else, property speculation, but debt had been eroding their standing for over twenty years. Mayakovsky was their knight in shining armor, coming in from Russia, and they pretty much threw Cecily at him. He wanted that English aristocratic life, the Savile Row suits, attending social events as if he was a count in a Tolstoy novel. Interviews with him were full of soulful Russian allusions to literature and poetry.

"I feel my soul is Russian, but the romance of the English spirit touches my heart deeply," he effused on Channel Four.

I remember that interview. A few million viewers must have vomited in disgust at the same time that evening.

But then there was the requisite scandal. No rich foreigner who put up sticks here with such a high profile was devoid of skeletons in his closet. Mayakovsky's first wife showed up with his young son. This was the upmarket reality soap opera for people who were tired of gossip involving footballers and their wives.

Irina Petrovna Mayakovsky kicked up a very loud fuss the moment she arrived in London, landing interviews with the papers and society magazines. She was the first wife, who had stuck with Mayakovsky through the thick and thin of the Cold War years when he traveled all over Europe and the US, holding down the fort back home in Moscow and raising their son on her own while he was doing spy stuff under the guise of diplomatic activities. He couldn't tell her what he was up to, of course, but he always sent money back and made sure she and little Sacha wanted for nothing, which was considerable in the dying years of the Soviet Union. She played the role of loyal wife as he weathered the fall of the Berlin Wall and the utter chaos of the perestroika years. She railed against his callousness, this woman who supported him in his leanest times only to be abandoned when he became prosperous, for a younger, more attractive model with a higher social standing. The media ate it up.

"That scandal was the shit," said Marcie. "I remember my old PR firm chomping at the bit to rep her. Every PR wanted in on that gig."

Of course, Marcie secretly being CIA meant that landing Irina Mayakovsky as a client would have meant acquiring a potential piece of leverage on her husband should the Company ever decide they had a use for him, like, say, propping him up as America's man to run for President of Russia . . . but that didn't come to pass. He was not a fan of America, and she refused all overtures to be represented by any PR firms. Perhaps she was sincere in her desire to just have her husband acknowledge her and their son, and then to live a quiet life after all.

Mayakovsky condemned the media coverage as a plot by his enemies to discredit and humiliate him. As a former spy, he certainly had his long list of suspects. It could have been one of the other media moguls out to take him down a peg, his former colleagues in the KGB-now-FSB running an op, someone in MI6 out for revenge, the CIA (though Marcie denied it). No one ever found out who paid for Irina and Sacha's air ticket to London. Mayakovsky couldn't marry Cecily Harkingdale because he hadn't yet divorced Irina. Mayakovsky then had to make a very public display of atonement, helping Irina and Sacha get British citizenship, setting them up in a decent flat in Bloomsbury, far less extravagant than the luxury penthouses and condominiums he had bought all over London, making sure Sacha got into a decent school, then finally getting his divorce with a generous settlement to keep Irina housed and fed and alimony for Sacha's upkeep. Now he could complete his fantasy of joining the British aristocracy by marrying Cecily. Then he set about his Great Project of being a patron of the arts, a donor to political causes for Mother Russia, supporting campaigns for reform there and even hinting he might run for president there, if there wasn't a warrant out for his arrest, and showing up at all the right parties and events with his newfangled Sloane Ranger wife.

His last five years had been a more muted affair, though. Failures and disappointment had set in. No matter how many overtures he made, the Russian government refused to lift his arrest warrant. His marriage to Cecily Harkingdale didn't pan out the way he had hoped, and gossip about their extravagant, furniture-smashing fights about not producing an heir were covered all the way from the tabloids to *Vanity Fair* to *Popbitch*. His football team didn't break out of a six-year rut of losing streaks and lackluster player acquisitions, and he considered selling it. The massive overheads of his sponsorships and his stock investments also incurred losses to the point where he was no longer a billionaire. There were reports that he was depressed, and no one rode that black dog like a Russian.

"Reminds me more of Thomas Hardy," I told Julia. "I used to teach my students *The Mayor of Casterbridge* for their GCSEs."

Then one day, six months ago, Mayakovsky died.

The butler found him in the bath that morning, his head submerged under water for far too long and without a pulse. The autopsy concluded that he'd suffered a heart attack and lost consciousness. His high blood pressure and the various medications he was on didn't help. His dreams of an English Happily Ever After turned out to be a chimera.

TWO

Do you think he really topped himself?" I asked.

"It's entirely possible," Olivia said. "The thing about extremely rich men is that they become obsessed with their legacies, what they're going to leave behind and all that. If he was looking at the loss of his power, status, and wealth, the sense that he was a failure in his twilight years, I wouldn't put it past him to just bump himself off out of despair."

"And in the bath, no less, like a Roman emperor," Mark said, ever amused.

"Not exactly the same despair of a pensioner on a council estate who can't afford to continue living because his benefits have been cut," Cheryl said in one of her rare contributions to our office chatter.

"The filthy rich have their own, more narcissistic versions of existential malaise and despair," Mark said.

"They really are an alien species," I said, shaking my head. "Worthy of their own nature documentary."

Mayakovsky's death was proving a huge inconvenience to his heirs and next of kin. It seemed he'd died intestate—that is, without a will. By law, his property should have gone to his spouse, so Cecily Harkingdale-Mayakovsky should have gotten it all, including the tens of millions of pounds' worth of properties all over London.

If you were wondering where we came in, chalk it up to David Okri.

David might be Golden Sentinel's lawyer, but he still kept in touch with his former colleagues at the practice where he had started out, and they used him as a contact when they needed the services of a prime private investigations firm like us. They happened to be Mayakovsky's lawyers, and they'd always thought the Harkingdales were well dodgy. Mayakovsky's lawyers were entering the discovery phase, taking inventory of his properties and assets while the Harkingdales were kicking up a fuss about getting what was their due as soon as possible. Cecily was merely the conduit through which they could claim all of Mayakovsky's goodies. And they believed they were due everything he owned. This should be their payoff for putting up with him and his louche Russian ways when they let him into their pristine English family.

Except there was the rather inconvenient matter that there *was* a will, after all. This threw the Harkingdales for a loop. Naturally, Mayakovsky had had a will drawn up years ago when he married Cecily, but it had been changed, revised, and redrawn over and over again, codicils added again and again to the point where the will was scrubbed and a new one was drawn up. The Harkingdales were insisting they get on with it and conduct a reading of the will, but there was another snag. They were surprised when Mayakovsky's lawyer announced that weeks before his death, he had had another will made without their knowledge, so the one that favored the Harkingdales could no longer be considered valid. Now the Harkingdales were tearing their hair out because they didn't know what was in the new will. The lawyers were insisting that Irina and Sacha should be present for the reading, which implied they were going to get a share of the estate.

The problem here was that Irina and Sacha had gone missing. Poof. Vanished off the face of the Earth. Without them present, there could be no reading of the will, and the Harkingdales were in inheritance limbo, their own debts piling up while they waited.

David told Roger that his old law firm wanted to hire us to find Irina and Sacha, and Roger, smelling money, power, and a chance to make friends and gather new gossip, readily agreed.

And I was made primary.

Julia still liked to see this as a kind of latter-day George Eliot novel where the Harkingdales accepted marriage to a dreaded foreigner, a former Communist no less, to keep the family financially afloat.

"How they must have chafed at the thought of lying back and thinking of England as they let this Russian into their vaunted English household," she said.

I was no raving leftie, but even I could see the Harkingdales were just the type who would be the first to be lined up against the wall if the proletariat ever rose up and revolted. You could sense the resentful class privilege and entitlement wafting off of the family even from looking at photographs of them. It was just as well we didn't have to come into any contact with them on this job. It was strictly research, paperwork, and basic old-fashioned footwork.

THREE

So far, so pedestrian," I said. "Find someone. Straightforward enough."

"I suppose it's a relief not to be dealing with cloak-and-dagger stuff," said Julia.

Once again, we had spoken too soon.

"Dude," Marcie said from her desk, looking up from *Hello!* magazine. "Mayakovsky used to be KGB. You might find out stuff you weren't expecting."

"Oh, Christ," I said. "Don't tell me there's bloody spook shit here."

"Don't rule it out."

Marcie, our resident American at Golden Sentinels, was in fact CIA, masquerading as a private investigator. You could say she was the real boss here, but Roger would take great offense at that. None of us believed she was just a former PR agent anymore. That was her cover, her legend as they called it. She was CIA through and through. If nothing else, she was Roger's handler, giving him assignments to dole out to the rest of us under the guise of simple work for hire, when her own masters had some off-the-books assignments they didn't want to be caught doing. The CIA was, after all, the Big Bad Boss of us all, no matter how much Marcie denied that and said we were merely contractors. Why else would she hang about here at the office instead of a desk in the bowels of the American Embassy? Granted, Golden Sentinels was a much nicer gaff. We could order sushi and Vietnamese for takeout and had better coffee, ergonomic chairs, and gossip, which Marcie thrived on.

Roger liked to show he had more power than he really did, and then desperately scrambled to get as much as possible to make it true. Marcie was an expert at wielding power by pretending not to have any. And she had more than she ever let on. She knew never to overplay her hand.

Of course I was terrified of her. She could disappear me with one phone call if she felt like it. I suppose I was lucky that she seemed to like me. Julia believed Marcie considered me her protégé, which was a mixed blessing even at the best of times.

"Nope, this one's nothing to do with me," Marcie said, barely looking up from her yogurt. "Mayakovsky was never my assignment."

"So why are you bringing this up?" I asked.

"I know you like things to be neat, Ravi, and I just want to remind you that when it comes to Russians, especially dead ex-KGB guys, it's never going to be simple or clean."

"Thanks for the warning."

"Dude, you're my peeps. I would never screw you over."

. . . *yet.*

"If anything interesting comes out of this, I want a piece," she said, as much a warning as a request.

This was just a missing persons case, I reminded myself. A first wife and a son who had gone to ground. No reason to suspect foul play. They'd simply dropped out of sight in the last few years. A cursory check of travel records indicated neither of them had left the country for the last five, so they were definitely still here in the UK. Neither Irina nor Sacha's passport had been used or spotted at any ports. Sacha was still in university, but had taken time off, and that was the last anyone saw of him. Irina had been living alone in a modest flat out near Russell Square when she seemed to drop out of sight around the same time. That raised a bunch of questions for which it was now our job to find answers.

FOUR

I took Julia with me to ask about Sacha's whereabouts. (A pretty blonde next to a dark-skinned Asian man always helped set people at ease.) Sacha was studying at the School of Pharmacy at University College London, and lived with his mum.

"I find all this concrete a bit depressing, no matter how many shops they have here," Julia said as we walked through Russell Square. "Imagine living here while her ex-husband was living large in Mayfair."

"It was her choice. Irina didn't want much from him, just what she felt she was due, which was a decent flat. She wasn't one for luxuries. She was a die-hard socialist at heart. Maybe all this gray concrete reminded her of their old digs in Moscow."

"At least they sent Sacha to a good school."

Mrs. McCree, the pensioner next door, told us Irina and Sacha were good neighbors, though Irina was a bit reclusive. Sacha was shy, gentle, and radiated thoughtfulness and intelligence, and he would recommend books to Mrs. McCree. "The Russian variation of the sensitive boy," Julia mused. They often went to see European films over at the Curzon together. Over the last year, Irina had had visits from a well-dressed gentleman with an accent: Mayakovsky. Still visiting his ex-wife. Interesting. Then a few months ago, Irina and Sacha left early one morning and hadn't been back since. Occasionally some men in suits would come and knock on the door and ask the neighbors the same questions we were asking right now.

"Sounds like they left after they'd heard the news that Mayakovsky'd died," I said as we left.

"So they ran?" Julia asked. "And went dark like that? What were they running from?"

Mrs. McCree had held some of the post that was coming to Irina's flat. Electricity bills, junk mail, unanswered letters from Mayakovsky's lawyers, no doubt to inform her and Sacha of his death, letters from a later date, this time informing them of the reading of the will, which had now been postponed because they couldn't be found.

"You're looking less bored now," Julia said.

"I wasn't bored."

"You were all ready to phone this in. Now there may be foul play. This may not be another boring search."

"Boring is good," I said. "Boring means I don't see any gods popping up."

As we walked to the car, my mobile rang.

A familiar number showed up on the screen as it rang.

"Heeey, babe. How's it hangin'?"

Oh, fuck.

"Hello, Ariel. You're not in town, are you?"

"Sorry, hon. I'm in an undisclosed location in the Middle East. I got bored waiting in this car, so I thought I'd touch base with you and Julia."

"Ariel says hi," I said to Julia, who raised an eyebrow.

Sleeping with Ariel Morgenstern might have been the second-biggest mistake of my life (the first was becoming a private investigator at Golden Sentinels). Yes, Ariel was well fit and a banshee in bed, her shock of red hair, tight black T-shirts, nipple rings, and Kali tattoo on her arm making her the most goth private military contractor you were ever likely to meet. Oh, she was good fun and had an appealing sense of humor, before you realized she was also a gleefully amoral and murderous sociopath with no boundaries whatsoever. Her company, Interzone, was also a contractor for CIA black ops, and Roger considered her boss, Laird Collins, his mortal enemy, but since Golden Sentinels and Interzone were both independent contractors engaged by the Company, we were expected to play nice and not step on each other's toes whenever possible. To do otherwise was bad for business. As a result of my original dalliance with her, our respective bosses appointed Ariel and me the liaisons for our companies. Then Julia had gone off and slept with Ariel as well, which cemented what Ariel liked to call our three-way personal bond. Ariel seemed awfully fond of us, sending us texts and selfies from her backpacking holidays, which she went on when she wasn't off in some hot spot doing horrible things for Interzone. She sent us Christmas cards and birthday cards, and often threatened to visit us in London, promising a threesome. Yes, that would be lovely, if having sex with a ticking time bomb was your thing. I was always relieved that work kept her from setting foot back in London. I had no doubt that if it she was ordered to, she wouldn't hesitate to shoot us in the head and move on to her next BFFs.

"So what can I do for you, Ariel?"

"Always so gracious," she laughed. "It's more about what I can do for you."

"I'm doing just fine, thanks."

"Not for long."

"What do you mean by that?"

"You're dealing with the late Lev Mayakovsky."

"How do you know that?"

"Please! We always keep tabs on what you guys in London are doing. We're on the same side."

"So what's this about, then?"

"I figured I ought to warn you."

"About what?"

"Dead ex-KGB oligarch? Lotta skeletons in a lotta closets. Lots of hungry spooks sniffing around. And what you're good at is finding those closets and opening them. That's what the gods compel you to do. You just can't help it."

"Are you suggesting there's espionage stuff going on?"

"Baby, Russians are like crack cocaine to all spooks. Your Marcie will never admit it, but nothing gets the CIA's juices going like Russians 'cause of all the nostalgic Cold War moral certainties that come flooding into the pleasure centers of their brains. There's gotta be some political angle to all this. There always is with Russians abroad. It's so quaint I could squeal."

"Thanks for the heads-up."

"Ariel!" Jarrod's voice came through in the background, probably on a radio. "What's the holdup?"

"Still waiting on the drone to ID them all," she said absently, then back to me. "Jarrod says hi."

"I don't say hi to Jarrod," I said.

I asked Marcie for Jarrod's file after our first encounter with Interzone last year. He and a squad had been sent to London to murder a bunch of hapless bankers who were suspected of stealing from a CIA-controlled investment account that they helped set up. Henry "Hank" Jarrod was a former sergeant in SEAL Team Six who resigned his commission when Laird Collins headhunted him for Interzone. He didn't enjoy killing, but did it with a cold and appallingly competent efficiency. What I hated about him was his unerringly polite demeanor no matter what he did, and the more threatening he got, the more polite he became. Ariel was often in his squad.

"Ariel, we're about to murder a roomful of people," said Jarrod with a hint of irritation in his voice. "Can you at least confirm it's the right people?"

"Chill, Jarrod," she said. "I'm just waiting for the facial recognition software to kick in."

Ariel chuckled. Just about every syllable from her and Jarrod sent chills down my spine. It was like receiving a transmission from a dark, murderous universe I never wanted to hear from.

"Do what you do, Ravi. Bring the chaos. You're Kali's beautiful monster, unleashing the chains of karma. Whoops, shooting's started. Gotta go. Later!"

And with that, she hung up.

I felt Kali's hand on my shoulder as she loomed behind me, listening in. Of course Kali would show up whenever Ariel did. We were both her children, after all. Her tongue was positively wagging at the chaos to come.

"We're never going to be rid of Ariel, are we?" mused Julia as I started the car.

"I think she might be Kali's harbinger."

"This should be fun," Julia smiled.

"Did you catch this taste for mayhem since we first met or did you always have it?" I asked.

"It's not always about you, love," she said. "It was in me long before I met you. Tell you what, let's stop by the Metropolitan Archives."

"For what?" I asked.

"A hunch."

FIVE

Julia and I spent nearly three hours looking up records and collating the Harkingdale family history. We headed straight for Roger's office when we got back to Golden Sentinels. Cheryl sensed something was up and joined us.

"The Harkingdales murdered Mayakovsky," I said.

"How do you reckon?" Roger arched an eyebrow.

"The circumstances of Mayakovsky's death were unusual and suspicious, even if the coroner declared it suicide," I said. "Add to that the missing will the Harkingdales want to contest the moment it's found. They're so desperate to claim the estate they might as well be wearing a 'WE TOPPED THE BUGGER!' sign on their chests."

"This is all very circumstantial," Cheryl said, scribbling notes. "How did you come to it?"

"We looked up the Harkingdale family history in the registers at the London Metropolitan Archive," Julia said. "For over a hundred years, the Harkingdales of Sussex had a history of bad financial decisions where they consistently lost their lands and properties bit by bit, but they always clung on by marrying up and marrying rich. And the spouses often died of some sickness or other. Consistently. And the Harkingdales would inherit the property. It happened once or twice a generation, and the intervals were long enough that no one would notice that spouses from outside the family would die after a reasonable number of years. Long enough to have children to continue the Harkingdale line. Men of means would marry a Harkingdale daughter, then end up dying soon after, and she would inherit his property and bring it into the Harkingdale fold. They assimilated any children as well, of course. Occasionally those children would die as well, but in the nineteenth century, people still died from so many illnesses and mishaps that no one would bat an eyelash."

"So property isn't the only thing that's the Harkingdale family business," Roger said, impressed. "There's also murder."

"We reckon it's poisoning." I said. "After all, no one conducted toxicology tests or autopsies in those days. Faking Mayakovsky's suicide wouldn't have been difficult. They could have slipped something in his wine before he got in the bath. It knocks him out, and Cecily comes in when he loses consciousness to just gently push him under the water and keep him there."

"Which brings us to Irina and Sacha Mayakovsky," Julia continued. "In the months before he died, Mayakovsky began to visit them quite regularly after only seeing Sacha just once every few months since the divorce ten years ago. He spent time with Sacha to keep in touch and help bring him up, but he and Irina avoided each other if they could help it. Then in the last year of his life, he started seeing her even when Sacha was away at school. I don't think he wanted to get back together with her."

"We think he knew something was up with the Harkingdales," I said, "And Irina was the only one in his life who would understand if he talked about it."

"He must have told her about his new will," said Julia. "If he was expecting the Harkingdales to bump him off, he might have decided not to give them his assets, so he would have another will drawn up leaving it all to Irina and Sacha."

"So he felt trapped," Cheryl said. "He saw his whole life crumbling around him. He was depressed. He saw no way out. Cecily wasn't going to give him a divorce because he was the Harkingdales' meal ticket."

"What I don't get," Roger said, "is why he continued to live with her, with her relatives coming and going in their house. He could have legged it, moved out and into one of his penthouses in London with extra bodyguards restricting access to him."

"Oh, Roger," Cheryl sighed. "You've never understood the mind of a fatalist. The poor sod was depressed and losing the will to live. He might have thought this was his fate, his punishment for his hubris and arrogance, for abandoning his first wife and son, the simpler life with purer love, for an illusion of glamour and status, and this was where it got him. He was probably at the end of his rope."

"Bloody stroll on!" Roger rolled his eyes. "If I ever get that way, Cheryl love, you have my permission to shoot me. Just blow my head off and get it over with."

"Might be too late for you by then," Cheryl said.

"I mean it!"

"I know," she said.

"Back to the case at hand," Roger said, suddenly rubbing his hands. "This could call for a nice earner for us. Lots of ways to play it. Lovely-jubbly!"

"So now our priority is to find Irina and Sacha before the Harkingdales do," I said.

"Too right! We are their new best friends," Roger said. "No, even better. We're their fucking guardian angels. Their *very expensive* guardian angels!"

Of course, this was all still circumstantial evidence and pure speculation. We didn't have any real evidence to support this. You might think we were awfully quick to jump to the worst conclusion about human nature here, but the way things went in this world, by the time Golden Sentinels was brought into the picture, there was already an expectation that awful shit was afoot. In the time I'd been at the firm, that usually turned out to be true. Murder cases were still not the norm, however. We usually referred such clients to the police, and if we were called to solve a murder case, we had to be extra careful. To be implicated as an accessory, to hide or tamper with evidence, to be accused of obstruction or perverting the course of justice were not charges the firm could shrug off. That was why Roger, Cheryl, Ken, and Clive took great pains to drum into us the old saying "Do what thou must, but for God's sake, don't get caught!" Words to live by.

I glanced at the sofa in Roger's office. Kali was dancing up a storm on the cushions, whirling like a dervish, tongue wagging, bouncing up and down in rapture, reveling at the coming madness. Bagalamukhi stood by, goading her on, anticipating the drama to come.

Great. Just bloody great.

SIX

We went up on the roof to have our usual communal spliff. Mark had a new strain he wanted to try out, one with less sting, more smoothness.

"What's landed gentry in the twenty-first century anyway?" Mark asked. "An outmoded form of aristocracy still leeching off the resources of the nation. And now we find out this family is evil? The Harkingdales have form as poisoners? That's just too rich!"

"Well, they got away with it for over a hundred years," I said.

"It's like something out of a Brontë novel," Julia said, taking a puff off the spliff.

"Charlotte, Anne, or Emily?" Olivia asked.

"Emily. More full-on death and melodrama," Julia said.

"This is kind of an interesting irony," Marcie smiled. "Mayakovsky was a KGB badass for twenty years before he got out with his billions, hoping for his happy ending livin' large in London, only to end up poisoned by a family of English aristocratic assholes for his money. My buddies at the US Embassy are gonna love this."

Marcie was such a gossip I could tell she couldn't wait to tell her mates in the CIA. And this would then spread throughout the entire intelligence community. Spies relied on information, and gossip was no less valid as intel. If knowledge was power, Marcie must have been getting a lot of street cred amongst her fellow spooks, justifying her staying here at Golden Sentinels to run us as a network of assets, and juicy morsels of potential leverage.

"I want to use drones," Benjamin said when the spliff was passed to him.

We all looked at him as if he was mad.

"For surveillance!" he said. "To get dirt we need on the Harkingdales! Roger won't get me access to weaponized drones!"

We all relaxed.

"Bloody hell! Do you think I actually want to kill people?"

"Sometimes we wonder about you, Benjamin," I said.

"I can't believe your opinion of me is that low!" He sulked. "Where's the lulz in killing people? Honestly."

"What's this about killing people?" David asked, arriving late.

We told him what Julia and I had turned up.

"Fucking hell!" David cried. "Another murder case?!"

I could sense the panic bubbling up from his stomach. The normal human reaction that the rest of us often sidestepped.

"David throwing a wobbly again," muttered Benjamin.

"I hate murder cases!"

"Me, too, David," I said. "Deep breath now."

David was the first person I'd ever met who had a genuine phobia of murder cases. I suppose it was a middle-class fear, that fear of chaos and the breaking of reason and the social contract, and of becoming tainted by that darkness.

"This was supposed to be a simple case of due diligence!" he cried.

"David, you know as well as I do that when it comes to fuck-off amounts of money, things will always get complicated."

"Fucking hell!"

I caught Ken and Clive glancing at David's panic attack when we went back down to our desks. Ken shrugged. Clive rolled his eyes. I could tell he thought David was such a wimp. Not everyone could be hardboiled like Ken and Clive. Actually, no, Ken and Clive were not hardboiled. They were concrete.

"Do they know we suspect?" David asked.

"The Harkingdales? No. They don't have any reason to, but once we find Irina and Sacha Mayakovsky, they might kick off."

"Like how?"

"I don't know. Off the top of my head, they might try to have them killed, which might mean coming after us first."

"So we might end up collateral damage!" David was losing it again.

"I'm glad you've had your weekly dose of medicinal libation, children," Roger declared, stepping out of his office. "Now I think the task is clear. Anyone with a spare moment, help Ravi find Irina and Sacha Mayakovsky before the Harkingdales do. I want everyone rested and fresh in the morning to talk strategy."

SEVEN

As Julia and I left the office, my dad phoned. I didn't need gods to forewarn me that this was coming.

"Come and pick up your washing," Dad said. "And please talk to your mother."

"About what?"

"She's been receiving stolen goods from that Dhewan gangster woman!"

"What?!"

The skies cracked open and thunder and lightning raged above us as I sped towards my parents' house. Julia didn't see any of it—Lord Ganesha raising his scepter above the clouds and goading Arjuna on as he led his troops forth in the great Kurukshetra War.

"I might be mixing up my stories, since Ganesha wasn't there," I said, my foot on the accelerator.

"Ravi, calm down," Julia said.

"I am perfectly calm. It's just the bloody *Mahabharata* is being reenacted above me as my parents go round the bend again!"

"What does a war have to do with your parents and Mrs. Dhewan?" Julia asked.

"I don't bloody know. My mother committing a crime and a gang war erupting?"

"That's ridiculous, Ravi. You know that won't happen. Mrs. Dhewan would never get your mother involved in one of her ventures. Your mum is too much of a loose cannon for her to take the risk."

"Julia, I appreciate you trying to calm me down. Really, I do, but I'm seeing a fucking big mythical battle going on up in the night sky as we drive to West London."

"Maybe it's telling you about something else, not your parents."

"What, then?"

"This case. You said the gods send you signs and portents, yes? Think about how big this thing we're on could blow up into. Tens of millions of pounds at stake, a murderous family, a mother and son on the run and facing a fight for survival."

"We really don't need to think about that now. We just need to find two missing people. And I just need to sort out my parents."

"You don't always need to be so stoical, love."

"I can't help it."

"Of course," she said. "*Singh* means 'lion.' You can't help but live up to your name. You just need to protect everyone because you feel guilty. Even when you don't have to."

Julia's literary perspective made her a unique investigator. Roger must have spotted that when he interviewed her. He didn't see her as just another pretty face as I had first thought he did. She and I complemented each other, and to my surprise, she was the only person in my life who could actually calm me down. We seemed to have that effect on each other, as if we were a complete person, but my worry was that we also enabled each other to do the outrageous things this job demanded, with no remorse and even a certain amount of glee. It was the perfect contrast to reading literary criticism and writing papers. Julia enjoyed this job much more than I did, as addicts chased dangerous situations to feel alive, and that worried me.

"Stop thinking you're responsible," she would say. "It's not about you, Ravi."

Meanwhile, my parents' living room looked like a food warehouse.

"What's all this?" I asked.

Boxes upon boxes of canned foods, pasta, sugar, jars of sauces, soups, biscuits, toiletries, and basic household cleaning products were stacked against the wall. Dad sat in his armchair, seething.

"I'm just holding them for Mrs. Dhewan," Mum said. "Her nephews are collecting them first thing in the morning to take to the food bank."

"It's not even an official food bank!" Dad grumbled. "These must be stolen! Or past their sell-by date! They might be poison!"

"They've been giving these away to the poor for months," Mum retorted. "Nobody's died. Why do you leap to the worst conclusions about everything! You've done nothing but complain!"

"Leave me alone, woman!"

"I have been leaving you alone! I should ask the same of you!"

"Listen to you two!" I said. "What are you? Children?"

"At least I'm doing something to help with the community," Mum said. "Instead of sitting around sulking all day."

I decided to leave Julia to look after my folks while I went over to see Mrs. Dhewan, whose house was only two streets down. I phoned ahead and asked to visit, a necessary formality, and she granted permission. Mrs. Dhewan may have looked like a Hindu housewife with airs, but she was really the local gangster and loan shark, with her son and nephews keeping the peace as her enforcers. I grew up with them, after all, under the veneer of respectable middle-class courtesy, since we never got mixed up in her business. That came later, after I became a private investigator, which brought my world uncomfortably close to hers.

"I understand work has been very busy, Ravi," she said as she received me in her living room. "How nice of you to come by to see Auntie."

"What's going on?"

Her living room was piled with even more boxes than my mother's. She formed a surreal juxtaposition against them, in her expensive gold-and-red sari and jewelry.

"A temporary situation." Mrs. Dhewan waved her hand away. "All these goods are donations from local businesses for the food bank."

"So they're actual donations? They didn't fall off the back of a bunch of lorries off the M4?"

"Of course not. Do you think we could get away with having this much in full view of everyone? They're a tax write-off for those warehouses and businesses. Did you think I would jeopardize your mother by telling her to hold on to stolen goods? She's a civilian, dear. You know as well as I do that we do not mix civilians with our business. They're woefully unsuited to cope."

"Well, as long as everything's kosher, but that doesn't explain why you and my mother are storing them at home instead of the food bank."

"Oh, you're such a good son, Ravi. Your mother is holding those goods precisely because they're not stolen."

"I don't follow."

"We've been having a spot of bother with thieves stealing from the stores in the back of the food bank itself. Since we're catering to the community, we had to hide the goods away from the shop and bring them in the next day so people will get their food."

"Here's the thing: I'm a bit concerned that my mother agreed to store them at home. In the past she would have kicked up a fuss about it cluttering up the house."

"Blame it on the tensions between her and your father."

"Oh God, don't tell me she told you about that, too."

"Women commiserate, Ravi, otherwise we would all go mad. If your father was performing his marital duties as a husband, she would be much more relaxed and happy."

"I'm not comfortable discussing this with you, Auntie."

"You're an adult now, dear. You and I both know your mother is prone to being highly strung at the best of times. She might even be bipolar if you want to get psychological. That might explain why she was so eager to accept so many boxes, but it wasn't my place to comment. I can only say that this situation between your parents needs to be dealt with sooner or later."

"I never thought of you as a marriage counselor, Mrs. Dhewan."

"I am whatever the community needs me to be." She shrugged. "Just like you in your day job."

"Do you need any help with the thieves? Like a line in finding out who they are?"

"I thought you'd never ask. I have my boys on the lookout, but they're hardly detectives. Be a dear, won't you? I would be ever so grateful."

EIGHT

I sent Benjamin over to Mrs. Dhewan's food bank warehouse in the morning to hide some extra surveillance cameras in the storeroom and RFID chips in the dozen boxes I got her boys to put there to attract the thieves. Benjamin never seemed to sleep. He was always happy for a chance to play with his toys. I could tell Roger I was "cultivating local relationships that might prove useful."

Then back to Golden Sentinels for the strategy meeting. Julia was off in class, since she was still part-time, but I would fill her in later.

"The Harkingdales are chomping at the bit to find Irina and Sacha Mayakovsky," David said. "Since as long as they're in the wind, the estate is in limbo. They can't execute the will, the Harkingdales can't touch the properties. They have millions in debt, so they want to sell them as soon as possible."

There we were, doing what we did. Open-plan office, everyone gathered around for a strategy meeting. Roger's Bright Young Things, us, acting like we were a trendy start-up when we were in fact dealing with literal life and death.

"If this was a murder inquiry," Ken said, "we'd be lookin' at the ex-wife and son leggin' it so soon after he snuffed it as highly suspicious."

"If we were still coppers," Clive added, "we'd be on the telly askin' the public for help and appealin' for Mrs. Mayakovsky and Junior to come forward."

"Highly unlikely for them to be suspects," Mark said. "Since they didn't have access to Mayakovsky. And we know the Harkingdales have form with poisoning and access to him."

"They're not the ones who've done a runner," Ken said. "That still makes 'em suspect."

"You think the kid might have killed his dad, then grabbed his mum with the intent to get rid of her, too?" Marcie said.

"Can't rule it out," said Ken.

"Wow," Marcie said. "You went to the dark place fast."

"It doesn't make sense if he killed his father and wants to kill his mother," I said. "Much easier if he just got rid of her at home rather than run off with her."

"So the missus and Junior have gone to ground," Roger said. "I take it you know how to set about finding them?"

"The usual," I said. "Scour social media."

"Sacha has a big disadvantage," Olivia said. "He's nineteen years old."

"And no nineteen-year-old doesn't keep social media accounts," I said as it dawned on me.

"So he's as good as found, then," Roger said. "Hop to it, children."

"Will we be putting them in danger if we find them?" I said.

"Not our concern," Roger said as he walked back to his office. "The job is to find them. Everything else is not our problem."

"Yet," Cheryl said.

Roger shrugged.

"Hang on," I said. "How do we know the Harkingdales haven't got people looking for Irina and Sacha right now?"

"Because they haven't hired us to do it." Roger grinned.

And so we set to work. Cursory searches for Sacha's social media accounts. Sure enough, he had all of them, all the ones a teenager would have had from the age of twelve onwards.

"What's with the pensive look?" Mark asked.

"We're still operating on a plane of uncertainty," I said. "I suppose I'm still hoping it's all just nothing, a misunderstanding. No murder, a harmless explanation for Sacha and his mum going off, like a quick holiday, the Harkingdales just a family that needs money. Wouldn't it be nice to have a dull case without drama?"

"Is this something the gods are saying to you?" Mark asked.

"No! I never talk to the gods and I certainly never do anything they say! They never tell me to do anything!"

"Steady on, son," Ken said. "Mark's just askin'."

"Sorry. Look, I just want to be clear. It's possible I'm schizophrenic, but it's never affected my work or what I do, all right? Schizophrenia is a thinking disorder, and if I have it, I need you lot to tell me. Does anything I say come off as the ravings of a nutter?"

"Not that we've noticed," Benjamin said with a shrug.

"Look, the gods are just extensions of my stress and hang-ups, all right? They show up when things look dicey because it's probably my mind's way of making sense of it all and making me feel guilty. They don't give me prophetic visions or advice. They're just parts of me, not visitations from the beyond. If I start to sound incoherent or stop making sense, I need you all to tell me. If I go completely doolally and need to be sectioned, I need you to do that for me, yeah?"

"Totally," Marcie said.

"Good," I said, perhaps a bit too emphatically. "Good."

A layer of storm clouds blanketed the ceiling of the office. Thunder and lightning, then a storm right there in the office, that only I noticed. Rudra stood in the center of the office, orchestrating the storm, sipping coffee from my mug.

"We might have another problem," Olivia said, not even looking up from her computer. "I looked up Irina Mayakovsky's medical records."

"Bad news?" I asked.

"She has early onset Alzheimer's."

"So we really need to find her, then," Julia said.

"Yeah," Clive said. "Duty of care and all that."

NINE

Once again, it was Olivia who compiled and collated Sacha Mayakovsky's digital footprints on the Web. She did it with her usual air of bored superiority. It wasn't even that satisfying for her since she could hack as easily as she breathed. I sensed she could use a proper challenge soon lest she got too bored, and then God knows what she might get up to in her hacker ways. Olivia, in her librarian glasses and black Gucci pantsuit, was punching below her weight and she knew everyone knew it. Even doing forensic analysis on a major finance company was small potatoes for her when she could hack her way into anywhere and take over everything if she wanted to.

"Clever boy, our Sacha," she said. "The day he disappeared, he locked down his accounts and made them private."

"So we can't see any of his posts?" I asked.

"Nope."

"We'll do this the hard way, then," I said.

It wasn't really that hard. We just did a search for any forums or blogs he might have shown up on. There was a Russian expatriate forum he posted on to talk about his life in London. There was a message board from his college he had an account on. Mark found a message board devoted to psychedelic and synthetic drugs that Sacha was especially active on, and read through his posts.

"Sacha's a talented lad," Mark said. "He's got some interesting ideas on combining certain compounds to boost memory and cognition without the negative effects of speed."

"To enhance learning and retention," Olivia said. "Very clever."

"Is he still posting?" I asked.

"Too right," Mark said. "I'm going to start a dialogue. Pick his brain."

"Still sloppy," Olivia said. "Typical teenager. Just can't leave his interests alone."

"Here's a thought," I said. "What if he's been brewing up some of these synthetics and selling them?"

"Go on," Mark said.

"He's in hiding. He's going to need cash to feed himself and his mum. He's probably used to dealing a bit to his mates at school."

"I'll start feeling him out on that," Mark said.

Olivia and I began to cross-reference all the people he communicated with on the message boards and blogs, and ran a search for their social media accounts. Sure enough, many of them followed him and he followed them back. We found photos of him and his friends at parties, on holiday, just down the pub.

And there was one girl in particular that he appeared with more than all the others.

"Girlfriend," Olivia said.

Her accounts were not locked down, and it was easy enough to see her real name. Tamsin Lowry. From there it was especially easy to find her contact information. She was one of Sacha's classmates. She still lived at home with her parents, because student housing and loans were through the roof so that was a way to save money.

"I doubt Sacha and his mum would be staying with them, then," I said. "But she probably knows where he is."

This worried me. If we could trace Sacha's girlfriend this easily, so might whoever the Harkingdales might have hired to do the same thing.

"Sorry, who are you again?" Tamsin Lowry asked, wide-eyed.

Her parents' house was in Hounslow. We knew she took the Tube to university in Central London every day.

"I'm the caseworker for Sacha's mum," I said, presenting the card that we'd printed up in the office. "We need to find her to make sure her treatment is continuing."

"I don't know . . . ," Tamsin muttered, stalling for time as Julia and I stood outside her front door.

"Have you spoken to him recently?"

"Yeah, but I didn't know his mum was ill. He just said he took her on a trip."

"Well, she's not really supposed to travel. He really should have spoken to us first."

"We just want to make sure she's all right," Julia said, offering sympathy. It was all about bedside manner.

"How did you find me anyway?" Tamsin asked.

"Sacha listed you as an emergency contact," I lied. "Have you heard from him recently?"

"N-no," Tamsin stammered. "He just said he was going on a trip with his mum."

"Did he say how long they'd be gone?"

"I don't know, a week, maybe two?" She was making up her answers as she went along.

"Tamsin," Julia said. "You're not in any trouble. We're just concerned about Sacha's mum, that's all."

"Did anyone else contact you asking about her?" I asked.

"Yes," she said, suddenly more confident. "Dodgy-looking bloke. Said he was a private investigator."

Julia and I exchanged a look.

"Did he say why he was looking for her?" Julia asked.

"Said something about her being owed money and he needed to find her as soon possible."

"Did he leave you a card?" I asked.

She went back inside and brought back a slightly crumpled card that read "Richard Boyd Investigations."

Looked like a small firm compared to ours. He must have been hired by the Harkingdales. He probably did a cursory Internet search for Sacha's social media accounts like we did and found Tamsin. There was a slightly beat-up Ford Fiesta parked across the street and two doors up that looked a bit out of place in this neighborhood.

"Tamsin," I said. "Are you all right? Have you felt like you were being watched or followed since this guy knocked on your door?"

"N-no," she lied. Poor girl.

Boyd must have been watching her, following her to and from school, hoping she might lead him to Sacha. Old-fashioned footwork. It's what we were considering doing. Question was, how far was he willing to go? Would he intimidate her? I didn't like that idea.

"Don't worry," Julia said. "We're caseworkers. We can sort this out for you."

We left Tamsin and walked back to our car. I glanced at the Ford Fiesta and the slightly puffy sod sitting in it, pretending not to watch us. He was actually scribbling into a notebook.

I got on my phone and called in. We told Roger and Cheryl about the man in the car.

"Hang on," Ken asked over the office speakerphone. "Did you say 'Boyd'?"

"As in Dickie Boyd?" Clive chimed in.

"You know him?"

"Oh, we know him," Ken said with a chuckle. "Leave him to us."

TEN

"ickie! Me old china! Awright?" Clive bellowed, a bit too friendly.

"Ken . . . Clive . . . long time no see," Dickie Boyd stammered.

Julia and I were back in the office by then. We were watching on our computers alongside Mark, Olivia, Marcie, Benjamin, and David. Roger and Cheryl were content to do their own thing at their desks.

Ken and Clive sidled up behind Boyd's car as he kept watch on Tamsin's parents' house, all in hopes that she might lead him to Sacha. Sloppy of him that he didn't even notice Ken and Clive coming up until they were right next to him. We were trained to spot danger better than that. We could see the terror on Boyd's face, a perfectly understandable instinctive reaction to being approached by big bastards like Ken and Clive. This was the fundamental lizard brain kicking in from back when our ancestors had to worry about being eaten by big fucking predators. Good to know Boyd was at least normal in that respect. I immediately felt sorry for him, as I would for anybody Ken and Clive went after.

Roger had taken to equipping Ken and Clive with lapel cameras whenever they went out on a case now, to document events for evidence. Benjamin was more than happy to fit them. I suspect even Roger wanted to make sure that if Ken and Clive kicked off on someone, he had the facts straight so as to sort out any legal ramifications. Ken and Clive were surprisingly compliant about it. In fact, they seemed to relish it, as if it was a chance to show off, to show they could play well with others.

I wondered what they were going to do here.

"Are they going to drag Boyd out of his car and kick the living shit out of him?" I asked.

"Of course not," Cheryl said. "That's a cliché out of private eye novels. What would be the point of that? It would only tell Boyd he was onto something."

"Why make new enemies when you can make new friends?" Roger said, cheerily.

Before we knew it, Ken and Clive had brought the justifiably nervous Boyd back to Golden Sentinels and into the comfy seat in Roger's office. I was very glad the video hadn't turned into a snuff film. Cheryl was even offering him tea and biscuits, the latter of which he palmed and put in his pocket for later.

"Richard." Roger put on the charm. "May I call you Richard? We're all friends here."

"We are?" Boyd whined. I realized then that the nasal quality of his voice was permanent.

"Ken and Clive told me a lot about you," Roger continued. "All the way back in the days in the Met."

Turned out Boyd was another ex-copper from Ken and Clive's days. Worked Vice but developed a cocaine addiction and was caught sampling the wares out of evidence. Turfed out on his ear, lucky not to be sent to prison, and with his pension withdrawn. Sacked in disgrace. Scraping by as a PI.

"So what's this about?" Boyd asked. "When I saw Ken and Clive comin' up to me, I thought I was a goner for sure. Unmarked pit in the middle of Epping Forest for me. No one'll miss me. Not the ex-wife, not the kid. Not even my pub landlord."

"Perish the thought! Ken and Clive's reputation for drastic population control is strictly the stuff of rumor!" Roger said.

"Could have fooled me, the stories I heard back in the force," Boyd muttered.

"They tell me you do good work as a PI," Roger said. "Small firm. Strictly solo, trying to make ends meet. Must be hard, the alimony payments, the bookies you owe."

"You seem to know a lot about me, Mr. Golden."

"Like I said, I've been watching you with great interest."

(More like a five-minute summary of his life and career from Ken and Clive before they drove out to get him.)

"Yeah? Give us a job here at your fancy firm, then," Boyd ventured, glimmer of hope in his eyes. "That'd be a good leg-up."

"I'm afraid my quota's filled here, old son," Roger said.

Boyd's shoulders sagged.

"However, I do need an outside contractor from time to time when my people are all booked up, and I could use an old-school geezer like you for some old-fashioned footwork."

"Well, Mr. Golden, that's very generous of you," wheezed Boyd. "Whatever you need, I'm your man. Yeah."

We could see the qualities in Boyd that would make Roger not put him on staff. The neediness, the desperation, the lack of finesse and politesse, as Roger liked to tell us when he wanted to flatter us.

"So, Richard old son," Roger pushed. "Tell us about your current case."

"Oh, I dunno, Mr. Golden. I dunno—client privilege and all that, you know?" Roger, fully prepared, handed a small envelope to Boyd.

"Client confidentiality! Of course! But you're one of us now, Richard. And we keep each other abreast of our caseloads so we can back each other up if need be. Consider this your first retainer."

Boyd opened the envelope. His eyes lit up at the five hundred quid in crisp £50 notes. This indicated to us that whoever had hired him to track down Sacha and Irina, they were paying him fucking peanuts. Poor sod. Of course, we were under no illusion that he would hesitate to sell us out if a better offer came along. But for now, Roger was the best offer he had.

"Classic missing persons case, innit?" Boyd said. "Find this kid and his mum. Summink about the readin' of his dad's will wot they need to get on with. Probably a lot of dosh involved."

"So who hired you?" Roger asked. "The lawyers?"

"Nah, the other family, innit? The second wife, Cecily Harkingdale and her dad, Sir Tobias Harkingdale. Right bunch of toffs that family, like their shit don't stink. Even haggled down my usual rate."

"Disgraceful." Cheryl shook her head in sympathy.

I was in awe watching Roger and Cheryl work as a team to charm, cajole, manipulate, bribe their way into the heart of a mark. I saw right there their shared history as scrappy PIs back in the day before there had been smartphones and the Internet, when Roger was less polished and Cheryl was a violent punk in leather; that shared dynamic was still there, even though they'd both cleaned up and learned to look respectable in the intervening decades.

"Did they approach you directly?" Cheryl asked.

"Yeah, yeah, they did."

"Not through any intermediary? Not through their solicitor?" Roger raised an eyebrow.

"Nah," Boyd said. "Cecily contacted me herself. Said I came highly recommended. Maybe their solicitor told 'em about me. Odd, that. She phoned, invited me out to their fancy gaff in Lancaster Gate, had the help show me in. It was as if they wanted to show off to me, make sure I knew my place."

"And how does that smell to you, my old son?" Roger said.

"Like a pile of pants. Keepin' me isolated, got me thinkin' they might set me up to take the fall for summink dodgy later on."

"Your instincts are probably spot-on," Cheryl said. "We have reason to believe the Harkingdales did in Lev Mayakovsky for his inheritance."

"Stone me!" Boyd cried. "You reckon they aim to snuff the kid and first wife as well?"

"Great minds think alike, Richard," Roger said.

From her desk, Olivia, who never looked up from her computer, stifled a giggle. She heard every word. She did enjoy her godfather Roger in action. I'm sure he'd taught her a thing or two growing up.

"So if I find them, they might do 'em in and pin it on me!" Boyd started to hyperventilate. "Wankers!"

"Here's where us lowly plebs have to stick together, eh, Richard?" Roger said. "We back each other up."

"Yeah, yeah, right you are, Mr. Golden—"

"Roger. Please, friends call me Roger."

"Right. Roger."

"Could you tell us what the Harkingdales are like?" Cheryl asked. "How that family fits together?"

"They're tight, they are," Boyd said. "Very cagey. There's Cecily, Sir Tobias, her father. Charles, her brother. They seem to speak in a kind of code or shorthand among themselves. Probably all kinds of secrets between 'em. Sir Tobias is a heavy drinker, even more than me. With him it's brandy. Charles was a gambler and speculator, always losin' money in bad stocks that I could never understand. Has a shrew of a wife with expensive tastes. Feels like Sir Tobias calls the shots in that family. They were gaggin' for me to find Mayakovsky's kid and first wife so the will can be read and the estate can be divvied up right and proper. No love lost between them and the first wife, I can tell ya."

"Here's what I propose," Roger said. "You continue to tell the Harkingdales you're looking and collect your daily rate from them. Leave the rest to us. Meanwhile, you keep an ear on the Harkingdales and tell us if they start acting strangely, if they start losing patience, if they get more nervous than usual."

"All right. Sounds like a plan."

"And not a word to them that we're in cahoots, eh?"

"Too right, Mr. Golden—Roger."

"Good man!" Roger clapped Boyd on the back as he walked him out.

"Epping Forest," Ken snorted. "As if we'd pick a place that fucking obvious for a dump site."

"Shows how much he knows," Clive sniffed. "Twat."

"Well played, boss." Mark slow-clapped once Boyd was out the door.

The gods clapped with him. It disturbed me how much in synch Mark was with the gods. I wished they would appear to him instead of me. At least he would really appreciate it. They would get on like a house on fire and leave me alone, but that was not to be.

"Right, my dears." Cheryl turned to us. "We just cleared the way for you. Time's a-ticking. Chop-chop."

ELEVEN

With Boyd out of the way, we could concentrate on our own efforts.

Tobias Harkingdale, Cecily Harkingdale, Charles Harkingdale—the whole lot of them. And their spouses and kids were complicit. This was a family for whom murder was a tipple, a few drops of tincture into a cup of tea or a glass of brandy, a casual chore. To hire a hit man was to enter a different league altogether, and they were probably ill-prepared for that. This suited our plans.

I could sense the air in the room get heavier. Ken and Clive. They were sitting stock-still, but the rage was radiating right off their bodies. I suppose this was what the Japanese called "killing intent" that combatants and martial artists sensed in an opponent ready to attack.

"What?" Clive asked, after my stare.

"You're not thinking about kicking off, are you?" I asked.

"Dunno what you mean," Ken said.

"The Harkingdales. Whole family of upper-class twats who might have got away with murder?" I said. "Just the types that get on your tits."

"What do you take us for? Couple of loose fucking cannons?" Clive said, rolling his eyes. "Do us a favor!"

"'Ere," Ken said. "You Hindus got a god that's all about vengeance?"

"Rudra," I said. "God of rage and storms. And righteous revenge."

"I like the sound of that," Clive said.

"Oh, believe me," I said. "He likes you."

Sure enough, Rudra stood behind Ken and Clive at their desks, grinning madly, nodding in approval at them, our office Rakshasas.

Ken and Clive smiled, satisfied, and went back to reading their tabloids.

"Sacha's talking a lot about how to keep a dementia patient lucid with ginkgo biloba," Mark said, reading the forums. "He's also doing research about breaking down the plaques that cause Alzheimer's. I think he's trying to synthesize something himself."

"That's ambitious," Olivia said. "But he's so typically careless for a clever nineteen-year-old. He hasn't masked his digital footsteps as much as he thinks he should have. He hasn't used a VPN to post on that forum. I can trace the IP address. Gotcha, you silly boy."

God, she was competitive.

I blinked. An ethereal Chinese woman, serene and elegant in a white shawl, stood patiently behind Olivia, watching over her shoulder as she typed. I knew who that was. Quan Yin, the goddess of mercy. I'd seen Olivia quietly pray to her from her desk from time to time.

"I'm in a discussion with him now about how protein is needed for the brain to retrieve memories," Mark said. "He's wondering if it's possible to synthesize specific proteins for dementia patients to help them remember things. I've been asking if he tried any combinations of psychoactive compounds."

"Mark, do you actually know biochemistry?" I asked.

"I dabble in my spare time," he said. "It's not just about getting high for me, you know. He's starting to get pretty hardcore, talking about gene-editing with CRISPR."

"You mean gene-splicing and gene therapy? For Alzheimer's?"

"It's the future of dementia treatment, Ravi."

"Surely he doesn't have access to actual gene-editing tools?"

"I seriously doubt it," Olivia said. "Look, he says he wishes he could run some kind of simulation software on his computer."

"All right. So is he actually conducting experiments?" I asked.

"Says he's mostly doing theoretical formulating," Mark said. "No opportunity to do it for real."

"And he's doing all this while in hiding," I said. "How's he feeding himself and his mum?"

"Easy," Mark said. "He's selling nootropics to his classmates. Smart drugs. Basic memory and cognition-enhancing supplements that aren't technically illegal. His own mixes. For the ones who need to be up all hours studying for their exams, writing papers, and whatnot. I gave him a few tips on dosages and combinations."

"Sounds like you should go into business with him, Mark," Benjamin said, barely looking up from printing out a new drone on the new 3-D printer he'd convinced Roger and Cheryl to let him buy. Benjamin was all about DIY, and what better prospect than untraceable surveillance drones that weren't purchased from known manufacturers?

"Tempting," Mark said with a wistful smile.

"Wouldn't he need a lab to do the combining?"

"Oo-er," Mark said. "So you're asking where he would find a lab to do that stuff in?"

"He must be sneaking into the lab at uni," I said.

"His big obsession is getting ahold of CRISPR tech to do some real gene-splicing," Mark said.

"I can do him something close," Olivia said. "A computer software simulation program that runs gene-editing and synthesizing models."

"Isn't that program extremely expensive?" I asked. "Only available to institutions?"

"Please!" Olivia rolled her eyes. "I have my ways. Someone's always going to leak it online."

I thought for a moment.

"Right, here's our play," I said. "Mark, send a private message to Sacha offering him a copy of this program on a drive, arrange to meet to talk about smart drugs and gene-splicing. Meet him someplace like a pub near uni so it's public and he can feel safe, but we can control the exit points so he can't do a runner easily."

"Oh, he'll well be up for that program."

TWELVE

As Mark took his correspondence with Sacha to Direct Message, Benjamin turned to me.

"'Ere, Ravi," he said. "You might want to check on your folks."

I logged onto the server to review the surveillance footage Benjamin had installed in my parents' living room and Mrs. Dhewan's food bank.

"You know," Benjamin said. "I would bet the food bank is a money-laundering front."

"I assumed as much," I said. "I don't think she does anything from just the kindness of her heart. She's probably getting some kind of kickback from the shops and warehouses that are supplying her, or it's a way to off-load stolen gear."

I clicked on the various feeds to make sure it was all kosher. Benjamin had told only Mrs. Dhewan he was installing cameras and where they were, just in case any of her own people were the ones nicking the supplies. She wanted to have whoever it was bang to rights.

"What the fuck?"

I fast-forwarded through hours of footage of my father sitting on the sofa in his living room, keeping guard over the boxes from the food bank, his trusty cricket bat in his hand.

Why wasn't he in bed with my mum?

I checked the feed to my parents' bedroom and found my mother sound asleep during the night. She tossed and turned in bed and occasionally got up to go to the loo. I clicked to the live feeds. It was late afternoon and my mum was back working the counter at the food bank, and my dad was sitting in the living room watching daytime telly, still with his cricket bat on his lap.

I called him on my smartphone.

"Dad, why are sitting around with your cricket bat?"

"Your mother has turned me into a nervous wreck! I must stand guard lest some ruffians break in."

"Did she say they would break in?"

"No, but since all these goods are here, it would stand to reason!"

"So let them take it. Why put yourself at risk?"

"It's a point of principle! I will not let my house be invaded by a bunch of have-a-go Henrys!"

"Dad, you look ridiculous."

"What you do you mean?"

"I'm looking at you right now."

Dad froze. He looked around, paranoid.

"Did the gods put you up to this?"

I winced. Lord Vishnu was standing over me, watching the screen.

"Dad, I told you Benjamin was going to install these cameras to keep you two safe."

"My life has come to this! Presiding over stolen goods and put under surveillance by my own son!"

"Dad, will you please talk to Mum and sort out whatever this tension is between the two of you?"

"If only it was that simple," he muttered.

"I can get you some pamphlets from the GP about intercourse after prostate cancer surgery."

"I don't need you to do that for me."

"Then what is the problem?"

"You know your mother is highly strung and demanding at the best of times. She's gotten even worse in the last few months."

"Isn't it because she's been getting, well, frustrated?"

"Well, you getting her in with that Dhewan woman again hasn't helped. It's made it worse!"

"Look, Dad, do you need to see the doctor about your situation? You're in full recovery. Normal sexual function should be back by now, or on its way back. It's all right if you're anxious and can't perform, and even if you don't have a prostate anymore, you can still experience orgasm. It might feel different—"

"Ravi, stop. You have your father under surveillance and you're trying to teach him how to orgasm."

Oh my God. This is what my life has come to.

Behind me, Vishnu and Shiva were laughing their arses off and gave each other a high-five.

I stammered some excuse and hung up.

Everyone in the office was staring at me with a mix of pity and bemusement.

"I set up a meeting," Mark said.

"Thank fuck," I said.

Anything to get me away from thinking about my dad's sex life.

THIRTEEN

One of Mark's talents, aside from his massive intellect hidden under a stoner façade, was his sincerity. He was genuinely interested in the types of research and experiments Sacha Mayakovsky was doing in nootropics and cognition drugs, so he wasn't lying when he said he wanted to meet so he could give Sacha a copy of the software. Mark made social engineering look easy.

Sacha had picked a café in Central London, not far from Tottenham Court Road station. Mid-afternoon. Crowded. If anything went awry, he would have plenty of options to do a runner—onto a bus, into the Tube, even vanish into the crowd in Oxford Street. He had clearly picked this with some care, displaying a basic grasp of tradecraft. Had his father taught him some basics of setting up meetings and avoiding tails? It wouldn't have surprised me if that were the case.

But we outnumbered him, and we were organized. Even with Olivia sitting this out back at the office dealing with her own case involving Hong Kong, and Marcie sitting this out because she was off talking to her friends at the US Embassy, we still had it covered. Only Mark was in the café waiting for Sacha. Ken and Clive were close by, within sight, but out of sight of anyone coming to the café, and even did a reconnaissance of the surroundings ahead of the meeting time. Benjamin had gone into the café an hour ahead of the meeting under the guise of buying an espresso and planted an insect-sized drone near the counter. He then retreated to the car around the corner and flew the drone above the heads of all the customers to record footage of Sacha when he came in. And just to be safe, Mark was wearing one of Benjamin's pin-sized cameras on his jacket.

Julia and I were in the electronics shop across the street, posing as a couple shopping for computer parts. The latter was actually legit— Benjamin had given us a list of accessories and parts he wanted for stuff he was putting together back at the office. We were in touch with Mark through our Bluetooth earpieces.

Trust Benjamin to find ways to milk side benefits out of an op.

"Pragmatism," he had said cheerfully, totally shameless. "Kill two birds with one stone. Besides, Cheryl already approved those parts for my gadgets budget."

We watched Sacha Mayakovsky walk into the café, approach Mark at his table, and shake his hand. Then they started talking. We heard them get well into it, jumping right into chemical compositions and cognitive enhancement, using terms and names that were way beyond the rest of us. This must be what it was like when two people with high IQs got together. The rest of the world was simply shut out. Sacha's London accent still had traces of Russian from the first ten years of his childhood. He also had the sad, soulful eyes of a lad who had seen some things while he was still too young, the types of eyes that broke girls' hearts.

"He's very Russian," Julia said, observing him.

He also had a bit of a black eye.

"What happened to you?" Mark asked.

"Got into a fight on the street last night," Sacha said. "Couple of blokes heard me speak Russian on the phone and thought I was Polish."

"I'm sorry you had to grow up here and experience British xenophobia," Mark said. "British racists don't just hate people with different-colored skin, but even white-skinned people who aren't English. Some of them are still racist towards the Irish and the Scots."

"And my father told me this was the most civilized country in the world," Sacha said.

"When we want to be, yes," Mark said. "But the British have always had the tendency to blame the Other for their woes. Poles and Eastern

Europeans just got on their radar recently because they were doing menial jobs like building work."

"In the end, my father's romanticism for England got him killed," Sacha said bitterly.

I had a decision to make now. We had set up a series of options. Ken and Clive could try to grab Sacha when he left the café. We could let Sacha go back to wherever he was hiding. The thumb drive Mark gave him contained not only the CRISPR simulation program but also a rootkit that would surreptitiously install itself on his computer and take it over, a nasty, insidious little present Olivia wrote. It would give us the option to track his computer by GPS, and we could just find him when he was next online.

Julia read my cue. We crossed the road hand in hand, shopping bags in our free hands, entered the café, ordered cappuccinos, and went over to sit at the table next to Mark and Sacha's. Sacha hadn't cast his eyes on us, which meant he was not used to tradecraft or watching out for surveillance. As Olivia said, he was still an amateur.

Julia and I looked at each other like a couple in love, which wasn't acting.

Then I turned to their table and smiled.

"Hello, Sacha," I said. "Don't run. We're on your side."

FOURTEEN

Of course Sacha was hiding his mother with his classmates in their flatshare not far from the university in Central London. The Harkingdales wouldn't have thought to find them there. Boyd might have cottoned onto this, given enough time. The flatmates didn't seem to bat much of an eyelash at having a Russian woman in her fifties with early onset Alzheimer's living in their midst. I would have thought it massively disruptive and stressful to their routines, but apart from her sitting around muttering to herself in Russian all day, they seemed used to having her around. I suppose Sacha had explained the stakes to them, that she and he were in danger, and they had risen to the occasion. They weren't wasters or layabouts. They were earnest students pursuing their degrees and worrying about their student loan debts. They reminded me of some of my secondary school students, the ones who would get their act together and go to university.

Irina was sitting quietly in the living room staring at the telly when Sacha showed us in. The flat was slightly messy, as student flats tended to be. Irina had been helping herself to the cigarettes the flatmates left around the place, and the ashtray was a blooming tree of spent fag ends.

Sacha kissed her on the cheek and she smiled greeting him, then said she was waiting for her son to come home.

"She thinks she's at the dacha in Crimea where her family took her on holidays when she was young," he said.

This was what it was like to have a parent with dementia: you lost them piece by piece, in slow motion, every day, until in the end there was almost nothing of them left.

"I'm trying to at least stabilize her with my formulas," Sacha said, "keep her calm, but it's difficult with her moods. That's normal for her condition."

This wouldn't do. I put in a call to Cheryl, who got Roger to sign off on putting Sacha and his mother up at one of the firm's safe houses in Pimlico, and we hired a twenty-four-hour nurse with experience caring for Alzheimer's patients. This was an extra expense, but Roger was gambling on getting into Sacha's good graces, since it was now quite likely that he was going to inherit a proper chunk of his father's fortune. Roger, ever resourceful, even managed to find a nurse who spoke Russian. Julia helped Irina get dressed while Ken and Clive helped Sacha pack their things. By the end of the afternoon, it would be as if Sacha and Irina had never been in this flat.

Once we got them settled in at the safe house, it was time to ask Sacha what was really going on.

"My mother was diagnosed with Alzheimer's almost a year ago," he said. "I told my father and he began visiting my mother every week. Maybe there was still some love there or he felt guilty. He promised me that he would take care of my mother. We knew this was a death sentence even if it could take years. Then six months before he died, he was different, depressed, like he was under a strain. He said he believed he was going to die soon. I thought he was ill, but he said no, it was the family."

"The Harkingdales," I offered.

"He had suspicions and confirmed them himself," Sacha said and nodded. "They have a history of marrying their daughters to rich men and then poisoning them to take their fortune."

I glanced at Julia, who closed her eyes for a second. No satisfaction at being right, only a sense of grim confirmation about the nastier side of humanity.

"My father told us he was changing his will to leave everything to my mother and me," said Sacha. "He wanted to make arrangements for bodyguards, security, but we refused. My mother wasn't in the present.

She still thought they were married. We couldn't just put her in a hospital or a home. The Harkingdales would have had a way to get to her. Father was too preoccupied with staying alive. Then he ran out of time before we could finalize a plan. When I heard he died, I took my mother and left our flat to go dark."

I looked at Ken and Clive, saw a mix of relief that Sacha was innocent and mild annoyance that he hadn't turned out to be the villain they had initially suspected.

Lord Vishnu sat by the bar counter and nodded his approval at the way this story was playing out. He was presiding over revelations, the outing of truth that brings in light. I was almost moved by the tenderness in his eyes as he looked at Sacha and lay a fatherly, godly hand on his shoulder, a touch Sacha didn't feel.

"Not to worry, Sacha," I said. "We'll keep you both safe here, and when you show up for the reading of the will, the Harkingdales will have lost."

Sacha was brooding.

"My mother put up with my angry bullshit and she was always there for me, even though she was alone with her own pain. It broke my heart when my father divorced her and sent me to boarding school."

"So what will you do now?"

"I want to look after her for the rest of her life. I want to start a company that manufactures legal, legitimate drugs that can prevent or even treat dementia and Alzheimer's. Drugs for the memory."

"Good on you, mate."

"What rankles me, what disgusts me, is those fucking Harkingdales. They killed my father to get at his money and estate, now they want to kill my mother and me for it. And they won't be arrested. They won't pay."

"Do you have a pound?" I asked.

"Yes. Why?"

"Give me a pound."

He fished a coin out of his pocket and handed it to me.

"All right, Sacha, you've just hired me. My colleagues and I are already committed to keeping your stepmother safe, but I have the extra job of making sure the Harkingdales get some form of comeuppance for what they've done and what they'll try to do to her."

He looked at me, full of questions.

"We're not hit men, Sacha. But there are things they fear more than death or prison. This is not just my promise now. It's my job."

FIFTEEN

Julia was smiling at me when we left the safe house.

"What is it?"

"I love it when you're righteous," she said. "It means things are about to get interesting."

"I suppose Sacha reminded me of one of my troubled students from back when I was teaching secondary school."

"Whatever wheeze you got in mind," Ken said, "we're in."

"It will be our personal pleasure to kick off on those upper-class fuckers," Clive said.

When we got back to the office, Boyd was waiting.

"He's awfully needy, that one," Cheryl said. "I'd hate to have been married to him."

"I told him you were running point," Roger said. "So he should talk to you."

I could almost smell the booze on his breath along with the overwhelming stress and anxiety. Honestly, how did he survive being a private eye? He could drop dead from a heart attack just from staking out a cheating spouse's hotel.

I introduced myself in the most reassuring manner imaginable, the way I usually spoke to clients to cajole them into some semblance of calm.

"The Harkingdales are starting to pressure me for a result," Boyd said. "They said I should get more people to do the search."

"Show them these photos," I said.

"Stone me! You found 'em already? That was bloody quick!"

We had photographed Sacha and his mum a few streets outside the safe house after I explained to Sacha what we were planning to do. I promised I would keep him and Irina safe, that we would control the narrative.

"Tell them you will need extra manpower to do some additional surveillance. And ask for more money to pay the people you'll need," I said.

Boyd looked uncertain, started to stammer something.

"And keep the extra dosh," Roger said. "After all, it's your job."

Boyd seemed relieved.

"Oh, cheers, Ravi."

I waited till Boyd was gone before I spoke.

"Let's assume the Harkingdales will want to bump Sacha and Irina off before they get to the reading of the will."

"Are you thinking of a wheeze, Ravi?"

"I'm thinking of a wheeze, Mark."

A wheeze was what Marcie liked to call an "op," what Ken and Clive would consider a sting, a social engineering campaign that the whole team set up, planned carefully with little margin for error. A wheeze was an op where we controlled the whole environment, the narrative. It came not from assumptions, but educated guesses based on researching the subjects and knowing how they would react, so that they did what we wanted them to do and we got our result.

We set about researching the Harkingdales. Julia, Mark, and Marcie took it upon themselves to suss out how they thought. The Harkingdales followed the direction of Tobias, the patriarch. They were all about keeping the family name going by any means possible and at the cost of anyone and everyone else. Their main MO was poisoning, and they could only do that if the victim was in their household. At the moment, Sacha and Irina were out of their grasp. That couldn't last forever, though. We had to do something to break the stalemate, and that would be when Sacha and Irina emerged from hiding. When that happened, we had to control the circumstances, especially with Irina in a state that could be legally defined as mentally incompetent. I also wanted to keep my promise to Sacha and use that opportunity to trap the Harkingdales.

"Fancy creating a website?" I asked Olivia.

"If I must," she said, shrugging. This was not even going to be a challenge for her. Indeed, I wondered what could *ever* constitute a challenge for her.

SIXTEEN

I really don't know what to say, Ravi," Mrs. Dhewan said.

"Auntie, this is well out of order," I said, trying not to shout.

Oh shit, Kali was there with us, wagging her tongue at the aftermath of the evening. I wondered if she'd anticipated the chaos, but caught myself: she was inside my head. She was a projection of my anxieties. How could I have known what would happen when I left my parents to their own devices?

"I never thought your father had it in him."

"Well, Dad can be a very passionate man," I said. "Especially when his ire is up."

"Indeed," she said.

We were in Mrs. Dhewan's living room, watching the surveillance footage on her laptop. My mother was closing up the food bank for the evening and my father had arrived to pick her up. The men in the balaclavas burst in the door before my mother could lock it, and before they could even menace my mother, Dad went completely batshit with his cricket bat. He was like a mad dervish as he swung the bat at the would-be thieves, connecting with their arms and torsos, doubling them over in pain.

"He's quite the hellion," Mrs. Dhewan said.

"My parents were not supposed to get mixed up in this kind of thing."

"I apologize, Ravi. I've had my boys remove all the boxes from your house by now. Having civilians like your parents involved in my business only makes everything more complicated."

"I told my dad he should have let them steal a couple of boxes. You can track them by the RFID chips Benjamin tagged them with."

"That's why I'm putting the boxes back in the storeroom of the food bank. Better location for the bait."

"Well, please keep them out of this," I said. "I'm going to tell my mum she doesn't need to come back to work at the shop."

I left and went back to my parents' house. My sister and Vivek were just coming out.

"How are they?" I asked.

"They're . . . all right," Vivek said.

"Why the pause?"

"They're more than all right," Sanjita said. "They said you don't need to drop in."

"Why? What's going on?"

"It seems Dad becoming all manly and heroic was the cure for their dry spell," Sanjita said. "A reaffirmation of his masculine identity, as it were."

"They've retired to the bedroom for the night," Vivek said.

"Do you mean—?" I couldn't finish the sentence.

"They're off happily bonking and don't need you to interrupt, Ravi," Sanji said.

I winced.

"Too much information, Sanji."

"It's brilliant!" Sanjita said. "It gets them off our backs at last! Now they won't be harping on about us giving them grandkids."

"And we can at least bonk in peace ourselves." Vivek beamed.

"Again, too much information," I said.

"All's well that ends well," Sanji said. "You might as well go on home. Isn't Julia waiting for you?"

I got back to my flat and told Julia what had happened. She laughed and laughed.

"This has the makings of another cosmic joke," Julia said.

"I've been on the receiving end of way too many of those."

"It's almost as if you planned it," Julia said.

"What? I would never send a bunch of thugs after my parents to jog their sex lives. There's no way I could have predicted Dad would become Rambo with a cricket bat."

"I'm just joking," Julia said. "You're wound up too tight, with the weight of the world on your shoulders, as usual."

"I could certainly use some relief."

"Well, seeing as everyone's having a celebratory shag tonight, it'd be churlish for us not to go along with it."

"Not sure I'm in the mood," I said.

"Why don't you lie back and let me help?"

It took a bit of doing on her part, but Julia finally took my mind off my parents. Sex when she was happy brought a kind of joy that almost made me believe in heaven.

And the gods left us alone.

SEVENTEEN

The next day, Boyd came into the office, sweaty and hyperventilating. Was he having a panic attack? Cheryl waved him towards Roger's office, and he barreled right in.

"You watch," Cheryl said. "He now thinks Roger is his rabbi. Or his confessor."

"Or his psychiatrist," Marcie said.

"Roger's silver tongue does have that effect on people," Olivia said.

We pretended not to watch while Boyd ranted and gesticulated wildly before Roger put an assuring hand on his shoulder and led him out to us.

"Tell everyone what you just told me," Roger said.

"Showed 'em the photos of Sacha and Irina Mayakovsky you gave me," Boyd said. "They were bloody chuffed, and not in a good way."

"You didn't tell them where Irina and Sacha were, did you?" I asked.

"I told them that my 'people' found 'em in London, no specifics just to keep 'em on the hook, yeah?" Boyd said. "Just like you said. I said 'we' were watchin' the place, and I could find out the phone number where they could just contact the kid and his mum directly. They said no need. They wanted me to go in and bump them off. They came out and fucking said it! 'We need them disposed of,' the buggers said, like they were asking me to take some rubbish out to the recycling bin on my way out!"

Boyd took a stiff drink, one Roger had poured for him, if a bit reluctantly. Boyd's hand shook.

"Said they wanted the kid and widow to be 'looked after properly.' "

"Well, we know what their idea of 'looking after' is like," Cheryl said.

"Do private investigators often get hired to bump people off?" I couldn't help asking.

Ken and Clive looked at me like I was stupid, then shrugged.

"If I wanted to be a bloody hit man, I'd have done it," Boyd cried. "You gotta draw the line somewhere. And I'm not a fucking psychopath."

"The sheer cheek of it." Roger sagely shook his head sympathetically at Boyd.

"Sounds like a psychopath is what the Harkingdales are desperately looking for," Cheryl said.

"So what did you tell them?" I asked.

"We told you this could happen," Roger said to Boyd.

"Fuck me," Boyd said. "They want to stick me well in it, don't they?"

"Did you turn them down?" I asked.

"I said they needed to think about this very seriously, that it was a criminal act, a big decision, and one there was no coming back from," Boyd said, voice quivering. "And I said it would cost 'em extra."

"Good man." Roger smiled. "You can keep that cash if they bite."

"Well, I said it wasn't really my field of expertise, and it might require a professional, someone we could trust. They asked me for a recommendation. I said I would make some inquiries. Fucking hell! This is all incriminating shit, and I'll be the one taking the fall, won't I?"

"Now now, Dickie," Roger said. "We have your back on this. Tell him, Ravi."

"Go back to the Harkingdales," I said. "Tell them it's best for you and them to put several layers separating you all from the act. That means you lot can't be seen to be anywhere near this. Then tell them about this website."

I handed him a piece of paper with a URL jotted on it, and how it could only be accessed through a Tor-style proxy server, which had really been set up by Olivia.

"What's this?"

"Something that removes all responsibility from you," I said. "Tell

them you want a commission for finding them the website and walk
away."

"I want to see what this is," Boyd said. "Ignorance won't save me if I
get hauled in for an interview."

Olivia handed Boyd a laptop and he linked to the site.

"Stone me!" Boyd cried. "This is some frightening shit!"

"That's the Dark Web for you," I said.

"I heard about sites like this, never wanted any part in 'em!"

"For them it's just business," Olivia said.

I then remembered we had all neglected to tell Boyd that this was a
completely fictitious site that Olivia had whipped up at my request. Mark
and Benjamin had written all the posts for contract killing services, and
took the darkest recesses of their imaginations for a walk as one would
the family dog.

Poor Boyd was shitting bricks at each advert he read from prospective
contract killers.

"*Disappearances guaranteed. Untraceable body disposals." "Defene-
strations a specialty." "Dismemberment fees extra." "The best use of
chemicals to dissolve a body." "Best deaths by drone—fees and payments
structure." "Arson specialist." "Top Beheading Experts—Special Rates.*"

Mark, Marcie, and Benjamin probably had too much fun writing those
entries, especially the descriptions. Between the three of them, a few tens
of thousands of words' worth of prose was on that site going into intimate,
technical detail about the various methods for murdering and disposing of
bodies, comparing the merits of leaving a corpse behind to be discovered
with disappearing someone altogether, and what kind of message each
act sends, which was also why there were different pay rates for every act
of murder, dismemberment, burial, chemical dissolution, burning, and
even mummification. It was indeed dark shit. I did not want to find out
how they knew all this stuff.

"This is ordering a murder as if you order a pizza!" Boyd cried.

Boyd was almost dry-heaving by the time he read the tenth entry. I
had to put the poor bastard out of his misery and tell him the site wasn't
real.

"The point is for the Harkingdales to hire Ken and Clive. It'll be Ken and Clive no matter who they pick. Then we get them bang to rights," I said.

"Hang on, that's entrapment!" Boyd said.

"We're not coppers anymore, Dickie," Ken said.

"And we won't get done for this," Clive added. "None of us."

"How do you reckon?" Boyd asked, still unconvinced.

"If they find out this is fraudulent," David said, stepping forward, "they're not likely to report you, are they? You would have been defrauding them for trying to arrange a murder for hire. We're in a territory where the police are not even part of the equation. It'll be the Prisoner's Dilemma. You'd only incriminate each other."

"And if you get picked up by Old Bill," Roger said. "David will have your back as your legal counsel."

"Quite," David said, wincing.

"Just stick to this plan and you'll be off the hook," Roger said to Boyd, the smile never leaving his face. "And remember, you keep the money you charge them for yourself. It's only fair."

"Still blood money, innit?" Boyd muttered.

"It's not blood money if you don't spill any blood for it," Roger said cheerfully. Roger and his moral calculations. The gods whistled in admiration. Vishnu was impressed.

Ken and Clive had to take Boyd down the pub for some stiff drinks afterwards, because Roger didn't want him burning through the expensive booze in his office.

Bagalamukhi was sashaying by our desks, smiling, stroking everyone's shoulder affectionately as she passed us, offering her blessing at this epic deception we were concocting. Lord Shiva, destroyer of worlds, was sitting in Roger's chair, laughing as he texted the other gods on his phone. I should have felt a lot more uneasy, but I thought I was in control of the situation. That was my hubris.

Kali was wagging her tongue and rubbing her hands, anticipating the delicious chaos I was about to unleash.

EIGHTEEN

Sure enough, the Harkingdales took our bait. Boyd phoned and told Cheryl that they'd accepted the Web address and paid him the finder's fee, and with that, he was out.

Since Olivia had set up the site on our server, we could see when they logged on and could track their IP address. If Boyd had done his job and only the Harkingdales knew about the site, they would be the only ones to log on to it. We could see when they created a username and password to register membership and gain access. We could even watch them browse the site in real time, looking over the different types of contract killings and rates on offer. They browsed the forum with the fake posts by clients discussing jobs for hire and how satisfied they were and how secure they felt in using the site, all written by Mark and Benjamin under sockpuppet usernames. They looked up the site's payment methods several times, and procedures for communicating with the "contractors," including which ones would meet with a prospective client face-to-face. Meeting in person would demand a further payment and certain steps to guarantee that the would-be client was not an undercover police officer or being followed.

Mark, Benjamin, and Marcie had certainly thought of everything when they wrote the site up in just one night. If you were to read the site, it would be like an interactive, nonlinear digital novel that took you on a tour of a dark, nihilistic world of death-for-hire as a cold, clinical business.

It needed Olivia's coding expertise and precision, of course, but it took Benjamin's mischief to make it pop. (No, I will not name the site, lest you look for it. And anyway, we've since taken it offline. It was only created for this particular case.)

"It's almost Ballardian in its literary tone," Julia said, fascinated.

"Shame we can't submit it for the Man Booker Prize." Mark smiled wistfully.

"I am constantly reminded that our lovely, cheerful colleagues are bloody scary people," I said.

The Harkingdales decided to pick "death made to look like random street violence" for Sacha and "death made to look like a burglary gone wrong" for Irina.

And it didn't even chill me that I'd predicted those were the likely options they would pick.

"You'd think they'd be more cautious than this," I said. "They're laying themselves wide open to exposure."

"The arrogance of the privileged," Cheryl said. "Roger and I saw this all the time when we were starting out in this job. You should ask Ken and Clive about their cases when they came on board."

"Look at this," I said. "They have the option not to meet the contractor in question, but they're actually requesting a meeting."

"How very old school," Mark said.

"Ken, Clive," I said. "Looks like you'll get to see some of the Harkingdales up close and personal after all."

I did not like the smiles that crossed Ken and Clive's faces. They were the smile of cats relishing the opportunity to slowly torture some mice to death.

"Please don't lay a finger on them," I said.

"Of course not," Clive said, without much conviction.

We messaged the Harkingdales back to inform them that to meet with a contractor would involve a payment just for the meeting. It was not an audition. It was a commitment to engage the contractor's services. Payment would be made in advance into an account that would be sent to them in a private message via this website (again so we could control and keep records of their communications). It could be in the form of bitcoins, bonds, gold bars, or cash.

We gave the Harkingdales every opportunity to back out of this. Legally, this could still be entrapment, but we weren't the police. We were gathering evidence for our client.

And at every step, the Harkingdales said yes.

NINETEEN

Up until this point, the Harkingdales, for all their awfulness, had been something of an abstract presence for us. More often than not, that was how the subjects of cases were to us. We didn't often need to have any direct contact with them, as we could investigate and research them from afar. Sometimes we didn't even have to leave the office, when we could just find out all about them from an Internet search. Murderers didn't often come up in our caseload, despite what you read in novels, and this was a chance for us to have a proper gander at some of them.

We picked the meeting place. As the contractors, who were more at risk than the client, Ken and Clive reserved the right to pick the venue where they felt safest.

Benjamin fitted them with pin-sized webcams on their jackets, disguised to look like buttons. This was like gingerly trying to fit a bell on a lion. They met Charles Harkingdale, oldest son of Tobias and brother of Cecily, in the basement of a pub in Holloway. Charles had his father's jowls but not the exploded blood vessels that made Tobias's nose look like a red, blossoming cauliflower, which were signs of the excessive alcohol abuse he clearly indulged in. That didn't mean we could underestimate the patriarch Harkingdale, though. He was the one who directed the children and probably decreed when they might poison a spouse. We were reasonably sure it was Cecily who had poisoned Lev Mayakovsky, since no one else in the family could have gotten close enough to tamper with his booze. Perhaps Cecily led Lev to believe she was the one he could trust, warning him that her family was plotting against him and that she was on his side. She was, after all, still his wife and lulled him into complacency. This would have made it easier for her to put something in his drink before his bath that led him to lose consciousness and then drown.

It was obvious that Charles Harkingdale was there as the family's mouthpiece. His mission was to lay eyes on the contractors they were hiring and report back to Daddy. The hire was already rubber-stamped when they agreed to send the payment to us.

The pub was one that Ken and Clive liked to use on their own cases. It was one that various informers and villains frequented. Ken and Clive used to meet their grasses there when they were still coppers, and never told the Met about the place. It was their place of power. One they could control. Everyone there knew them and was absolutely terrified of them, even more so after they had been thrown out of the force and were now untethered by any rules.

Charles Harkingdale, with his expensive Savile Row suit and tie, looked well out of place in that gaff. Ken and Clive wanted it to be as uncomfortable for him as possible. He might not have realized that the patrons at the pub would remember him, that in agreeing to meet with Ken and Clive he was already implicating himself and his family.

They sat in the darkest corner at the back of the pub. We laid eyes on Harkingdale from Ken and Clive's button cams. They frisked him, lifted his shirt in full view of everyone in the pub to make sure he wasn't wearing a wire, and confirmed he didn't bring his phone since it could be used to listen in.

"A Russian lady and her kid," Ken said when Charles showed the photos of Irina and Sacha. "Punching below our weight here."

"I shan't tell you our reasons," Charles said, trying to sound in control, his posh accent perhaps overly pronounced, betraying his uneasiness at having to sit in a pub full of dangerous oiks. "But we do need them taken care of."

"Job's a job." Clive shrugged.

"Of course, we would expect proof," Charles said.

"Photos," Ken said.

"Unless you have a better idea," Charles said. "I'm under the impression you're professionals. It's rather outrageous, I must say, that we had to pay just to meet you."

"Listen here." Clive leaned forward. "You're not auditioning us. We're auditioning *you*. You insisted on a meet, which places us at risk already. That's why you pay for the privilege of meeting. It's danger money for us. You think this business is fucking easy?"

"I don't think it's easy," Charles said. "Otherwise we'd take care of it ourselves, keep it in the family, as it were."

My God, the murderous intent was radiating from Ken and Clive. Even watching them on the video feed, I could feel the sheer hatred coming off them, filling the room. The other people in the pub must have felt it, too, as they were giving Ken and Clive the widest berth possible. It must have been like having two angry, hungry sabertooths sitting in the room.

"We offer a premium service," Ken said. "Satisfaction guaranteed."

"The fact that we're here now and not in prison is proof of our expertise," Clive said.

"Er, yes," Harkingdale stammered. "Quite."

Who would have thought that Ken and Clive being slightly well spoken would be even more menacing than when they were their usual sweary, informal selves, which was already more than menacing enough?

I couldn't stop repeating this mantra in my head:

Please don't murder him . . . Please don't murder him . . . Please don't murder him . . . Please don't murder him . . . Please don't murder him . . .

Rationally, I knew Ken and Clive wouldn't kill Charles Harkingdale there and then. They were in a public place with too many witnesses, they knew this trap had to be baited for his whole family, but I was still irrationally anxious that they might snap and do it anyway.

"So will you take the job?" Harkingdale asked. "It is imperative that you do. Or we'll have to find someone else. But you came most highly recommended. You had the highest scores and the most reasonable rates."

"On the website," Clive said.

"On the website, yes."

"Most reasonable rates," Ken said, voice dripping with contempt.

Ken and Clive just sat and stared at him a good long while. They let the deep silence linger on, causing him to shift in his seat. They wanted the bastard to sweat, and they were going to enjoy this.

"Now we've met, face-to-face," Ken said. "Means we're committed to the job just as you're committed to us."

"Our mutual obligations align," Clive said. "Occam's razor."

"Yes, yes, quite," Charles Harkingdale said, relieved, eager to end the meeting as soon as possible.

"Do you want it quiet or public?" Ken asked.

"Sorry?" Charles blinked.

"There are two types of jobs," Ken said. "The type where they disappear forever. No one hears from them again and no one's the wiser what happened to them."

"Then there's the public display of the aftermath," Clive said. "Made to look like random street crimes, robberies gone wrong, muggings, accidents. They're found. They make the news. Become public."

"Public," Charles said without hesitation. "We need them to be public. For it to be on record."

"Then it's agreed," Ken said. "Once you leave here, you will arrange the first half of our fee. That's the down payment. Once we see it in our account, we set to work."

"Here's how we play it," Ken said. "In a day, you will receive in the post a clean smartphone. Wait for our call. Don't use it for anything else."

"We won't talk," Clive added.

"We will send you pictures once it's done. That's your proof."

"After today, you won't see us again," Clive declared.

By the time Ken and Clive left the meeting, I realized I had kept my mantra running in my head even as I concentrated on everything else.

"Did you get all that?" Clive said.

"Yup," Benjamin said.

"They want us to bump off Dickie Boyd while we're at it," Ken said. "No witnesses, no loose ends."

Ken and Clive were laughing.

I doubted Boyd would find this quite so amusing.

TWENTY

Staging a scene, building a drone, planting a bug or a camera—these were the activities Benjamin felt most at home with. He had always been a tech head. A Chinese kid who grew up in Peckham, so he always knew how to take care of himself, as he built cheap computers from spare parts to sell to friends and neighbors. Olivia, who was unfathomably sleeping with him, said she wasn't even sure if he spoke any Chinese. His parents might not have taught him. Benjamin spoke in a broad "Sarf Laaaandan" accent, and if you only heard his voice, you wouldn't know he was Chinese. He and Olivia probably had similar IQ scores, but he was all about hardware, gadgets, mics, and cameras, anything tactile. Olivia's expertise was in computers, Internet security, and hacking. She could probably build her own computers and had probably done so, but she didn't know how to build or fix the engine block of a car, improvise a remote listening device with a cheap Bluetooth earpiece, or assemble a working drone from 3-D-printed parts. The latter were more in Benjamin's wheelhouse.

Benjamin's biggest problem was boredom, so Golden Sentinels suited him because of the different types of cases that called upon his skills. One day, he would leave Golden Sentinels if he got the right idea for an invention that excited him, and form his own tech start-up company. For now, he was more than happy to cause all kinds of mischief for Roger. To him, money was just a means to buy the parts and gear to build devices for causing mayhem, and a tech company didn't exactly offer those opportunities.

Thus, it fell to Benjamin to take the faux murder photos as proof of deed for the Harkingdales. He was both director and cameraman here, creating tableaus that would do the Grand Guignol proud. Did I mention he took very good surveillance photos? He was an expert at composition, a deft hand at picking just the right angle and lighting. So staging a murder scene was not only a piece of piss but also an absolute joy for Benjamin. He'd seen more than his fair share of Eighties Italian slasher films and previously banned gorefests, and on top of messing with gadgets had spent his teens extensively researching the forensic realities of bloodletting and grotesque wounds.

He worked with Ken and Clive here. You could say they were the writers of the scenarios. First was Sacha's, and he went along without a fuss, since I'd explained to him what our plan was.

And Bagalamukhi followed us through all three photo shoots, watching us approvingly and taking photos of her own on her phone. This got awfully meta. In the last few months, she had taken a shine to Benjamin, standing over his shoulder as he took photos, waving her cudgel over his head as if anointing him with her approval. I think she may have decided to be his patron god. Truth and deception were spells he cast, after all.

"This ought to be simple enough," Ken said. "It could be claimed he was set on by a pack of racists who heard his accent, followed him to this little corner of the street out of the sight of surveillance cameras, and kicked him to death."

Sacha lay on the ground against the wall, his face covered with lumps of mortician's wax molded to look like horrendous swelling over his left eye and cheek, from vicious blows to his face. Olivia applied blue and purple makeup to make the lumps look purple and blue like hematomas and heavy bruising should.

Sacha closed his eyes and lay limp while Benjamin snapped about a dozen pictures on a burner smartphone. Then they cleaned his face up and headed back to the safe house.

Next was his mother.

"Make it look like a burglary," Clive said. "Found her in the bedroom. She must have woken up and they panicked and stabbed her to death."

They waited for Irina to go to sleep that evening and Benjamin simply snapped some photos of her in bed, completely oblivious. Best not to disturb her or tell her what they were up to.

The nurse wondered why we wanted photos of Irina sleeping. Sacha told her he wanted some photos of her at peace.

"I'm going to photoshop the stab wounds and smears of blood in later," Benjamin whispered. "Best to leave her be."

Last but not least, there was Dickie Boyd's demise to stage. No surprise that he would be the one who had to kick up a fuss.

"You're not gonna kill me for real, are ya?" he pleaded.

"Don't tempt us." Clive glowered.

"Just lie down under that car," Benjamin said.

"Oh God, don't drive over me!"

"It's a fucking parked car, arsehole!" Ken growled. "It's not even ours and the door's locked!"

"Now get down and act dead before we go hands-on with you!" Clive added.

Boyd complied. We'd picked the car completely at random on that quiet street not far from Boyd's office near Bethnal Green. He positioned himself as Benjamin directed and lay under the front fender of the Vauxhall hatchback, wedging his chest by the wheels so it looked like he was crushed under the car. Benjamin made sure to have his head and face in the shot, and framed it close enough so it didn't show that the car was parked.

"Could you half-open your eyes, mate?" he asked.

"What for?" Boyd sputtered.

"So it looks more horrific."

Boyd shuddered and did as requested.

They bought him a whiskey down the pub afterwards as a reward.

They texted the photos of Sacha and Irina from the burner smartphone to the phone Ken and Clive had given the Harkingdales. Then they waited a day and texted the photo of Boyd under the car.

The family authorized the rest of Ken and Clive's fees within minutes after they received the photos.

Bagalamukhi glowed even more golden as this went on. She was one of the ten forms of the goddesses of wisdom, after all. She cooed over Benjamin as her newest child even as he worked away at his desk on his 3-D printer.

"Smashing deception with deception," she said and smiled. "A most elegant contradiction."

At least she was leaving me alone, but she was really speaking to me, since I was the only one who could see or hear her.

"All the better for the changes to come," Bagalamukhi said, and sashayed out the door.

Changes? What was she talking about?

I hated it when the gods spoke to me, because it was always something cryptic and never good. I put the thought out of my head. It was me; they were manifestations of my psyche. I was only making things complicated for myself thinking about changes and Prophecy.

At least, that was what I told myself.

TWENTY-ONE

Mayakovsky's solicitor scheduled a reading of the will a week later. Tobias and Charles Harkingdale accompanied Cecily to lend her support through this difficult time.

"He's your father's lawyer, not yours," David said beforehand.

"I know," Sacha said.

"You need to get your own lawyer to work with him, and protect you and your mother's interests," David said. "And you'll want to disclose your situation, including the attempt to have you both killed."

With that, Sacha engaged David as his lawyer, tying Golden Sentinels to his protection and interests. Roger was well chuffed. Being on the payroll from Sacha's inheritance meant more pay, especially given how much we'd acted to help him.

"It's all thanks to you, Ravi," Roger said with pride. "You always bring that little something extra to a case."

"And all for just a pound," Mark said.

I shrugged.

We gave Sacha all the evidence we had gathered against the Harkingdales.

"You could just turn the evidence over to the police," I said. "Let the law take its course."

"Thank you," Sacha said.

With that, David accompanied Sacha and Irina to the reading of the will. Ken and Clive went along to provide muscle, and send a message. Sacha wanted them to see Ken and Clive.

"Don't drink anything they're offering," Mark quipped.

David shuddered and glared at Mark as he walked out.

"He's like a character out of Dostoyevsky," Julia said. "The angry, sensitive boy who knows more than he would like, whose innocence is gone forever, looking at the world with darker eyes."

Sacha reminded me of some of my secondary school students. Maybe this was why I wanted to help him. Back then, if a student showed signs of distress or trouble at home, we would try to talk to their family and then call in Social Services. This was several worlds away from that. This was probably much worse. We were in a gray world where justice wasn't always served and no one was truly safe. I wanted to at least save Sacha and his mother, strike some universal karmic balance for a change.

David, Ken, and Clive were wearing Benjamin's pin-cameras on their jackets so we could watch the proceedings.

The look on the Harkingdales' faces when Sacha and Irina walked in alive and well was definitely worth the cheers we threw. Ken and Clive stood protectively by Irina, who was quite chipper and lucid from the supplements Mark and Sacha had mixed for her. Mark and Benjamin did a Mexican wave and the gods followed suit, which I found disconcerting.

The Harkingdales had to sit and quietly shit themselves while Mayakovsky's solicitor read out the will. As we expected, they had been cut out. Cecily, as the widow, was given the penthouse flat in London she lived in. Other than that, she—and by proxy, her family—got fuck all. The properties, holdings, and money all went to Sacha and Irina. Much of it was placed in a trust to take care of Irina's care and pay for Sacha's living expenses and education.

"This is an outrage!" Tobias Harkingdale cried. "Trickery! We'll file an appeal!"

No one in the room took him seriously.

David proceeded to play the recording of Charles hiring Ken and Clive to murder him and his mother.

"We have multiple copies backed up to various servers," David said. "Should anything untoward happen to Sacha or Irina, or me or my colleagues, the recordings and screencaps of the Harkingdales trying to hire contract killers will be automatically released to the police, blogs, and the media."

So that was the play. David had discussed the pros and cons of whether to release the evidence to the police. There were possible liabilities, accusations of entrapment, not to mention that the Harkingdales' lawyers could tie up proceedings so the case would take years to come to trial, and even then, there was no guarantee of a conviction. There was no way to charge them for Mayakovsky's death, and Sacha decided it was better to continue to hold it all over them to keep himself and his mother safe. Releasing the evidence to the media would be a scandal the Harkingdales couldn't survive even if they were never tried.

Sacha and Tamsin threw a party at his flat, inviting his classmates who'd helped shelter him and his mother, and us. Roger and Cheryl, Ken and Clive begged off. Olivia was busy with whatever she was up to, and Benjamin wasn't into it. Marcie had her own party full of A-List celebrities to go to, so it was just David, Julia, and I. It was an odd sight, a bunch of private investigators and Hindu gods nobody saw but me, mingling with a bunch of university students while Irina sat quietly in the corner, smiling absently at childhood memories she was reliving. Julia remarked that Sacha and Tamsin were a cute couple, though who knew if that relationship would last. Mark was having a grand old time hanging out with fellow enthusiasts for the ultimate high and sharing a spliff.

"I'm going to sell most of the properties," Sacha said. "My mother and I already have more than enough money from the trust."

"Well, the Chinese are on a buying spree for London properties," I said.

"They can have them. I don't care. I can use the money from the sales to form my start-up."

"Are you going to be all right, then?" I asked.

"Don't worry about me," Sacha said. "I will never forget what you did for me."

TWENTY-TWO

So ended this particular case. Justice was sort of served. As usual with us, nobody was arrested. The police didn't come within spitting distance. That would have been that, if Ariel hadn't called me three weeks later.

"Babe!" she said. "I never thought you had it in you."

"What are you talking about?"

"Wiping out the Harkingdales. That was a masterful op."

"What? I did nothing of the sort."

"No, that's what's hot about you. You weren't anywhere near this. You let the Russians do it?"

"Russians? What?"

"That Marcie bitch didn't show you the intelligence briefing from this month? The Harkingdales are literally no more."

My stomach began to fall.

"Ariel, tell me from the start. What's this about the Russians and the Harkingdales?"

"Look it up, babe. It's okay. I'll wait."

I'd been busy and hadn't paid that much attention to the news. Tobias Harkingdale collapsed at his club after a night of heavy drinking and died of heart failure days later in hospital. Charles Harkingdale went for a drive out to Dover with his wife and children and never returned after that weekend. Their car was found near the White Cliffs. Cecily Harkingdale, seemingly distraught, took some pills and cut her wrists while soaking in the tub, virtually mirroring Lev's demise. Signs of a family that finally fell apart?

"Think about it," Ariel said. "Who do you think would want them gone?"

"Sacha."

"Think the kid had it in him? Nah. This was hardcore. It was Russian spooks. Ask your Marcie."

No wonder I had seen the gods waging war in the sky when I took this case. No wonder Shiva, Kali, and Bagalamukhi had been hanging about when we went after the Harkingdales. Shiva the destroyer of the world was overseeing the destruction of the Harkingdales' world. This was their apocalypse.

I searched the deaths on the Internet. The Harkingdales' deaths were made to look like accidents and suicide, and weeks apart to avoid suspicion. No wonder I hadn't noticed, since I was busy on other cases. The Russians were experts at that. Just like how the Harkingdales made Mayakovsky's death looked like suicide. This was karma.

Kali stood behind me, smiling.

"Haven't you forgotten, my son?" she said. "You are an agent of Chaos, bringing change. You are my lovely monster."

I hung up my phone and showed everyone the news.

"Yeah, that fits," Marcie said.

"What fits?" I asked.

"My buddies at the embassy noticed a bunch of Russian spooks were coming and going an awful lot in the last few weeks. Not a lot of chatter about what they were coming to London for."

"KGB? FSB?" I asked.

"They were all former KGB, gone private. We've known these guys for a long time. These Ivans, Sergeis, Evgenys. They were hardcore Soviets before the Wall came down. Way before I joined," Marcie said. "Both the Brits and our guys were wondering what they were up to, since we didn't know about any major ops the Russians were pulling in London."

"So they all came to London to get the Harkingdales, then?" Benjamin asked. "A few weeks of surveillance and planning, then swooping in and Bob's yer uncle."

"This is like a fantasy of the Revolution," Mark said. "How many old-school Communists get to actually wipe out a bunch of upper-class wankers these days? It's the execution of the Romanovs, updated. It's like a dream come true for them."

"Not every day you get to wipe an entire family of posh villains off the map, Ravi," said Roger. "Quite a result."

What was my karmic tally now? I didn't want to think about it.

"How do we know this for sure?" I asked.

"That's the thing about deniability, isn't it? It's impossible to be sure," Cheryl said.

"Are you worried the cops are going to come knocking? Do you think you're a suspect?" Marcie asked me.

"No, but—"

"There's nothing that ties them to us at all," David chimed in. "No reason the firm would be questioned."

"So the Harkingdales have literally vanished off the map," Olivia said, the first time in months I'd seen her impressed. "Scorched earth."

I looked at Julia, who watched the screen intently. She returned my gaze and merely raised an eyebrow.

"This is one for the books, eh, Ravi?" Ken said.

"Not even we ever dreamed of knocking off a whole family of villains," Clive said. "Respect."

TWENTY-THREE

Sacha opened the door to his mother's flat. He'd gotten a decent haircut. His clothes were more formal now, a white dress shirt and black trousers, not the hoodie and dirty jeans I had last seen him in. He handed me a check. The amount shocked me. It was in the five figures.

"It's a small percentage of the first property sale. From the Chinese conglomerate that bought my father's building in Holborn," Sacha said. "It's not very much, but I wanted to compensate you for what you did for me."

"Or to buy my silence."

Hurt, he looked at me.

"I didn't order their deaths, Ravi."

"I can't accept this check. It's blood money."

"It's my appreciation for your work, Ravi, for helping me get justice. You trapped the Harkingdales for me."

"I didn't mean for them to get killed."

"Neither did I. It was part of my father's legacy."

"You didn't call those men from Russia?"

"No. They came to London on their own. And I'm not sorry they did."

"Did they tell you they were here to get the Harkingdales?"

"I didn't know they were here until after the deed was done," Sacha said. "They contacted me *after* it was done and said my father could rest in peace now. That the scales were balanced. Then they went back to Moscow. I had no objection."

"So that's it, then?" I said. "Your mother will be looked after. You can start a company to develop legal drugs and gene-editing to improve memory, cognition, cure Alzheimer's."

"Isn't there an old Buddhist saying?" Sacha said. "There is no need to take revenge. If you wait long enough, you will see the corpses of your enemies float by in the river."

"If you can live with all that."

"Deposit the check, Ravi," he said, resigned.

TWENTY-FOUR

My head was spinning when I left Sacha's flat. How had the Russians known the extent to which the Harkingdales murdered Lev Mayakovsky? If Sacha hadn't contacted those ex-KGB men, there was only one other person who could have gotten word to them.

Marcie.

"Did you—?"

"Put a hit on the Harkingdales?" Marcie said, surprised. "Why would I? And I don't have the power to do that. They were already finished. It served no strategic purpose to get rid of them. They have no real impact on geopolitical policy. By our standards, they were a bunch of petty criminals, not threats to national security."

"Then how did this happen?" I was still fighting to stay calm. Lord Shiva was sitting on the office sofa, gingerly picking dirt out of his fingernails in a particularly unnerving manner. He looked at me with pity.

"Well, I wrote a report as I always do. This consequence of Lev Mayakovsky's death was of some academic interest to the intelligence community."

"Wait, by 'community' you mean the whole—?"

"Dude, we trade gossip like anyone does. Spies are like schoolgirls when they chat with each other in private."

"So does that mean MI5, MI6 know this? And the Russians would know it, too?"

"Yup."

"So those Russians decided—?"

"To go on a mission that was totally off the books."

I dragged Marcie into the soundproof conference room.

"Marcie, did you plan this outcome all along?"

"Hell no! I had no skin in this game, and I had nothing to gain from it."

"Why would they even avenge Mayakovsky?" I asked. "I thought they hated his guts."

"Spies may disagree with each other," Marcie said. "Be on opposite sides, even try to kill each other from time to time, but spies have an understanding: they're in a priesthood together. It's the most exclusive club in the world, and they're loyal to that ethos."

"So, what, it's a point of honor?"

"For a bunch of ex-KGB dudes, totally. Deep down they're still Communist true believers. They can't stand the idea of some English aristocrats taking out one of their own, and for something as petty as money. That made it personal."

"And I caused it to happen. Fuck. Fuck!"

"Ravi, chill. You couldn't have known."

"I should have!"

Marcie scoffed.

"Oh, come on, Ravi. If you could predict that a routine case about an inheritance and a will reading would end up with a bunch of Russian spies wiping out a whole British family of blue bloods, you would not be toiling away as a private eye. Dude, you would be the God Emperor of the World."

The gods were standing behind Marcie, all looking at me with pity and tut-tutting at my hubris. Shiva took a photo of my ashen face with his phone.

The conference room was getting too crowded. I excused myself and walked to the loo, where I bent over and vomited the entire contents of my curry lunch.

What have I done?

Lord Vishnu stood over me as I huddled at the sink to splash water in my face. I really had been getting too comfy in this job. That was when fate stepped in and kicked me in the arse.

Through the glass walls of his office Roger saw I was unhappy, and he was already pouring me a brandy when I came out of the loo and walked towards his office.

"Good result, Ravi," he said, offering me a glass.

I downed it in one gulp.

"How can you say that? I wiped a whole family off the map."

"Well, technically, not you. And good bloody riddance to them. Those Harkingdales have been a plague on the land for over a hundred years. In one fell swoop, you've made the world safe for hapless rich bastards hoping to marry into a titled family that wouldn't murder them for their dosh. It's almost like you're an antibody that rose up and eradicated a long-running infection in the body politic."

"I am not a vessel for class revenge! Or a harbinger of karma!"

"Don't sell yourself short, old son. You just happened to say the right thing to the right person at the right place at the right time, and got a result."

"I don't know if I can keep doing this."

"You're not doing anything other than your job, and then the worl reacts accordingly, sometimes in spectacular fashion. Perhaps that's wl the gods like hanging around you so much. You're guaranteed to give 'e a good show."

"I don't see how you could carry on saying I'm a mensch."

"Of course you are. That's what makes you not only a good investig here, but interesting to me. You're a *weaponized* mensch."

"If this is the real nature of the cosmic joke, then I'm not sure I sl keep being a part of it."

"I don't think we get to choose, old son."

Roger looked at me with a mixture of pity and what look comfortably like admiration.

"Ravi, my boy," Roger said. "Perhaps you'd like to get out of t a bit, out of the country, even?"

ONE

The light was different in Los Angeles.

I couldn't get used to it.

People told me it was the smog. It served as a kind of filter for the way sunlight seeped through the air and onto the city, giving it a kind of almost hallucinatory sheen. At dusk, as night descended, the dying glow of the day was particularly surreal and vivid. No wonder the entertainment industry was headquartered here. Fantasies could only be born out of a city that wasn't quite real, a city that had been brought into existence through sheer will and desire. Los Angeles was like a mirage forced to take solid form at the hands of men who imposed their vision on the otherwise desolate desert landscape. I was fascinated by the cracks in the road that always needed to be mended, the continuing shift of tectonic plates, the erasure of the city's own history as old buildings were constantly demolished in favor of the new. Like its inhabitants, this city was obsessed with always appearing young. Its permanent default state was a battle against entropy. All it took was money and power. I'd swapped the gray, wet dystopia of London for the blazing, sun-blasted dystopia of LA.

"What's that you're writing?" asked Julia, glancing over my shoulder. "It's awfully purple."

"It's just some poncey thoughts I'd been having since we got here."

"Ravi," she laughed. "You've caught the bug!"

The "bug" she was referring to was this impulse to write. I'd never been one to keep a diary, but lately I'd had the urge to jot things down. Maybe I just needed to capture my thoughts because of how batshit insane my life had become since I started at Golden Sentinels—and it wasn't getting any less so. Julia's hobby since we'd arrived was to immerse herself in books and novels about the city. She was obsessed with the mythology of Los Angeles. It wasn't old like London. It was ethereal, a chimera in the heat-haze, and she took to that in a big way. In fact, she bloody loved it because it was so unlike London. It was naked in its dishonesty, without the pomposity with which the City of Fog liked to coat its deceits and hypocrisies due to snobbery and embarrassment. This was a city with no sense of embarrassment or need for dignity at all, and Julia found that liberating. With her English Rose looks and accent, the city took to her in an equally big way. Rooms stopped when she entered them. Some people remembered her supermodel sister Louise and would tell her they were big fans. This touched her. Louise was never far from her, from us. We kept mum that Louise was trans, though in this day and age, that would probably have gone down a treat and given her career a massive boost. It was a shame Louise hadn't lived to see this. Julia wept for that.

As I held Julia in my arms during the night, I saw Bagalamukhi standing on the balcony of our rented apartment surveying the city. Roger had put us up in a one-bedroom condominium just off Sunset Boulevard in West Hollywood. It was no surprise she would like it here. It was full of deceit and façade. As she texted and tweeted about it on her phone to the other gods, she looked like she fit right in.

That was the thing about the gods, they fit in everywhere now. A god for every occasion. I had hoped they might have stayed behind in London, which had enough chaos and strife to keep any deity occupied, but of course they followed me, watching, being amused. They were *my* gods, after all.

TWO

"Morning, Ravi." Marilyn the receptionist greeted me cheerfully, as usual. "Would you like some water?"

"I'm good, thanks."

Offering people water seemed to be the thing here in Los Angeles, the first courtesy in every meeting. I wondered if this had anything to do with the city's having been built in the desert.

Chuck Feeney, the head of the firm in LA, ran the place with a laid-back, distinctly Californian air of casualness and a variation of Roger's silver tongue. His charm was less abrasive than Roger's, his tan a direct contrast to Roger's paler London skin. Chuck had grown up in show business, a surfer dude in Malibu who had enjoyed a brief stint as an actor back in the seventies and eighties, done detective work as a favor to friends, and when the acting work dried up, been persuaded by Roger to get a license and run the LA office for job security. Apparently, a good health insurance plan was a huge incentive for them here, along with something called a 401(k), which someone would have to explain to me later.

"Listen up, kids," Chuck announced to the staff the day Julia and I arrived. "Ravi and Julia here are from the mother ship in London. Roger sent them here to shadow us and watch how we do things out here, kind of a fact-finding tour. They're not going to get in your way, just ask a few questions and pick up some pointers. Let's make 'em feel welcome in the Golden Sentinels family."

This was a busman's holiday. Julia and I were here as Roger's people from London, here to learn how the Los Angeles office did things. We didn't have a license to practice as private investigators in California or the US, so we couldn't officially work any cases. What was unspoken was that I was assessing whether they were slack or incompetent at the office here. They were kind enough to fix up a desk for Julia and me to set up our laptops. These were clean laptops that they kept at the office, part of a policy that Olivia had implemented for all the Golden Sentinels offices. Julia and I had flown into LAX with clean smartphones that didn't have any social media apps installed, or contacts lists filled in, so the US immigrant officials couldn't get any information off of the phones—and they certainly tried, after asking to inspect them. They let Julia in without a hitch since she was white, blond, and had a posh accent, but they kept me back at the airport to ask if I was Muslim. Even when I told them I wasn't, they eyed me suspiciously. It wasn't my British passport and the Visa Waiver rules, but whatever Very Special List Marcie Holder had put me on, that persuaded them that I wasn't some enemy terrorist trying to infiltrate the country. The immigration officer took my passport and whispered something to his colleague, who typed something into his computer, then looked at me again, before they let me through without any further hassle. The Muslim couple who were in line behind me didn't look quite so lucky. As I walked through Immigration, I glanced at them being led to the interview rooms and didn't fancy their chances.

"I thought they were going to clap you in irons and that would be the last I saw of you," Julia said, half-jokingly, when I met her out at the baggage claim section.

"This trip is still young," I said.

The first thing that struck me about Golden Sentinels Los Angeles was how pretty everyone who worked there was. Oh, Roger liked to hire good-looking people whenever possible. Apart from Ken and Clive, who looked like bruisers and ex-coppers of the old school, Roger made sure the rest of us were at least easy on the eyes when we wore business suits. The Los Angeles investigators were in a completely different league— their bodies were toned and athletic with not an ounce of fat, and their teeth were so white they could reflect the sun and provide lighting for the room. Julia recognized the signs of cosmetic surgery in some of them—a chiseled nose here, some cheek implants there, breasts so pert they could only have had the aid of medical science. Cheryl had told me a third of the staff were struggling actors earning a decent wage on investigations in between auditions, hoping to land a TV show during pilot season, which made sense, I suppose. And at least half the staff here were ex-coppers *and* struggling actors.

And despite their unreal, fantastical looks, Julia still turned their heads. The way she didn't play up or make extra effort to draw attention to her looks drew attention wherever we went in LA. I also wondered if people here in the most oversexed city in America could detect the dangerous air of sex that Julia carried with her due to her addiction. At the end of the day, natural, unself-conscious, biodegradable beauty still trumped plastic perfection.

The LA office was in the most unreal and expensive part of town, of course—Beverly Hills—because it needed to be, to reassure clients the company was top of the line. It followed the same open-plan principles our London office did, looking more like a trendy tech start-up office than a private investigations firm. It had even more natural light and big windows, with desks arranged not as cubicles but a circle to encourage the investigators to engage and share with one another. The dress code here was much more casual, mainly tight T-shirts, polo shirts, and khakis for the men, shirts, denim jackets, and jeans for the women. The biggest difference from the London office was the recreational area, which had a mini gym with barbells, a treadmill, an elliptical machine, and exercise balls. The investigators there seemed to take breaks to do chin-ups and core exercises on the balls several times a day.

"Helps them think," Chuck said, but Julia and I just thought they were obsessed with keeping their bodies fit for appearances, the ones that were addicted to the burn and endorphin rush. Back in London, everyone went to the gym on their own time and never bothered talking about it.

Hector and Dave from the New York office had told me a while back that private investigators in America needed licenses in order to operate legitimately as businesses. That suited me just fine, since I was still reeling from the Harkingdales case in London and wasn't really up for working anyway. I was still seriously considering chucking it all in, but what was the alternative? I still had bills to pay and wasn't really qualified for any respectable, middle-class job now. Thanks to Golden Sentinels' training, I was good at social engineering and illicit information-gathering and a whole range of illegal skills. Working at a McDonald's was not going to do. Marcie also told me that I was an investment, for Roger on one hand and her on the other. They'd trained me very well and I was paying off in spades. It would be a waste for me and my skill set to drop out of the game now. And this was my break. I was perfectly content just to follow and observe the Los Angeles office on their cases. They had their groove going here. It wasn't as if they would need the advice of a parochial Londoner in the unreal madness of Los Angeles. No, Julia was right. Best to treat this as an adventure, a book unfolding before our eyes, or better yet, a movie playing out just for us. She was on break from college, so she wasn't even losing any time on her course work. She was reading Los Angeles novels and could get a paper out of it, so on top of spending time with me, this was a win-win for her. We both needed a change of scenery from the gray skies and gray morality of London. The vivid blue of the sky and the unfiltered sunlight was a harsh blast of culture shock that our systems seemed to need.

"Mad dogs and Englishmen go out in the midday sun," sang Noel Coward. If that were true, we could expect to go completely barmy here. According to Noel Coward, us Hindus should be able to sleep through it, but I was also British, and madness was still too close for comfort for me.

"You would like that, wouldn't you?" Kali whispered in my eye, her fingers brushing my shoulders lightly.

I shuddered at the thought. Going psychotic this far from home was not my idea of a fun holiday.

Julia was particularly taken with *They Shoot Horses, Don't They?* by Horace McCoy and *The Day of the Locust* by Nathanael West. For an airbrushed, sun-drenched playground, Los Angeles seemed particularly given to apocalyptic narratives even a century ago.

THREE

Darrell Chestwood was one of those men who looked like he worked out to within an inch of his life. There was not an ounce of fat on him, just hard lines all over his body. He was not untypical amongst the specimens in the office at Golden Sentinels LA, but he seemed to be the poster child. And yes, he was an actor, going on auditions and taking acting classes in between jobs for the agency.

"Darrell," Chuck said. "Why don't you take Ravi and Julia along when you go see your A-list client today?"

"Sure thing, Chuck."

I still hadn't decided if the pervasive amiability around the office was forced or not.

Darrell was a chatty one. So was Chuck. The whole LA office was, as if this was the law of the land. We liked Darrell well enough, but I imagined his overall affability was one of the qualities for which he'd been hired at the LA office. The first thing he did when we were introduced to him was give us his headshot.

"You never know," he said, indicating that this was not a new practice for him. It was his version of giving us a calling card. His was a flawless postcard-sized photo with contact information and his résumé on the back.

"Nobody's going to carry a letter-sized headshot in their pocket," Darrell said as he drove us down Melrose to the movie studio.

"How do you like working at Golden Sentinels?" I asked.

"It's cool," he said. "Like, really cool. Beats working as a waiter or bartender, you know? The hours are even more flexible. I can make time for my classes and auditions, and some of the clients put me in touch with casting calls. I landed a commercial once from that. Too bad it was local, not national, or I would have been made."

"So what's the percentage of clients who are in show business?" Julia asked.

"According to Chuck, sixty to seventy percent," Darrell said.

"And he doesn't have a problem with you getting leads on acting jobs from the clients?" I asked.

"Nope. That's stuff on the side, and outside the agency, so he's cool with it, as long as we fill him in on any scheduling issues."

When we got to the studio (which lawyers won't let me name, but you can probably guess if you know Los Angeles), the guard waved us in because Darrell and Golden Sentinels were known to them by now. Darrell parked his Prius and we got into one of those golf carts to drive to the star's trailer.

The client was filming his latest superhero sequel here at the studio in LA rather than a studio in London or Romania, a rare occurrence since so few films were even shot in Hollywood anymore. Darrell explained this to us. Tax incentives in other states and Canada made it cheaper to shoot almost anywhere but Hollywood. That was ironic. Hollywood had become a façade of itself; the movie factory didn't make movies in its factories anymore. That was surreal enough, but what was even more surreal was that punters like me knew this, too, by now.

We arrived outside The Client's trailer, and Darrell was about to knock on the door when he heard something from inside and refrained. (Lawyers have made me omit the client's name.)

"He's, er, getting serviced," Darrell said. "We better wait till he's done."

"Serviced" made it sound like he was a car being worked on, but of course what it really meant was the A-list movie star was getting a blow job. As we waited, Darrell shook hands with Sean's assistant, who stood by a small team of people Darrell told us were from the wardrobe department.

"Is my boy Darrell out there?" The Client cried from inside the trailer. "Get in here, bro!"

"Comin' in," Darrell said. "You decent? I brought some colleagues of mine."

"They with you? Great! I need all the help I can get!" The Client cried.

"Hey, Sharon." Darrell greeted the girl with the tattoos wiping her mouth and getting up from the floor of the trailer.

"Darrell," she said curtly.

"Darrell, man, I relapsed."

"Where is it?" Darrell asked.

"Drawer."

Darrell walked over to the dresser and retrieved a few Baggies of white powder. I had thought his relapse was Sharon, not the white powder, or perhaps both. But no, it was the cocaine.

"Now I'm going to have to talk about this at AA and not get my anniversary medallion," The Client whined. He was adjusting the compartment on the crotch of his superhero armor. The wardrobe department had seen fit to build a hatch to allow him easier access when he needed to pee. This had proved useful for when he needed to get "serviced" by his groupie Sharon. According to Darrell, she was originally the case. She had been stalking The Client, sending him emails, gifts, finding out his personal mobile phone number and directly texting him, to the point where his wife felt the need to hire Golden Sentinels to sort her out and see if she might harbor homicidal impulses towards him or his wife. She was an überfan, and fortunately for him, she was well fit. Or "hot," as the Yanks might say. The Client and his wife, herself an A-list actress, were known around town for having an open marriage, but he didn't tell her his stalker had become his latest bit on the side.

"Last chance, dude," Darrell said.

"Do it!"

Darrell flushed the gak down the trailer's toilet. The Client winced; his mouth pursed and grimaced at the sound of the waters swirling his favorite addiction away. Just as well he kept his second favorite addiction—sex outside his marriage—on tap.

"Think of your better and higher self," Darrell said.

"Better and higher self," The Client chanted like a mantra.

"Dollars to donuts he's going back into rehab once this shoot is over," Darrell whispered to me, the flushing toilet hiding his words from The Client.

Lord Vishnu stood in the trailer with us, looking on sagely. I glanced out the window and saw the other gods milling around, looking every bit like they belonged here, on a film set, completely at home. Kali dancing down the lot. Ganesha sitting in the back of another golf cart cruising by. If you asked me, the gods had been even more at home on Hollywood Boulevard when Julia and I took a walk down there on Sunday, milling and mixing with the superheroes and the Jesus Christs. Mark once idly said superheroes were modern gods. The difference being that these modern gods were corporate-owned and served to make them billions in profits in movie ticket sales and toys. This was all from my head, of course. I was projecting my own apprehension about the world onto the gods appearing before me. That was what I kept telling myself.

"Consider that the modern-day version of the tithe," Mark said. "After all, worshippers of gods give their dosh to churches and temples, 'donate' money for prayers, charms, and mantras. How is that really different?"

"I think there are differences in nuances of faith," I said.

"That's mainly semantics," Mark said, puffing on his spliff.

"Superheroes began as heroic fantasies for children," I said. "And given how fucked and chaotic the world is, a lot of people grow up and cling onto tokens and idols that give them succor and comfort."

"That's not so different from worshipping or praying to gods, is it?" Mark said. "It's all a form of magical thinking at the end of the day. You're the only bloke I know who's stuck with his gods and wishes it wasn't the case."

"So Hollywood is the place where the modern gods' stories are now being produced and enacted in the form of movies?" I asked.

"Think of it all as part of the continuum," Mark said, taking another puff. "More magickal rituals, grist for the mill. Punters will make use of stories and gods as they will and as they need. I envy you, mate, Roger sending you out there so you can witness it firsthand. I'm sure your gods will have a very pleasant holiday."

From what I could gather, Darrell served as a fixer, confessor, confidant, and unofficial therapist to his A-list clients. Marcie probably played a similar role to her clients back in London, but here there was a sense of much higher stakes, if that was even possible.

"Would you mind if you gave Sharon a lift home?"

"Sure. Why not?" Darrell said.

As we walked out of the trailer, the wardrobe department went in to make sure the superhero armor was properly cleaned and spruced up for the set. It was the stuff of millions of dollars' worth of toy sales, a metallic monolith of black and gold and thorns, and the costume itself had been insured by Lloyd's of London for over a million dollars. Once this sequel was finished, it would be auctioned off as a Special Edition. The next sequel would feature an upgraded design for The Client to wear.

"I'm not a pimp," Darrell said to me quickly as we left the studio. Sharon sat in the back with Julia, who engaged her in small talk.

"I'm getting certified as a personal trainer," Sharon said. "That way I get to earn my rent. I know I can't keep blowing him forever."

This was LA, where even the celebrity stalkers had long-term life goals.

"It's good that you have plans, Sharon," Darrell said.

"Have you thought about going back to school?" Julia asked. "Earn a degree?"

"Wow!" Sharon cried. "Are you, like, British? Your accent is so cool. Can you, like, teach me how to talk good like that?"

FOUR

How's it going, Ravi, old son?"

Roger's smiling visage beamed on the computer. It was early morning here but it was already afternoon in London. They were eight hours ahead of us. This was our morning ritual in our apartment before we set off for the office, to report in and tell Roger and Cheryl all we had observed of the goings-on at the LA office.

"I think they're trying to dazzle us with Hollywood glamour bullshit," Julia said.

"No different than what we get up to in Blighty," Roger said.

"So what's the point of having us shadowing them?" I asked. "There's no way they don't resent us sniffing around like that."

"I'll tell you why, Ravi," Roger said. "I've been thinking about changing things up a bit in the US offices, maybe put more Londoners in."

"Like me?"

"What do you think, Ravi?" Roger said. "London was getting a bit claustrophobic, don't you think?"

"It's not the claustrophobia that was getting to me, boss. It was the chaos I was raining down on people. How's sending me abroad all the time going to help me?"

"Just think about it, old son. You and Julia seem to be looking refreshed out there."

"No, that's just the excessive sunlight," Julia said.

"Do you think they might be skimming off earnings for the firm out here?" I asked.

"Everyone earns on the side," Roger said. "I don't hold that against them. I just want you to see if anyone's abusing the company name."

"Ah. Now I get it."

"Golden Sentinels is a brand," Roger said. "And you're there to make sure the Los Angeles chaps are keeping it polished spick-and-span."

"Well, 'polished' is certainly the veneer here," I said.

"We've taken up time. I'll give your love to everyone here at the office," Roger said, and walked off-camera, leaving Cheryl.

"Ravi," Cheryl said. "Stay there. Olivia's going to call you after we get off."

"Will do."

And she rang off.

Curious. What did Olivia want? She never usually asked for anything from me.

The teleconference app rang again. I noticed the symbol on-screen that indicated this line was going to have extra encryption on it. Typical Olivia.

I answered and Olivia's face came on the screen, immaculate as ever.

"Ravi. I hope Los Angeles is treating you well."

"As well as can be expected."

"Good."

There was a window in the background and I saw that it was pitch dark outside.

"Is that Chinese I hear in the background?" I said. "Where are you calling from?"

"I'm in Hong Kong, darling. The old hometown."

"What are you doing there?"

"My own case. I told Roger I had to deal with this one. He was a bit iffy since I might risk pissing off the Chinese government, but this is a personal matter, though it might also net Roger a major contact."

"So what can I do for you, Olivia?"

"You're working from the laptop we gave you, yes?"

"I'm talking to you on it right now."

"You've followed my instructions for how to use it, kept the firewall and VPN on all the time?"

"Of course. You read me the riot act about not getting hacked from the moment I was hired."

"Good. I want you to go into Documents and go to the folder marked 'OWW.'"

"I see it. The one you told me to keep around just in case."

"Now, there's one labeled 'HKS.' There should be over a dozen documents in it."

"I see them."

"I'm going to text you an FTP address to upload those files. I want you to switch the VPN to a Finnish server before you do the transfer, all right?"

"Will do. Olivia, what's this about?"

"You know those reports about book publishers who have been disappearing, snatched by the Mainland and forced to confess to crimes because they've been publishing books that air dirty laundry about the Chinese president and officials?"

"Don't tell me you're mixed up in that."

"Not me personally, but the latest bloke who's disappeared is a friend of my family's. His wife is going spare. My mother asked me for help."

"So is this an official case for Roger and the firm?" I asked.

"Yes and no. It will be when Roger sees some benefit."

"Typical Roger, hedging his bets," Julia said.

"Hi, Julia!" Olivia cried.

"So why are you asking me to send you these files when you can ask any of the others in the firm?" I asked.

"Because you're the only one I trust on this, Ravi."

"What did I do to warrant that?"

"Oh, please! You think I would trust Marcie, who would love to play CIA spook games on this? Or Mark, who could use it for mischief?"

"What about Benjamin?"

"He's not available. He's got his own caseload, and he's out of town."

"Where did he go?"

"Just flew into Los Angeles last night."

"Ah. He's here?"

"He's got a few things going on, all techy and industrial espionage-y," Olivia said. "Don't be offended if he hasn't called you. The client whisked him off to his hotel and had him working immediately."

"Who hired him? Google?"

"He signed a nondisclosure. Let's say Roger was awfully excited. He's likely to be there for a while, so if you get lonely, call him up."

"So you're in Hong Kong, Benjamin is here, Julia and I are here. Is Roger undermanned?" I asked.

"Roger and Cheryl are holding down the fort; David is still there dealing with the legal stuff. Mark is there with his caseload. Ken and Clive are there. Marcie is there with her celebrity clients, plotting away and lording it over Roger," Olivia said.

"That's all well and good, Olivia, but are you all right? Are you at risk?"

"You're very sweet to be concerned, but don't worry about me, darling. I'm playing on home ground here, and you know me. I've always covered my tracks."

"All right. I won't even ask what these files are."

"You can ask. 'HKS' stands for 'Hong Kong Stuff.' 'OWW' are my initials, of course, but it really means 'pain.' I didn't want to be caught with them when I arrived, and I didn't want anyone else to have them. They're all encrypted so you couldn't open them anyway."

"I might have guessed."

"There are programs embedded in those documents that will be time-released to certain parties. That's all I'll say for now."

"Got it. If you need anything, just email me or call."

"I prefer not to put anything in writing, darling."

"Fair enough."

"Oh, one more thing. One of the links I left you in your personal folder is access to some audio I'm recording while I'm here."

"Audio? Of what?"

"My case. It's my record of what happens. If . . . anything should happen to me, you and everyone back in London will have access to it."

"So it's a kind of insurance?"

"You should think about leaving some kind of record yourself, Ravi."

"Why? Am I in trouble?"

"Not at the moment, but you never know with the kinds of silly buggers Roger has us all get up to, and the kinds of people he has us breaking bread with."

For some reason, I had a vision of the goddess Quan Yin accompanying Olivia as she walked down the neon-lit streets of central Hong Kong. I suppose it made sense that the goddess of the moon, the goddess of mercy, was her patron deity.

"I'm not making you paranoid, am I?"

"I'm already paranoid. It's not making me any less," I said.

"Good man," Olivia said. "Now, it may be morning to you, but it's well past midnight here, and I need to catch up on my beauty sleep."

She said good night and signed off. I hoped Quan Yin was looking after her.

FIVE

The next few days were spent settling into a kind of routine at the office. We sat in on client interviews and briefings. We shadowed the investigators as they worked for a woman trying to get her under-age granddaughter away from the parents who were pimping the girl out to producers for sex to land her a role in movies and television. We observed the investigators as they traced the contents of a bank's safe deposit box to a real estate mogul's wife and mistress in a love triangle that became a battle over property deeds, which brought back unpleasant memories of the Harkingdales and London. The LA office did a lot of discovery work for law firms over inheritances and wills. Again, bad recent memories. There were the usual celebrity clients and stalking cases, but they were more restrained than we were at the London office. No beating up or intimidation, more turning over evidence to clients and lawyers so they could get restraining orders. From time to time I'd see some of them cleaning their guns at their desks. They had open carry licenses, yet they were so much more constrained than we were in London.

Benjamin seemed busy. He was knocking from one assignment to the next, all with NDAs signed. It struck me that he was loath to sign the Official Secrets Act, but had no problem with signing NDAs with tech companies. Go figure. I would get sporadic texts from him, something about testing a virtual reality prototype and introducing haptic shocks to anyone who molested female users in VR. He seemed awfully gleeful about that. There was another cryptic text about "Cool drones, bro!"

We finally met Benjamin for dinner at a venue we came to regret picking. It was a former hardware store whose new owners had converted it into one of those appalling hipster bar-restaurants they were so fond of in West Hollywood. It was the type of place whose acoustics were bloody awful and you had to shout to be heard. Darrell had explained to us that this was so people got parched from the constant shouting and would be forced to order more drinks, since the real money to be made was from selling booze more than food.

Benjamin had shown up in a prototype driverless car. When we arrived, he was showing it off to the valets and they were all oohing and aahing over it.

"You don't need to drive it, just tell it to park where you want," Benjamin said. "The AI's in learning mode."

It was more than twenty minutes before we were shown to a dimly lit table.

"I'm testing the car," Benjamin said. "Actually, I'm supposed to fuck with the AI as much as possible to see if I can break it."

"And is that when you take over and drive it manually?" Julia asked.

"That's the job."

"So let me get this straight," I said. "Instead of making sure it gets things right and doesn't get into an accident, you're mucking about with it to see if you can drive it round the bend? That seems to sum up your whole lot in life."

"You can hire anyone to sit in the car to make sure it's kosher," Benjamin said. "You spend the money on me to find a way to throw a spanner in the works. I'll always find a way."

That was Benjamin's genius, after all, to be the prankster, the coyote, the mischief-maker.

"When it's tech, I'm there," Benjamin said. "Like a rat up a drain-pipe, me."

"Long as you're having fun, mate."

"I'll drink to that." Benjamin clinked his glass to mine.

"Have you noticed your accents are even more pronounced since you got here?" Julia asked. "Mine, too."

"Maybe," I said.

"Too right," Benjamin said. "We're British and we're in a strange land. We double down on what we are."

"It's as if we're feeling insecure and need to reassert our cultural identity," Julia said over the din.

"So, what," I said, "we're playing up our accents as a kind of crutch or mental security blanket?"

"And we think we're superior to the Yanks," Benjamin said.

"Even as we have less and less justification to believe that," I said. "Given how bad things are getting back home."

"Have you noticed the way they perk up when they hear our accents?" Julia asked.

"Well, it certainly got us decent tables at the posh restaurants," I said.

"We'd sound awful trying to put on American accents anyway," Julia said.

"Here's another thing that gets to me about these clubs in Los Angeles," Benjamin said. "Why are they so bloody dark? We need flashlights to read the sodding menus."

"This is a trendy gaff," Julia said. "Celebrities come here. They keep it dark so people don't see them so easily and paparazzi can't take their photos."

"Celebs," I said. "Another thing this city is beholden to."

"Americans envy us having a Royal Family," Julia said. "Celebrities are the aristocrats of America."

"Never mind the actual billionaires and monied families," Benjamin said.

"They're not as pretty or glamorous," Julia said. "All they have is money, which they hide, and power, which many people don't have."

This wasn't the only job Benjamin had here in LA, and the undisclosed tech company with the self-driving car was not his only client. Apparently, he was working for at least six tech companies, each with a different assignment for him, and some of them even entailed some investigative work. He wanted to get a look at some new drone technology, some new surveillance gear, virtual reality development, that we might end up using for investigative work in the future, as well as a couple of cases of industrial espionage, sabotage, and employee harassment—a full dance card all said, and of course, NDAs signed with each of these clients.

"Since we're all here," Benjamin said. "Why don't we back each other up when the need arises, eh?"

"Julia and I aren't working any cases here, but sure, why not? Couldn't hurt."

"You never know, right?" Julia said.

"You never know."

We drank to our pact.

In the days to come, we would be extremely glad we'd agreed to it.

SIX

Olivia's Hong Kong recordings:

"So here I am, back in Hong Kong. Called Mum and Dad and told them I was in town. Dad was his usual distant self. I think he was a bit suspicious about why I came. I said I was here to support Marie since her husband was grabbed by the Chinese authorities. Mum asked if I was going to stay in the house, but I said I would be staying at a hotel in Causeway Bay. I didn't want them to get nosy and start poking around my computer. I had to promise to have lunch and dinner with them when I wasn't out at 'meetings.'

"Hong Kong is changing. A lot of the local businesses and cheap restaurants have disappeared, priced out by nouveau riche Mainlanders who just bought up the properties and jacked up the rent. Chatted with my friends, who were all depressed about Chinese rule. Well, not all of them were depressed. The ones working in banks were still earning their bonuses and quite chuffed about the Chinese stock market despite the slowdown. The ones investing in property were a bit nervous about the bubble on the Mainland, what with all those empty skyscrapers standing there without a buyer. Then there's the pro-democracy demonstrators and everyone worried they might kick off something. Of course, the gangs that have deals with the Mainland government are doing their bit to intimidate the protesters. All par for the course.

"Marie was beside herself since Derek disappeared. He was the fifth *book publisher to be snatched this year. He was probably somewhere across the border in China being sweated and interrogated, being forced to confess. All he did was publish a vaguely gossipy book about the expensive lifestyles of the senior politburo and their wives in Hong Kong. Derek just left for the office one morning and never came home. It's been more than a week, and when Marie tried to file a report with the police, a friend who was a senior detective whispered in her ear that Derek had probably been snatched by agents from the Mainland and taken back for interrogation, leading up to a televised confession before they let him go. Who knows how long that could take. It might be a few weeks or a few months, depending on how much they want to break him and how strong they want the message they're sending to other publishers to be. Publishers are already running scared. Three major bookshops have already closed, including the big one in Kowloon that was part of my life for as long as I can remember. Never thought it would ever go away.*

"Marie and her lawyer had been trying to find out where Derek was being held but got no joy. She was vaguely aware of the work I did for Golden Sentinels back in London, and finally called me. We have a branch here in Hong Kong as well. I helped Roger and Cheryl pick and vet the investigators here. When I told Roger that I was coming to Hong Kong, he immediately sussed out that I was here to look into Derek Hong Kam Fong's disappearance. I discussed it with him and Cheryl, and we decided this should not be an official Golden Sentinels case, since it would put the agency on the radar of the Chinese authorities, and Roger didn't want to piss them off, since he still wants a good relationship with them. Roger had bought stocks in quite a few Chinese companies, after all, and had a few clients from the Mainland. We definitely did not want Golden Sentinels to end up on a Chinese government blacklist.

"So I'm on my own.

"Marie wants me to help get Derek back in one piece. How can I do that without being detected by the Chinese government? Roger thinks I might have some protection because of my dad and the fact that his bank does a lot of business with the government. That's up for debate since if I fall under

any suspicion or get arrested, the scandal could prompt dear old dad to wash his hands of me forever, which would make my life a bit more difficult.

"No pressure.

"I'll start making my plans in the morning after I visit the spa, make an offer to Quan Yin for protection, and pray to my grandparents."

SEVEN

The news announcer on the radio was talking in great detail about the Santa Ana winds blowing over the hills of Hollywood, Santa Monica, and the San Gabriel Mountains during the next few days, stressing the risk of brush fires in the mountains that could rage across the city. Even with the car windows shut, I could hear the gushing of the wind outside. It sounded like LA was about to be invaded by banshees.

"Is this a regular occurrence here?" Julia asked.

"At least once a year," Liz Calderon said. "Usually, some douchebag on a hike in the hills lights a cigarette, and whoosh, the hills are on fire for the next week."

"Is it on purpose?" Julia asked.

"Sometimes," Darrell, who was driving, said. "A lot of times. It could be just some moron lighting a cigarette. It could be a pyromaniac out to get his kicks. It could be some dumb kid who didn't mean it."

"Bloody hell," I said. "So on top of earthquakes, a drought, and riots breaking out, you face the risk of an annual ring of fire that threatens to engulf the city?"

"We're used to it," Darrell said. "Small price to pay for living in paradise."

Julia and I exchanged glances in the backseat.

"An awfully apocalyptic paradise," I said.

"We don't see it that way," Liz said. "We're too busy with work and trying to get our careers going."

"They call the Santa Anas 'the devil winds,'" Darrell said with some pride.

"Seriously?" I blinked.

"Poetic." Julia was delighted.

I could hear the gods laughing.

It was morning. We were driving out to watch Darrell and Liz sort out a case. Liz was another of the investigators at Golden Sentinels LA, also a struggling actor. She was quite unlike Marcie, Olivia, Julia, or anyone at the London office. She'd served two tours in Afghanistan before her honorable discharge and come back to Los Angeles, where she was headhunted by Chuck while serving as a technical advisor on a movie she didn't get to act in. She used her actor training to put on whatever persona the client needed, and her default personality was of a competent professional investigator. On the occasions where she got a walk-on in a network TV show, she often played a cop or an FBI agent in the background. On a good spot, she might even get a line of dialogue, and that was how she'd gotten her SAG card. She also had firearms training, so she could hold and fire a gun convincingly on screen.

My phone rang. Ken and Clive.

"Awright, Ravi?" Ken said.

"Did something happen?" I asked.

"Just reportin' in," Clive said. They were on speakerphone mode. "We've been watchin' out for your mum and dad from a distance, like you asked. All's quiet on the Western Front."

"That's good."

"So far."

"Sorry?"

"Your mum is still working at the food bank. In fact, she's been cooking meals for the mums and kids," Ken said.

"So she's shifted to even more volunteer work, then?"

"And your dad is helpin' serve 'em," Clive said.

"I guess he decided not to let her out of his sight," I said.

"Listen, mate," Ken said. "We don't want you to be alarmed."

"Why? Is there a reason I should be?"

"We looked into your Mrs. Dhewan and her operations," Clive said.

"Do I want to hear about this? I'm the one who has to deal with her when I get back."

"She runs a tight firm, doesn't she?" Ken said.

"Are you saying you're impressed with her?"

"I wouldn't go that far," Ken said.

"No criminal record. Low-level loan sharking. Mild protection rackets, slightly dodgy DVD rentals of pirated Bollywood films to the local community," Clive listed. "Her nephews are a bit thick as far as muscle is concerned, so no danger of them trying to grab her patch. If we were still coppers we'd be cultivating her and her lot as part of the information network."

"At least she doesn't deal drugs," Ken said. "That's probably why she never got on the radar of the law."

"Hate to admit it," Clive said, "but she does some good work for the community."

"Ah. Grudging respect," I said.

"Operative word is 'grudging,'" Ken said. "Don't you forget that."

"Anyhow," Clive said. "Your dad's earned quite the reputation as a hard man with his cricket bat since that story got out."

"Oh? I thought that'd die down," I said.

"And there's a rumor of a little gang war brewing between Ms. Dhewan and the West London posse wot tried to rip off her food bank," Ken said.

"'Little'?" I said.

"They're small fry. So the posse might think your dad was part of Mrs. Dhewan's posse and come after him and your mum," Clive said.

"Oh, shit."

That drew concerned looks from Julia, and Darrell and Liz.

"Don't you worry, Ravi," Ken said. "We got our eye on 'em."

"Ain't nothing gonna happen to your folks on our watch," Clive said.

"Thanks, I owe you one," I said.

"One day, we might collect on that, mate," Ken said.

And they hung up.

"Trouble back home?" Darrell asked.

"It's under control," I said. The term was used loosely given that this was Ken and Clive.

Gossamer Rand Ross was one of Golden Sentinels LA's top priority A-list clients. Whenever he had a problem, the firm dropped everything to cater to his every need. I'm sure you've heard of him. He directed some of the biggest blockbusters of the last two decades. Ross was a director who liked to flaunt his connections. He liked to hobnob with presidents, had a love of sports cars, expensive watches, and, most of all, guns. He loved to go out shooting with small arms, rifles, and assault rifles, and had a large collection of vintage guns. This had led to Darrell and Liz's case. Ross was in Romania shooting his latest $200 million action blockbuster with half a dozen A-list stars, a lot of cars to crash, and enough explosives to make Eastern Europe look like the aftermath of World War II. That's not even including the tens of millions of dollars' worth of CGI effects that would be added in postproduction to actually depict cities being leveled.

It was while Ross was away that the case had arisen.

"This is how it went down," Liz said. "Ross left the care of his five-million-dollar house in the Hollywood Hills to one of his assistants, Keith Doyle. Now, Keith, like any twenty-something hipster with the keys to the kingdom, likes to party, so throws one every Saturday in the house. Ross doesn't give a damn as long as the place is kept clean and nothing goes missing. Keith is there to let the gardeners and cleaning staff in to tidy up the place every Monday."

"Well, last Saturday, something did go missing," Darrell said. "An antique Flintlock Duval pistol from 1765 that used to belong to Alexander Hamilton. Taken out of its display case in the living room while everyone was doped out of their minds and having sex."

"So Keith woke up on Sunday afternoon all hungover, and the first thing he saw was the empty case," Liz said. "He freaked out because it's probably worth millions. Ross has Golden Sentinels on retainer, and Keith called us up to clean up this mess, track down the pistol."

"It wasn't that hard," Darrell said. "Ross had cameras installed all over the house, so all we had to do was review the footage of the party. Saw who took the pistol out of the case with a time stamp and everything."

And that was who we were driving out to see.

EIGHT

We had come all the way out to a chop shop in Malibu. Even here, the winds were howling. The temperature was low for Southern California and we were all in coats. Dix Coolihan was the one we were meeting. He had sandy hair and a sandy beard. He could have been a surfer dude if he hadn't been so twitchy. This wasn't even his shop. It was his cousin's. He just happened to deal drugs out of it when clients like Keith didn't call him out to make deliveries. Liz said that they received stolen cars here, then repainted them for resale or stripped them for parts. Dix didn't work here, but his cousin grudgingly let him use the garage as a meeting place and informal office.

"Uh-oh," Liz said when she saw Dix come out to greet us. "He's totally tweaking."

"Think he's packing?" Darrell asked.

"Stay sharp," Liz said.

"Tweaking?" I asked.

"He's on meth," Liz said. "That makes them unpredictable."

We got out of the car and walked towards Dix. We all stepped out in the lot, a fair distance from the garage entrance. His cousin must have told him he didn't want any of Dix's business being done inside. I looked around. This was largely an empty lot, with the hills in the background. Not a lot of cover if guns were drawn and things kicked off. I'd just remembered that I'd never been in a shoot-out before and had no desire to be.

"You two might want to hang back," Darrell said. "He could fly off the handle at anything."

Liz kept her hand on her holster as they got closer to Dix.

"What the fuck, man?" Dix said. "You brought a whole party out here?"

Liz and Darrell stopped, keeping ten feet between them and Dix while Julia and I stayed near the car.

"Now, Dix," Darrell held out his hands, "we told you. We need to see the Flintlock. These guys are from Christie's to inspect it."

"Not too smart, Dix," Liz said. "It's not something you just fence. It's a specific kind of antique. You don't have the certificate of authenticity, you got jack."

"Yeah, so what I'm thinkin'," Dix said. "You go back, and you bring me that certificate of whatever, yeah."

"That's not what we discussed, Dix," Darrell said. "We got you on video lifting it at Gossamer Ross's place. We said we'd keep LAPD off your ass if you give us back the gun."

"Yeah, yeah, I go down, I take Ross's boy Keith down with me, and we both sing about what your fancy client Ross has in that fancy house of his."

"You don't wanna go talking like that, Dix." Liz's tone got harder.

"Yeah? Or what? Huh? You wanna draw down on me? I got a piece, too. You wanna see? Huh? Let's do it! Let's dance."

Suddenly, Dix glanced my way and went wide-eyed with terror.

"Whoa! Whoa! Who the fuck are these guys?"

"Dix, chill," Liz said. "We told you. They're the people from England who are here to check the gun for damage."

"Not them! The other ones! The ones with the arms and blue skin!"

What the fuck?

Kali and Rudra were advancing on Dix and he could see them? What was going on here?

"Are they even human? Stop smiling at me!"

Liz and Darrell looked in my direction, perplexed, and saw only Julia and me.

Dix pulled the small .22 pistol from his belt and pointed it at them.

"Whoa!" Darrell cried. "Chill, man!"

Liz drew her Glock and pointed it at Dix, her hands steady where his shook.

"Dix, put the gun down."

"What are they? Keep them away from me!"

"They're gods," Julia said.

"Please, don't you start," I whispered.

"Dix, put the gun down!" Liz cried.

Darrell stayed calm but tense, held out his hands to show he was open, no threat.

"You're seeing them because you're ready," Julia continued.

"You're shitting me!"

"If you can see them, it means you've hit a point in your addiction," she continued.

"Fuck you! Get them away from me!"

"Dix, listen to me," I said. "You're seeing them because it's time."

Dix was backing away. I slowly walked toward him.

"Time for what? Am I gonna die? I'm not gonna die!"

"It's your call," I said, holding out my palms as I approached him. "Time to think about your life."

"Poor boy," Kali said. "All the karma spilling out of you."

"That's Kali," I said. "You heard of her?"

"She's like a goddess or some shit?"

"She's your chickens come to roost," I said, walking closer. "She can't hurt you. You can only hurt yourself here."

Kali loomed over him, smiling. She was enjoying this. Gods tended to enjoy their power.

Dix's gun hand wavered.

"Are you going to shoot a god, Dix?" I said. "Think carefully. Nothing good ever comes from that."

"Just tell me what to do, man." He trembled, clammy with sweat.

"For starters, put the gun down," I said.

He fell to his knees and started to cry. Kali had that effect on people. She towered over him, her tongue wagging.

Liz approached him, gun aimed. He let the gun go. She kicked it out of his reach.

"This is your chance to clean your slate," I said. "Just give us the Flintlock and we'll be off."

And he did. And we were.

"Well," Liz said as she started the car. "That went a lot better than I could have hoped."

Dix had taken the Flintlock out of a toolbox in the chop shop. It was wrapped in a dishcloth. Julia was holding it in her lap as we drove out of Malibu.

"Dude," Darrell said. "That was some amazing improv. How did you come up with it?"

"It's a knack Ravi has," Julia said. "He reads unstable people in a certain way and comes up with a way to wrong-foot them. Quite astonishing, really."

"Your boss told Chuck you were the magic sauce when things threatened to go south," Liz said. "We thought it was just hype. I'm impressed."

"We all wondered what Roger meant when he said 'throwing Chaos at chaos,'" Darrell said. "Now we know."

"Er, thanks," I stammered.

"And you used to teach high school?" Liz asked, her eyes suggesting she was assessing me anew. "Huh."

The radio was reporting that the fire department was on high alert for the first hint of a fire in the hills. The wind advisory was still in effect. Traffic all over town was starting to jam up because people were rushing home, especially those who lived in the hills, to take precautions, hose their roofs down with water, and so on. It took us forty-five minutes to get to Ross's house up in the hills, which Darrell said was in a prime real estate spot.

As we drove towards the house, both Darrell and Liz's smartphones rang.

"My manager," Darrell said.

"Mine, too," Liz said, answering with her Bluetooth earpiece so she could keep driving.

"Yo," Darrell answered. "Yeah? Seriously? That's awesome, man! Yeah, yeah, I'll be there!"

"Really?" Liz said. "Today? Okay. Okay. I'll make it."

They hung up at the same time.

"Callback!" they cried in unison.

"Sorry, what's happening?" I asked from the backseat.

"A part I've been dying for!" Darrell said. "Every guy in town's been after it! This could be it! They want me back today for a screen test!"

"And I'm up for the female lead!" Liz said.

They both got out of the car, hugged, and jumped up and down.

"They want us down there ASAP," Darrell said. "Everyone's gonna want to finish this early 'cause they all wanna get home to fireproof their houses."

"Shit," Liz said. "And I gotta pick up my kid from school after that."

"Do you need to go now?" Julia asked.

"Yeah," Darrell said. "But we gotta go in there, talk to Keith, put the gun back in the case, square things off."

"And Keith is gonna want to talk because he's such a nervous nelly." Liz sighed. "That's gonna take time."

Julia nudged me.

"Julia and I could do that," I said. "You can go to your callbacks."

"You sure?" Darrell said.

"We're just returning the gun," I said.

"We can get a taxi back," Julia said. "Go on."

NINE

Darrell called ahead and told Keith that Julia and I were getting dropped off at the house with the Flintlock. Darrell and Liz practically screeched off in the car once Julia and I got out at the front door of Ross's house.

It was an impressive piece of architecture, all glass and steel, perched over the hills for a full view of the city. We pushed the buzzer at the gate and Keith unlocked it electronically. It was one of those big, sturdy gates that rolled slowly open.

"Aren't you going to talk about what happened?" Julia asked as we walked up the driveway.

"What do you mean?"

"That Dix bloke saw Kali."

"He was completely off his face, Julia. Obviously hallucinating."

We reached the front door and I rang the bell.

"But to see *your* gods . . . none of us saw anything, just him freaking out. You obviously saw what he saw."

"I don't want to think about it," I said.

"Why not?"

"Because it means the gods aren't just in my head, and I'd rather not deal with what that could mean."

"It could mean you're not mad. You're not stressed out—"

"Julia, not now."

"Why not now?"

"Because," I stammered. "Because it could change everything."

"It could mean you're not mad," she repeated. "Isn't that what you always wanted? You're terrified that you might be mentally ill. What if you really are channeling the gods, or something from outside yourself?"

Of course she was right: this was entirely new territory, and it was territory worth exploring, worth thinking about. But between my recent arrival in LA and Dix's wild behavior, I needed to focus on the matter at hand and worry about the gods later.

"Julia, this doesn't make it better. It could make things worse. Much, much worse."

"How?"

"Don't you see? It makes the world, hell, the whole universe even more terrifying. It's one thing if I'm just chemically imbalanced. That we can all understand. If it's all real, that means something else is going on. For starters, if the gods are real, what do they want? What are their plans? Gods always have plans, and if they've chosen me to be their instrument or their conduit, where does that leave me? It means they won't leave me alone. I'm their shaman or their tool, and I'm supposed to carry out their plan in some way that I don't know. It means I don't have free will."

"So you *have* thought about it," Julia said.

"Yes, and it scares the shit out of me even more!"

The front door opened. Saved by the Keith.

"Hey, guys." He looked extremely relieved, and also a bit stoned. "Sorry it took so long. I have some people here. Make yourselves at home."

There was already a party under way when Keith opened the door. Everyone was wearing leather and corsets. I spotted a cat-o'-nine-tails as well.

"Heeeey, guys." He was already sloshed. "You have saved my life. Literally."

Keith wore glasses, had curly dark hair and an awkward, lanky body. He looked more like a graduate student than the assistant to a Hollywood director. He had the geeky air of someone desperately trying to hide that he was out of his depth and flailing. Darrell had said he wasn't a bad guy, just a bit hapless, lucky (or unlucky) enough to have been hired as

Ross's second assistant to hold down the fort while the first assistant went overseas with the boss while he shot his new film.

"Let's just get the gun back in the case, shall we?" I said. "We'll feel better about it then."

Keith showed Julia and me in. Keith's friends were all smoking joints in the living room and watching the seventy-inch flat-screen TV. It showed live helicopter footage of a fire starting in the Santa Monica Mountains, not far from where we were earlier.

"Looks like we had a narrow escape," Julia said.

"It's, like, sooo apocalyptic!" the guy with the cropped bleached hair and chiseled body cried.

"You have a soul mate, Ravi." Julia winked at me.

"Please don't start," I muttered.

"Would you like something? Beer? A water?" Keith asked.

"I'm fine, thanks," I said.

"I could use some water," Julia said.

I carried the Flintlock over to the glass case, turned the key and opened it, put the gun back on its pedestal, and shut the case.

"All done."

I looked at the TV and saw the plume of gray smoke rising from the mountains, then looked out the window. They were massive and gave us a panoramic view of the city, including across town towards Santa Monica, and I could see the same growing cloud of smoke rising in the distance. Everyone at the party just kept looking at the telly when the real thing was right outside the window.

"You know, Keith, we ought to get going," I said.

"I hear ya," he said. "I'm just here to hold down the fort, batten down the hatches, and wait for Gossamer to call from Romania so I can give 'im a status report on the fire. Probably gonna have to hose down the outside of the house in case the fire gets to this side of town."

"Do you think the fire will reach here?" Julia asked.

"The wind's blowing in this direction," Keith said. "Don't think the fire department's gonna be able to contain that fire, so we can expect major chaos. I don't wanna be here when that hits."

"Where do you live?" I asked.

"The Valley," he said. "Traffic's already gonna be chaos, even before rush hour hits."

"Then maybe we should just call a cab or an Uber and get going ourselves," I said.

"Dude," the goth-looking girl in the leather bustier said, holding up her smartphone. "Ain't no cabs or Ubers comin' up here. They're stayin' the fuck away from the hills, on account of not wanting to be caught in a brush fire and all."

"Bugger," I said.

"Look, why don't you hang out a little?" Keith said. "Once the boss calls and I finish up here, I can give you guys a lift."

"That's very kind of you," Julia said.

"Least I can do considering you saved my ass getting that gun back."

"Cheers, Keith," I said. "But is it going to be long?"

"Ravi, don't worry," Julia said. "If the fire reaches this side of the hills, it won't be for a few hours. The news on the TV just said that."

"Right," I said, unconvinced. "I'm just not so keen on sitting on my arse here for a few hours doing nothing."

"But you're not doing nothing, Ravi," Julia said. "We're having an experience very few people get a chance to. Look at all this, the surrealism, the mysteriousness of it all, as if cosmic forces are converging. Just sit and take this all in."

I looked around. The gods were here, milling about the house. Shiva sitting on the sofa with the leather kids. Kali dancing in the middle of the living room. Ganesha standing outside near the ledge, looking out at the city and the smoke. They were happy to mingle at this party. Or was it just mingling? Was someone else going to see them, too? So far, the human guests seemed completely oblivious to their presence. More than half of the guests were drunk or stoned, and still didn't see them. That meant it took more than intoxication to see my gods. More questions. More frightening implications for me.

Lord Shiva met my eye, as if he read my mind.

He smiled. Not a smug or malicious smile, but with a hint of sadness, as if he sympathized. He nodded at me and turned back to the conversation on the sofa. They were talking about some government conspiracy or other, mainly about how the Right wanted to criminalize marijuana again.

"So what am I really doing here taking all this in?" I asked.

"Why, bearing witness, of course," Julia said. "Isn't that what the gods always wanted you to do?"

Damn. Julia had my number there. Again. She always did.

"Bearing witness it is, then." I sighed. "Keith, I'll have some water after all."

"Good idea," he said, handing me a bottle of expensive mineral water. "Stay hydrated."

TEN

From Olivia's recordings:

"I contacted Golden Sentinels' Hong Kong office to let them know I was in town. If anything were to happen to me, they would at least let Roger and Cheryl know. Everyone in Hong Kong was freaked out that Derek Hong Kam Fong had been snatched off the streets by the Chinese authorities. It was still headline news, and pro-democracy activists were protesting about China's increasing erosion of freedoms in Hong Kong. Some of the chaps at Golden Sentinels' Hong Kong office offered to help me out, but I had to turn them down because Golden Sentinels could not be seen to be working on this case. Besides, they weren't getting paid. The other thing is, the office here is split between the boss, who just wants to keep his head down and keep getting big money clients, and the younger investigators, who want more democratic rights and representation in Hong Kong. I didn't want to throw a match to those tensions.

"Derek's office was not far from the red light district of Wan Chai. I went over and found that the office had been closed since Derek disappeared, so I tracked down his employees, who were all holed up at home. They told me the morning he disappeared, he never made it to the office. Derek didn't take the car to work because traffic was bloody awful. He usually took the bus. Whoever grabbed him had to have observed his daily routine before they decided the best time and place to make their move. I didn't have the names of any Mainland Chinese agents who could have been operating in

Hong Kong, and they may not have used any. They could have used local talent, and that meant the Triads. The next step, then, would be to find out which gangs operated in Wan Chai, especially near Derek's office. Wan Chai had seen its share of gang wars when I was a girl back in the nineties. I remember hearing about murders, police raids and skirmishes, but things had been fairly quiet in the last few years. The area is divided into different turfs overseen by branch gangs. I had to find out which ones had a deal with the Chinese authorities to keep the peace and gather information, particularly on Derek.

"Here was where I could use my family's connections."

ELEVEN

Julia and I stood out on the balcony, an elegant structure of steel and wood perched precariously over an abyss. The fall down the ravines of the Hollywood Hills would feel almost bottomless. We watched as the plume of smoke from the other mountains across the city grew bigger. The sound of helicopters in the sky was ubiquitous and endless. Every now and then another police helicopter would buzz by overhead. We even spotted the odd black drone flitting in and out of the vicinity. Police and ambulance sirens echoed in the distance.

"They're saying it could become a ring of fire around the whole city," Julia said.

"That's comforting," I said, not comforted at all.

"You really should try to enjoy yourself," she said, her hand stroking my neck.

"It's hard to do that when the world keeps looking like it's on the precipice of disaster," I said.

Ganesha was up above, looming large, sitting on one of the few clouds in the clear sky and looking down on the city with interest.

"Which gods are you seeing now?" Julia asked.

"Ganesha, as usual," I said. "Up there in the clouds. But then he's the god of travel, after all, and everyone has to drive here in LA, so that makes sense. I'm sensing some tension in the air because the fires are going to cause traffic to jam up. Wait, is that—?"

"What is it?" Julia asked.

"Over the hills. Vayu is there. God of winds. He's in casual wear, and he's just blowing away. It's as if he's sending the Santa Ana winds."

"You heard what some people say about the Santa Ana winds," Julia said. "That it's a kind of purifying wind that blows through the city a few times a year."

"So the brush fire that's carried by the wind might be part of the gods' process?"

"Didn't you tell me Vayu, or Pavana, was about purification?" Julia asked.

"I never thought of him quite like this," I muttered. "As in, this literally."

Vayu had a cocktail in his hand, and took a sip from it between puffs. It was a piña colada. I never liked piña coladas. Too sweet.

"I might start to resent the fact that the gods are having a much better time than me," I said. "But then, they're gods. Of course they would."

"We're quite the pair," Julia said. "People don't quite know what to make of us. You should be living large with it."

"Whatever do you mean?"

"People think you're some mysterious bloke from England with special abilities," Julia said. "I'm just the eye candy with the posh accent. I can live with that. It's how I hide in plain sight and find out people's secrets. Roger knew that from that start, and you know that."

"Don't sell yourself short, love," I said. "People have been going gaga for you everywhere we've gone in LA. To them, you're practically Princess Di."

"Being compared to the martyred royal broodmare doesn't exactly inflate my self-esteem." Julia smirked.

"You know what I mean."

"Ravi, what gets me is how you can't even enjoy any of this. You have so much guilt and angst about what you do and what you're afraid you might do. You still worry that you're going mad when you haven't done anything of the sort. We all witnessed something extraordinary and you won't even acknowledge it."

"It happened. I admit it. I just don't want to think about it."

"Why not? It means the gods aren't something that's just inside your head. Why don't you want to think about it?"

"Because it would mean they're outside of me. Dix was completely off his face on crystal meth and I wasn't, yet we both saw and reacted to Kali in the same place. We saw where she was and heard what she said. You couldn't see her. Darrell and Liz didn't see her. That means there's something out there, and everything my dad said, everything Mark has been saying, about me channeling something, that I might be some kind of modern-day shaman, that's not what I want my life to be. I almost wish I was just a seedy private investigator in a seedy little corrupt world."

"You're obsessed with some platonic idea of 'normality.'"

"All right, I suppose I am. Is that too much to hope for?"

"And yet you're with me."

"Julia—"

"You could have found yourself a nice girl who doesn't have an addiction or depression problem. Instead you chose my brand of damage."

"If you're damaged, I'm every bit as damaged," I said.

"So we might as well be damaged together?"

"It's better than living with the damage alone."

"Sometimes I see Louise," she said. "But it's more like I imagine she's there watching me, saying something to reassure me. I know I'm the one imposing the image of her there. She's not actually there. With you, it's different. I wish she really was there watching me. I like to think of her as fully transitioned, healthy. Her hair is fabulous, she's wearing a stunning Yves St. Laurent dress, she's got a set of marvelous tits, and she's happy."

"So I have my gods and you have your sister."

"Except I'm not worried that I'm going mad. I'm an addict, after all. That's already a form of madness."

"You're being too harsh on yourself again. You're not mad, Julia."

Her eyes welled up; the wetness glistened in the light of the monitors.

"I love you so much, Ravi."

"And I can't imagine my life without you," I said.

"Hey, guys." Keith came out of the living room. "I'm gonna call Gossamer now."

TWELVE

Gossamer Rand Ross's white walls were lined with photos of him with various A-list stars he had worked with (and the A-list women he had slept with), which was nearly everyone who was anyone in Hollywood, given that he had made eighteen movies over a twenty-five-year period. The pictures that took the more prominent pride of place, though, were the ones where he was posing with politicians, generals, presidents, and heads of state. The photos with movie stars said "This is me with Fame!" The photos with politicians said "This is me with Power!"

And given the antiques, paintings, and sculptures that adorned the house, you could safely assume that Gossamer Rand Ross was a man obsessed with wealth, status, power, and the finer things in life. He had a particular fondness for antique weapons and busts of military figures. It would stand to reason, then, that he might want to safeguard this house and its extremely expensive contents from a brush fire that threatened to turn it all into ash and scrap if it hit this part of the hills.

The party was winding down. Keith's guests in leather were drifting away, getting in their cars to beat the traffic and get home. The faint whiff of weed was still in the air from the joints that had been smoked.

Julia and I waited while Keith dialed Ross's number in Romania. It was late over there by now.

"Okay, Keith, what's the status?" Ross had never been in the military but was a major groupie for military-speak and war porn, as many of his movies indicated.

He sounded wide awake and alert, no hint of sleepiness at all while he listened to Keith give him the weather report and the brushfire warnings from the news.

"There's no way I can get movers in now to take all this stuff someplace safe," Keith said, his voice quivering slightly. "We're going to have to prioritize, Goss. What do you want me to save?"

"The guns! Get the guns!"

"Er, which ones?"

"The goddamn guns! Get them out of the house! The hell with the art! It's all insured! Just get the guns out of the house!"

"Goss, what are you talking about? I haven't seen any guns other than the antique Flintlock and the handgun in your desk."

"The ones in the panic room!"

"But it's locked. I haven't been in the panic room before."

"Oh, for—! Goddamnit! I'll give you the code! It's 467452!"

"Okay, got it."

"Go to the panic room now," Gossamer said. "It's at the end of the hall, the door next to the bedroom. Keypad's behind the framed picture of me with the Dalai Lama."

We followed Keith down the hall as he kept the phone on speaker. The picture of Ross with the Dalai Lama was on a hinge, and Keith entered the code into the keypad behind it. I noticed there was a small camera installed at the top of the wall, housed inside a protective glass dome, the type Benjamin liked to use to keep tabs on people.

We heard heavy locks grind and the door on the wall opened.

Virtually every mansion in Los Angeles has a panic room. Gossamer Rand Ross's was state-of-the-art. The air-conditioning system automatically kicked in and a gentle breeze blew the stuffiness away. The room was spacious enough to accommodate a bed, a desk, an armchair, a sofa, and a coffee table.

There were shelves of tinned foods, the most upmarket kind, like caviar, gourmet soups, and bottled water, canisters of protein powder, plates and utensils. There was a large flat-screen TV and entertainment center. There was a communications desk against the wall that consisted of six TV monitors, with feeds from surveillance cams positioned in and out of the house, and a telephone.

"There's about six big cases by the gun rack." Gossamer's voice came over the cordless phone in Keith's hand. "Open them up."

"Holy shit!" Keith cried.

Inside the sleek metal cases were not the usual semiautomatic handguns and hunting rifles that were on the gun rack against the wall. No, these were military-grade weapons: fully automatic combat rifles with laser sights, pistols converted to full auto; one case held an M-50 sniper rifle. These were not weapons a civilian would ever be allowed to possess. There must have been at least fifty assault rifles in the cases.

Keith started to hyperventilate. Was he terrified or excited or both?

"Listen to me, Keith!" Gossamer said. "I need you to get all those guns you into the car—"

"What? What? Hold on—"

"Those are not my guns, okay? I've been holding them for someone," Gossamer continued. "Now I need you to get them to the people they're due to before they're found or burned up in the brush fires."

"Wow," Keith said. "Oh, wow."

"Keith, I need you to focus, damn it! I'm shooting a whole war with a hundred extras blowing up all over the place tomorrow and I need you to do this little thing for me so we don't land in the shit when I get back."

Even in his state, Keith couldn't resist pulling out his phone and taking a selfie of himself in front of the guns.

"Is that such a good idea?" Julia asked.

"It's proof that this is all real," Keith said, uploading the photo to his Instagram account. "That I'm not dreaming."

"Who is that?" Ross said. "Keith! You're not alone? You brought people into my panic room?"

I took the house phone from Keith and we led him back to the living room.

"Mr. Ross, this is Ravi Chandra Singh." I put on my most professional voice. "We're from Golden Sentinels."

"Golden Sentinels, huh? Did Chuck send you?" Ross said. "Is that an English accent?"

"Julia and I are from England, sir. We're from the London office. Keith called the agency when he heard about the brush fires and wanted us to help him secure the art and antiques in your house."

There was a pause.

"Good thinking, Keith," Ross said, grudgingly.

Keith mouthed "thank you" to me.

"So back to the guns," I said.

"Yeah."

"Who were you holding them for? Where do you want them delivered?"

"Okay, this is strictly hush-hush, okay? I was keeping them safe as a favor for my friends in the CIA. They're going to some freedom fighters in the Middle East."

"I see."

"So we can't risk losing those guns if the house burns down or looters break in, you dig?"

"Of course."

"So the CIA has a safe house down in North Hollywood. Best thing to do is load up the guns in one of the SUVs in the garage and drive it down there till the fires blow over."

"That's, like, down in the Valley," Keith said. "Traffic's gonna be all jammed up."

"So what are you waiting for?" Ross said. "Get going!"

"But with the fires, there's going to be police checkpoints," Keith said.

"Might I suggest we take care of this so that you and Keith don't get implicated if he's stopped?" I said.

"Oh, yeah, yeah. You guys are the professionals, right? Keith, I hate to say it, but you're out of your league with this one."

"I agree!" Keith said eagerly.

I wrote down the address of the safe house.

"So, Keith, you can go home and write your screenplay or take care of your cat or whatever you do with your sad, desperate life. You're off the hook for this one," Ross said.

"Thanks, boss," Keith said and ran out.

We watched him jump in his Prius and speed away.

"Before we go," I turned back to Gossamer Ross on the phone, "is there anything else we ought to look out for? Does anyone else know about the guns? Is there anyone who might be after them?"

Ross paused as he seemed to be thinking.

"Maybe a couple of people," he finally said. "My buddies in the Company said the Armenians might want their hands on those guns since they can either sell or use 'em. Some of the gangs that are linked to the cartels."

"How might they know about these guns?" I asked.

"Word got out when my buddies managed to requisition them from some surplus at the manufacturers. They're hard to come by on the black market, so all the gangs want their hands on these guns. It's a status thing for them to have the latest military-grade arms. That's another reason to get the guns out of my house. They might use the brush fire as their chance to break in and grab 'em."

"I'll bear that in mind," I said.

"You guys are the best," Ross said. "Tell Chuck I'll pay a bonus if you pull this off."

And he hung up.

. . . *If?*

"Are we really doing this?" Julia asked, raising an eyebrow.

"I went into default professional mode before I knew I was doing it," I said.

Or did the gods compel me?

"We should just call Chuck at the office. He can send some of the others to deal with this."

"Good idea, and they can give us a lift back to our apartment."

I dialed Golden Sentinels.

"*You've reached Golden Sentinels Private Investigations and Security. I'm afraid no one is here to take your call. Please leave your name and number, and an investigator will call you back regarding your request.*"

Beep.

"Where the hell is everybody?" I said. "Even the receptionist is out."

I dialed Chuck's smartphone.

"Chuck here."

It sounded like he was driving.

"It's Ravi. I just tried calling the office and got the answering machine. Is that normal?"

"Nothing's normal today, Ravi," Chuck said. "It's the damn Santa Ana winds, makes the whole city go nuts. Everyone's either out helping a client or off making sure their house isn't going to get caught in the brush fire."

"Is it that bad?"

"It might get there. This is a big one. I have to go hose down the roof, get my wife and dog to a hotel for the night if the fire reaches my neighborhood."

"So is anyone at the office available for a client?"

"Which client?"

"Gossamer Rand Ross."

"One of our A-listers. Didn't Darrell and Liz take care of that case earlier?"

"They did, and they're off now. This is something new."

"Can it wait?"

"It's time-sensitive. He needs us to get a bunch of guns out of his house and into a safe house in the San Fernando Valley."

"Did you say guns?"

"Said he was holding them for the CIA."

"Oh, hell." Chuck groaned. "Ross playing amateur secret agent again, and he's not even in the country."

"And Julia and I aren't licensed to operate in the US, so—"

"Right, right. I don't know what to tell you, Ravi. Gossamer Rand Ross is one of our biggest clients, and this is way above your pay grade. Hell, it's way above *our* paygrade. I might ask you to do this as one of us, but at the same time I don't have the right to put you in that position."

"So what would you do if you were us?"

"Get in a car and just leave. Running guns as a favor for the CIA? That's just asking for troub—ou—on't—it—"

"Chuck? Chuck? You're breaking up."

"—to a—ad re—eption—I—it."

The line went dead.

"We should just get into one of his cars and drive away, Ravi."

"That's what Chuck said," I said.

We found the car keys on the coffee table in the living room. Lord Vishnu didn't look eager to leave. In fact, he stood in the hallway, beckoning to me. Kali was dancing in the living room with Ganesha.

"Er, Ravi," Julia said. "Keith left the gate open when he drove off."

"Just as well. We need it open when we leave anyway."

"There are people driving in," Julia said. "I don't think they were invited."

I looked out the window, down towards the driveway. Two, three black sedans were coming into the estate. They stopped in the parking area and about half a dozen men got out. They wore a mixture of colorful T-shirts, cheap jackets, and sunglasses. They hadn't seen us yet as they walked towards the house.

No wonder the gods were here partying. They'd been anticipating something like this would happen. I should have guessed.

"Into the panic room," I said.

THIRTEEN

From Olivia's recordings:

"I wasn't completely at a loss for where to start. Hong Kong is a small place where everyone sort of knows each other. Connections and gossip are the social currency here, just like anywhere else, but you need to be an insider to make proper use of that.

"I wondered why Derek would publish a book about the shopping habits of the Chinese elite and their wives to start with. On the surface, it might seem like a gossipy bit of fluff, but the information in it must have got up the Mainland's back, which prompted them to grab him off the streets of Hong Kong.

"I had questions: Had he just published it as another quickie cash-in? Where had he gotten the information from, which circles? Was the book a deliberate provocation in a larger game? Was it published under the aegis of the CIA through some front company that paid for it as some kind of propaganda tool to fuck with China? I wouldn't put it past them since they still don't really understand China at all and treat it like an old-school Cold War game, like they still do with Russia. Bloody spies and their games. Perhaps that's why they grabbed Derek—to sweat him and see if he's a CIA asset. This was why I didn't tell bloody Marcie back at the office. I didn't want her sticking her oar in. She could end up making things worse.

"My mission was to get Derek released and not be seen sticking my neck out. I still had to know who I was dealing with and how to get to them. I grilled his wife, Marie, to see if she was in on the book. She swore up and down that she didn't know anything. She would have tried to talk him out of publishing the book if she knew he was going to piss off the Mainland authorities. She was on her last nerve since he'd been snatched, and the kids weren't having a great time of it either.

"First port of call was tea with Uncle Ko. I've known Ko Chi Wan all my life. He was one of the old-school Triad leaders who went legitimate, parlayed his cash into proper, aboveboard businesses to get out of the game, though he still knew everyone in the Triad world. They treated him with respect and came to him for advice, even though he wasn't officially in the Jiang Hu anymore. Uncle Ko had accounts with my dad's bank and they socialized frequently, of course. He came to our house to play mahjong with my dad and his exclusive circle of friends every week.

"I brought Uncle Ko and his wife gifts from Harrods and had a pleasant tea where I asked him about the lay of the land. I asked about how the Jiang Hu was with the Chinese government. Uncle Ko confirmed that many of the bosses did deals with the Chinese to act as their eyes and ears on the ground in Hong Kong and Kowloon, and occasionally did 'jobs' for them.

"I asked Uncle Ko about the Wan Chai district, and he told me the area was overseen by Brother Bull and his men. Brother Bull was in his forties, been in charge for the last ten years, a gregarious bear of a man who enjoyed gambling, betting on the horses, and getting massages from the hookers in Wan Chai, many of whom he ran anyway.

"Brother Bull.

"Hm.

"That was a start."

FOURTEEN

We watched the men go through the house, overturning furniture, going through the cupboards.

"They don't look like ordinary burglars," Julia said.

"They're trying to make it look like a random break-in. Like they're looters and vandals from the chaos of the brush fire," I said.

Via the surveillance cameras, we watched them go through the house, picking up expensive items and perusing the artwork, which was too large for them to just drive off with, so they left them on the walls. There were at least four of them, and they didn't look like the wannabe hipster kids who targeted the homes of stars after following them on social media. All in all, they were doing a rather halfhearted job of tossing the place. Their body language indicated they weren't interested in just nicking cash and the telly. They had bulges under their jackets, which meant guns, and probably knew how to use them, though I suspected they weren't all properly trained. These were, if not necessarily professionals, hardened criminals. Just what we needed. They were after something specific, which had to be the guns here in the panic room with us.

"They don't seem to have found the door to the panic room yet," Julia said.

"Thank fuck for that," I said. "The way they're going about it, I don't think they're going to leave until they find the guns, or suss out there's a panic room here."

"Or the brush fire reaches this part of the hills and they're forced to leave," Julia said. "Traffic back into town is going to be packed, and people will be stuck on the roads and freeways for hours."

"But if this house is safe against the fire, they might just wait around here until nightfall," I said. "There's plenty of entertainment and food here to keep them amused for days."

"Same goes for us in here," Julia said.

I finally looked around.

"Christ. This panic room is larger than most flats in London," I said.

There was a large bed in here, since Gossamer Rand Ross might have brought a girlfriend or mistress in here if he ever needed to hide out.

I took out my smartphone and dialed London. It wasn't midnight there yet, so I didn't feel bad about waking anyone up.

"Ravi," David said. "What's up, mate?"

It sounded like he was in a quiet drinking club, probably his usual place in Soho, just off Frith Street.

"David, I'm calling about my will."

"You're what? What's happening out there?"

"I may have gotten myself in a spot of bother, and, well, if things go completely pear-shaped, you may have to execute my will. It's all in order, yeah?"

"You're not joking, are you?"

"Wish I were, mate. I just need you to make sure my money goes to my parents and my sister."

"What about Julia?"

"She's here with me, and she doesn't think it'll get that bad. I'm not so sure."

"What's brought this on?"

"Well, there's the Santa Ana winds causing a brush fire in the hills, a stash of military-grade guns and weapons the client was holding on to for the CIA that he now needs us to move, and a bunch of heavily armed bastards who would probably kill us for them."

"Hang on, is this Golden Sentinels business?"

"Sort of."

"So why aren't the LA guys dealing with it? Why you? You're not bloody authorized to work cases there."

"Because of the brush fire in the hills. The LA office is all MIA. They're either off helping clients put out fires, some of them literally, or they're off trying to save their own homes. Suffice to say, they're scattered all over the city."

"So, what, you're trapped?"

"Julia and I are holed up in a panic room. We can probably wait them out, but . . ."

"Oh, bloody hell. Ravi, just call the police."

"David, I'm a dark-skinned foreigner in a gun-ridden part of America in possession of enough guns to start a war in a small country. The police tend to get a bit trigger-happy in this type of situation, especially if they start thinking I'm a terrorist. There is no way this would go well for me."

"You know, Ravi, what really worries me here is you're not known for exaggerating things."

"If anything, I may be downplaying some of this."

"Right, I'm calling Roger. He needs to know about this."

"What's he going to do from over there? Who's he going to call?"

"All right. You know what? I'm calling Marcie as well."

"Why?"

"You said CIA, didn't you? She's got to know something about this. In the meantime, stop thinking about dying and just hide."

He hung up.

"What?" I said to Julia as she looked at me.

"I think you should have a bit more faith," she said.

"I like to think being practical is better than having faith," I said.

"We always find a way out of these binds," Julia said. "I'm not worried. If anything, I'm excited to see how you do it."

"Me? You're giving me far too much credit, love," I said. "But I appreciate the thought."

"Do the gods have any suggestions?" she asked.

"Please don't start about the gods," I said and winced.

I looked around. Yes, they were all milling about in here with us, lounging around in the chairs, looking in the wardrobe, and watching us intently.

"What's this?" Julia opened another wardrobe, which was painted red and black, making it stand out from the standard cupboard with the normal clothes and shoes.

Inside were some leather corsets, stockings, cat-o'-nine-tails, chains, fur-lined handcuffs, vinyl boots—all for women. Julia shook her head and laughed.

"So Ross's tastes are on the usual naughty schoolboy side after all," I said.

"Well, we might as well enjoy it since we're going to be stuck here a few hours," Julia said, picking up an expensive leather corset.

My smartphone rang.

"Marcie," I said, answering.

"Talk to me," Marcie said.

FIFTEEN

I gave Marcie the rundown on what had happened in the last few hours, without the bit about the gods, of course.

"Okay, I knew about this," she said. "It was in one of the briefings. Roger kind of knew about it, too, but it was never supposed to be a Golden Sentinels job. The LA office just happened to know about it because Gossamer Rand Ross told Chuck about it before he left town to go shoot his movie."

"So this is a CIA–Golden Sentinels thing?" I asked.

"Kind of," she said. "Golden Sentinels isn't the go-to for running guns. Ross just volunteered to give us a hand with this to earn brownie points and have a story to tell. Total coincidence that he's a client of Golden Sentinels, really. The firm was never going to get involved."

"Why is a Hollywood director playing amateur spook to hold guns for you lot?" I said. "So why don't you—I mean, they—send some proper agents to deal with it?" I asked.

"Ravi," Marcie said slowly. "Contrary to what all those dumb movies and TV shows have you believing, it is illegal for the CIA to carry out any operations on American soil. The Company's jurisdiction is strictly overseas."

"That explains why you like being in London so much. You get to do all your crazy shit there."

"Right, so what the Company does is subcontract to proxies. Like, you know, Golden Sentinels or Interzone or whatever security company we have on the books."

"What I don't get is why the guns, which are going to a bunch of US-backed rebels overseas, are here in the US? Shouldn't they be shifted all over foreign soil?"

"They will be, but they have to start from somewhere," Marcie said. "And those are some of the latest state-of-the-art arms hot off the factory floor and only available to the military. The type of guns that the NRA and all the gun nuts dream of, that are only rumors right now. They're not even in the gun magazines yet, but they talk about them on social media and message boards where they all have orgasms over them. You're not going to find them over the counter at Walmart or a gun store or even those gun shows in the Deep South."

"That's just great," I said. "So how do I get out of this situation with those arseholes outside who will probably just shoot me and Julia and make it look like a home invasion, and the police won't even know these guns were ever here?"

"I put in a call for backup," Marcie said. "They're on their way."

"Who?" I said. "Who's the backup? These are serious bastards out there, with guns."

"Oh, don't you worry," Marcie said with a chuckle. "I picked some serious bastards of our own. They're more than qualified. You've met them."

"What? Who could it be?"

"Who do you think? How many 'qualified' people have you met on the job?"

It finally clicked.

"Oh, no."

"Don't be an ingrate, Ravi. Turns out a couple of them were in town on another job for the Company," Marcie said. "Mostly a babysitting gig for Somebody Important. They can spare a couple of people to come pick you guys up."

"You say I already know them?" I said.

"Yup, so you won't be dealing with strangers here."

That didn't particularly make me feel better.

"So just sit tight, wait it out till your backup gets there," Marcie said.

"Then what?"

"They pick you guys and the guns up, drive the guns to a safe house in North Hollywood, San Fernando Valley, which isn't that far from where you are."

"So once we get to the safe house and drop off the guns, Julia and I can leave?" I asked.

"That's the idea."

"Hang on," I said. "Might these guns be connected to that babysitting assignment our 'friends' are dealing with? That seems too much of a coincidence. Am I going to get drawn deeper and deeper into this mess?"

"Just stay in the panic room and sit tight."

"Easy as that?"

"Easy as that."

"Except for the fact that there's a brush fire spreading across the hills towards us, and traffic is completely jammed on all the highways in Los Angeles," I said.

"How many times have we brought up the traffic now?" Julia said in the background. "I swear this is all everyone talks about here in Los Angeles."

"You can't say you're not getting the full Crazy America Experience, Ravi," Marcie said, amused, which pissed me off.

"Thanks, Marcie. I've always wanted to experience a different type of apocalypse in a different culture."

"Chill, Ravi," Marcie said. "You're not alone in this. We got your back. Call me if you need anything."

She hung up.

"So what shall we do next?" Julia said, her voice oddly low and smoky.

I looked at her for the first time since I'd been on the phone. While I'd been talking, Julia had changed out of her clothes and helped herself to the dominatrix gear from Gossamer's S&M wardrobe. Black leather corset. Black lace knickers. Thigh-high boots with six-inch heels.

"Um," I said.

"You look like a deer in the headlights," she said.

"What is this?" I stammered.

"I got bored," she said. "We're going to be stuck in here for a bit. Might as well find something to amuse ourselves with."

"But we have men outside who want to kill us," I said.

"All the better reason to have a fuck," she said. "To remind ourselves we're alive."

"Julia, this is your addiction talking—"

"Ravi, I'm trying to initiate some kinky sex with the man I love, not some sweaty arsehole in a bar." She picked up the cat-o'-nine-tails and smacked it loudly against her hand. "Now, how does Daddy like it?"

"Oh my God, Julia, this is getting too Freudian to turn me on!"

"So how would you like it, then? Would you like a spanking?"

"No, thank you."

She pushed me back on the bed and straddled me.

"Shall we keep it vanilla, then?" she said.

"Julia—"

She shut me up with a long, slow kiss.

I admit it calmed me down.

"Feeling better?" she asked. "You've been getting more and more wound up since Dix."

"All right," I sighed. "We can stay trapped in here, but if the fire reaches these hills and engulfs this house, we could burn to death or suffocate in here. That's if those bastards outside don't find a way of getting in here and shooting us."

"I thought these panic rooms were supposed to withstand explosives and fires," Julia said.

"There's a possibility that a fire outside could turn this room into a furnace and we'll be broiled like eggs," I said. "Or those arseholes could find the ventilation system and pump in poisonous gas. Or the fire could melt the foundations of the house and either we get buried under it or the house falls down the hills, taking us with it."

"Ravi, you're panicking."

"I'm not panicking, just thinking out loud."

She laughed.

"If we're going to die here, I'm glad we're together," Julia said.

"I'm beginning to think we might make it out of here," I said. "All because you're on top of me."

"Ravi, shut up and enjoy the sense of danger," she said, and kissed me again.

We fell onto each other and out of our clothes. There was a desperation here, born from the drink and the prospect that we might not survive this. A fire was going to rage over the city and there were people outside with guns who were after us. Under the glare of the TV screens, we tangled and tumbled, a mishmash of limbs, our lips melding. She licked and clawed and sucked at me as time dropped away from us.

We ignored the men on the screens, still running around the inside and outside of the house trying to find the guns that were in here with us.

If you ever thought an English Rose in bondage gear was a thrill, getting her out of it was even better.

SIXTEEN

From Olivia's recordings:

"I was still in intel-gathering mode. I needed names, and I wasn't
ready to approach Brother Bull in Wan Chai just yet. I still had to keep
up appearances, after all, so I killed a few birds with one stone. I agreed
to spend time with my mum. I went shopping with her, had lunch with her
at the Yacht Club, all those places that were the usual haunts of Ladies
Who Lunch. My mum showed me off to her friends, the gossipy aunties
who asked why I wasn't married yet, what kind of work I'd been doing in
London, when I was coming back to Hong Kong, offered to fix me up with
their sons. Thankfully I could say Benjamin was my boyfriend, a brilliant
techie and inventor in London who's going to start up his own company
any day now. Mum also introduced me to the new women in her circle, the
ones from the Mainland who were married to the tycoons and politicians
on the way up in China. Mum and her friends slagged them off behind their
backs, as snobby Hongkies were wont to do. Mum thought they were crass
and had bad taste, spending money for the sake of it and making awful
fashion choices. I made note of their names, especially the politicos' wives.
I spoke Mandarin better than most Hongkies, so I could speak to them and
agreed to hang out with them. We would go shopping together and work
out together at the gym, all the better for me to get the lowdown on them
and their husbands. I got the distinct feeling they were spending quite a bit
more money than their husbands, as government officials, were supposed

to earn. They definitely all went to the same plastic surgeon, since they all had the same nose job and the same cheekbones and eyes. But I wasn't going to judge.

"I find Hong Kong these days a bit depressing. The old haunts of my childhood, the shops, the cheap coffee shops and restaurants, were disappearing because Mainland billionaires were buying up property all over town and pushing them out with higher rents or demolishing them to make way for new luxury flats that the locals couldn't even afford. The locals bloody hated the tourists from the Mainland who came across the border to buy designer goods. One thing about being a former British colony was that Hongkies had long been conditioned to stand in line for buses, food, and services, possibly the last vestiges of Britishness that we still possessed that the Mainland Chinese did not. That, and our preference for democratic rights. You could tell who the Mainlanders were by the way they cut through a queue, which often resulted in rows. As if Hongkies didn't have enough to complain about already. I had come home to a culture war between Hong Kong and China. It wasn't just that Hongkies feared the Mainland strengthening political rule over Hong Kong, it was also that they were afraid of losing their cultural identity, what made them Hong Kong, which is a vastly different culture from the Mainland's, a different worldview, a different attitude. Hongkies were afraid of getting absorbed into China. I couldn't feel smug that being in London would keep me out of all this. China was starting to make inroads into the UK, after all, what with companies' property being bought up, and the British government only too eager to welcome any influx of extra cash into the country. We're all too bloody connected now, no matter what country we're in. This only reinforced my belief in keeping to the shadows, never getting caught doing what I do, which is pulling people's secrets.

"Just the first week of lunches, spin classes, yoga, and CrossFit at the gym with my new friends yielded some interesting clues. Hua's husband was a bigwig in the Ministry of Agriculture. Bee's husband was in Public Morals, and he was in Hong Kong keeping an eye on what kinds of content they have here that was prohibited in the Mainland but might be smuggled or digitally *pirated for Mainlanders to consume. Fay worked in property, but her husband was an investment banker who commuted back and forth across the border. Ling's husband was in the Ministry of Land and Resources.*

"The wives did love their designer clothes, and spent a lot of money on the latest Gucci, Christian Dior, Versace. As long as they stuck with the matching dress suits, they were fine. It was when they tried to mix and combine different tops and dresses that they tended to come a cropper. That and their tendency to wear the chintziest jewelry with it. Nothing spelled 'Mainland Nouveau Riche' like fashion faux pas such as these. And they were definitely spending more than a top official's salary could keep up with. I gained favor with the wives by helping them with their fashion choices. That put me in their good books. I was their Hong Kong bestie who helped them navigate the waters of Hongkie society. I was sure they would dump me if someone better came along, but nobody knew the highways and byways of fashion and shopping better than I.

"Back in my room, I consulted Derek's book. They and their husbands were probably the ones depicted there, which might have implicated their colleagues and bosses as well. The book was a compilation of rumor and gossip, a compendium of tabloid journalism with a bit of investigative vigor. I imagined the book must have caused a bit of a stir when word of it got to the Mainland. No one there could buy it unless they crossed over into Hong Kong, and only if they knew to look for it in the shops. The Mainland government certainly didn't want it smuggled in. Someone over there must have gotten pissed off enough about it to order Derek's presence across the border to aid in their inquiries, or make a confession about his corruption of public morals. How long before they got enough out of him, before he finally confessed to what they wanted, then trotted out in front of the TV cameras to read the confession out loud before they let him go? It was my job to make sure that happened sooner rather than later.

"Once I had enough names, I could begin to compile a list, and compare that list to the characters mentioned in the book Derek had published. That might give me a clue to who had decided to have him snatched and taken across the border for interrogation. I needed to suss out what game they

were running, what they really wanted. Without them detecting my presence in any of this. I don't want to get picked up and taken across the border to be interrogated in an unnamed facility. It would do my beauty regimen no good at all.

"Right then, that's enough for tonight. Time for bed."

SEVENTEEN

After the third time we made love, Julia and I lay exhausted together on the bed. The endorphins must have settled us into a contented stupor.

"Ravi?" Julia said, stirring.

"Hmm?"

"Look at the screens."

"What is it?"

"I think all those men are dead."

"What?"

I looked at the monitors. On all six screens, the men in the ski masks lay sprawled and broken by the door, the fence, the garden, next to the pool. Julia and I seemed to have fucked our way through a shoot-out without noticing it. Probably just as well. The gods hadn't been in here with us. I saw that Kali, Rudra, Vishnu, and Ganesha were all milling around the dead bodies, chilling and looking on as if admiring artwork at a gallery opening. Then I realized that Lakshmi, goddess of wealth and happiness, was in here with us. She seemed to enjoy hanging out in the panic room. She smiled and winked at me, gave me the thumbs-up. Yeah, thanks. I really needed to have her here to show me the fantasy of hanging around wealth. As far as I was concerned, she was still a projection of my unconscious. That made them all manageable to me.

A familiar monster stood over the one by the pool, black mist of bloodlust wafting off him as he holstered his semiautomatic pistol and dragged the dead man by the leg out of shot. His name was Jarrod. Our rescuers were a team of four—Kevlar vests, casual back T-shirts, ammo belts and khakis, and dark glasses, your standard PMC attire. The other two men I hadn't met before, one a Latino, the other a redhead with a large, exuberant beard.

The men all had the dark, shadowy skin and blazing red eyes of Rakshasas. Of course they would be the demonic entities from Hindu mythology. I had to blink to see them as human again. The woman never took on a demon's skin, but Kali stood behind her like a watchful parent.

The woman holstered her pistol and approached the entrance of the panic room. She looked up at the camera and smiled.

Ariel.

She removed her aviator glasses and waved cheerfully.

"Come on out, guys," she said. "All clear."

EIGHTEEN

By the time we came out of the panic room, Julia had changed back into her own shirt and jeans.

"So you were gettin' it on in there while we were cleaning up out here?" Ariel asked, smiling. "Good call! Cool juxtaposition of sex and death here."

Jarrod rolled his eyes.

"Do you always see everything in terms of symbolism and metaphor?" Julia asked Ariel.

"Just my way of getting through boredom," Ariel said cheerfully.

"Or deflecting from the killing," I said.

"Ehh." Ariel shrugged. "That's just the job."

"And that's the problem," I said. " 'Just a job' should not be about shooting people so casually."

"Maybe," Ariel said, "I'm just covering up my own inner darkness and emptiness with forced cheer, because otherwise I'd eat a bullet."

Julia and I looked at Ariel, then we saw that Jarrod was shaking his head.

"Uh-uh," he said. "She really doesn't feel a thing about shooting people. What you see is the real thing, brother."

Julia reached over and lightly brushed Ariel on the cheek, an odd gesture of pity and tenderness. Damage recognized damage, and Julia could only offer kindness where Ariel might not be capable. Ariel closed her eyes and purred like a cat. Or a panther. I still remembered that Julia would not hesitate to slit Ariel's throat the moment she posed a danger to us.

Jarrod introduced the other two men as Reyes and Mikkelford. They went into the panic room and carried out the crates with the guns.

"You did the right thing, brother," Jarrod said. "Took cover while the professionals took care of business."

"Yeah," I said. "It's a relief to be patronized by a private military contractor."

Jarrod grinned behind his mirrored sunglasses.

"Guilty Prince and People's Princess are secure," he declared to his earpiece.

"I'm sorry?" I said.

"That's the code names we have for you two," Ariel said.

"That's what you call Julia and me?"

"We have a code name for everybody," Ariel said. "Marcie Holder's 'the Siren.' Mark Oldham is 'the Stoner.'"

"Too easy," I said

"Olivia Wong is 'Dragon Digital.' David Okri is 'the Scholar.' Benjamin Lee is 'Chaotic Tech.'"

"Sounds like you got everyone's number," I said. "What about Ken and Clive?"

"The Thompson Twins," Jarrod said.

"I'm almost afraid to ask what you call Roger," I said.

"Nothing printable," Jarrod said. "Colonel Collins personally thought of that one for your boss."

"Somehow, I'm not surprised," I said.

"So what does he call Cheryl?" Julia said.

"The Muse."

So Collins still carried a torch for Cheryl, the one that got away. Everyone had their unrequited love. I almost felt for Laird Collins there. Almost.

Reyes and Mikkelford gathered in the living room to regroup.

"I need you to clean up the blood and take the bodies out of here," Jarrod said. "We were never here."

"So you're taking the guns and the car, then?" I asked.

"Our mission is to escort you," Ariel said.

"Sorry, what?"

"You drive the SUV with the stash to the safe house. We're your guard. Once we get there, stand by."

"Wait, once we drop the guns off," I said, "Julia and I are done."

"Where are you gonna go?" Ariel asked. "With the fires in the hills, the 405, the 105, and all the roads are gonna be jammed up. You won't be getting out of the Valley for hours, if not overnight."

"That's just terrific," I said.

"You'll be safer cooling your heels at the safe house until the freeways open up anyway," Jarrod said.

I did not want to hang around these professional killers longer than I needed to. There was the possibility that we would be drawn into something else.

"Hang on, you're the professionals in this top-secret black-bag bollocks."

"Sorry, babe," Ariel said. "You took the job. You're part of the deal now."

"Oh, for fuck's sake!"

Behind me, Kali laughed and clapped her hands.

"We'll want to exfil ASAP," Jarrod said. "Brush fire's spreading and heading this way. The hills are going to be covered in smoke by sundown. Traffic's going to be a bitch, and you can forget about getting a cab or an Uber to come pick you up anywhere tonight."

"Look at it this way," Ariel said. "This is your only ticket out of here. With us riding shotgun, you're safer in all of LA than the President in a motorcade down Pennsylvania Avenue."

Reyes and Mikkelford loaded the guns into the back of the two black SUVs.

I didn't trust Interzone with our safety. I took out my smartphone and dialed one of our own.

"Ravi, how's it hangin', mate?"

"Benjamin, I may need your help."

"Can it wait? I'm between locations right now."

"Where are you?" I asked.

"Still out in sunny, airy Venice," he said. "The winds are making everything a bit odd, I have to say. Colder than usual, smell of ash in the air from the brush fires."

"What happened to the self-driving car?"

"I crashed it."

"You what?"

"I finally narked off the AI. Gave it so many complex commands it finally kacked itself, and the car drove into a wall. Air bag deployed and everything! Stonkin' good time!"

He sounded awfully cheerful.

"Mission accomplished!" he declared.

"Isn't crashing the car in a wealthy neighborhood a bit drastic, what with the public hazard and all that?"

"I picked a secluded spot."

"Aren't you in trouble?"

"Nah, mate! This is the job I was hired to do! And I bagged a bonus because I did it sooner than they expected! Result!"

"Why this self-driving AI, though? Loads of other carmakers are doing them."

"Well, they were considering this one for military and governmental personnel. It has to be foolproof and hack-proof, and we all know there's no such thing."

"Ah. So what happens now?"

"They go back to the drawing board. Me? I'm waiting for my ride and the crew to come recover the car, take it back to the lab, and review my diagnostics to unpick all the shit I put the AI through. What do you need?"

"Julia and I are stuck with an SUV full of military-grade guns with Interzone as our escort."

"Wa-hey! My kind of jam!"

"We need backup."

"Say no more, mate. Where are you now?"

"About to leave the Hollywood Hills."

"All right. Once you do, keep driving. Have Julia text me the make and registration number of the car. I'm going to track you. I'll get back to you when I'm back at my computer."

"What are you going to do?"

"Drones, dude!" His enthusiasm was over the top. "And not just any drones. High-altitude drones with satellite imaging! I get to field test them for this other company. Ultra surveillance! Give you a heads-up where you're going."

"Don't take too long."

"Word of advice: keep the radio on as you drive. Keep the traffic news on. Some nasty jams all around 'cause of the brush fires."

"Yes, I know. That's all everyone's been talking about for hours."

"Race the devil wind, mate!"

I saw Ariel approach the S&M wardrobe and look at the corset and boots Julia had worn to seduce me. She held the corset against her face and inhaled. *Was she sniffing for traces of Julia and me?*

"Ariel," Jarrod called from the living room. "We're leaving, you freak."

Ariel took the corset, knickers, and boots Julia had worn and slung them over her shoulder as she came out.

"Souvenir," she said, winking.

NINETEEN

From Olivia's recordings:

"Time to go clubbing in Wan Chai.

"I found out where Brother Bull's favorite club was and arranged to go with some of the wives. God knows they were bored enough to want to get out of the house while their husbands were off at some meeting or seeing their mistresses or usual chickens.

"Oh, when I say 'chickens,' that's Hong Kong slang for prostitutes. Sorry for the confusion. And of course the wives hated them, but not as much as they hated the mistresses. God forbid that the husband fell in love with his favorite chicken and threatened to leave his wife. No, the risk of that lay with the mistresses. These wives lived in their own states of war, against their husbands, and against any woman who threatened to steal their husbands and their money and status. Is it any wonder that I'm reluctant to get married? My parents despaired, but I'd rather be financially independent first, thank you. Benjamin I can at least predict and control. I'm out of his league, and he's so shocked and grateful to have landed me that he would never cheat on me, no matter how much we rib each other. The more he jokes about finding someone else or a bit on the side, the more I feel confident that he won't. He finds my kind of controlled chaos too much fun, and he's not going to find it anywhere else. I chose Benjamin for his loyalty, no matter how much of a troublemaker he likes to be. He enjoys me driving him around

the bend with confused lust, and I enjoy his attempts to ruffle my feathers. It's all very perverse, I know.

"Anyway, we dressed to the nines, in our tightest dresses and shortest skirts, and showed up like a posse of bored rich women from Central in the mood for a bit of slumming. Here was where I began to draw both threads of my inquiry together without anyone on either side noticing. This was a club where pop stars, actors, and yuppies rubbed shoulders with gangsters, dealers, and hustlers, where hard liquor and cocktails flowed, joints were lit, coke was snorted in the loos, and bonding was achieved through copious karaoke matches. Brother Bull recognized some of the wives I was with, which means he knew their husbands. Good to know. Mental note made.

"Brother Bull was in his early forties, had the stocky body of a boxer, with a round, friendly face—because not all gangsters looked like snarling comic book villains—sported a polite crew cut, and wore sunglasses even at night. He had risen up the ranks ever since he joined the On Wah tong at the age of eighteen, and had seen his share of gang wars and upheavals. He was a bit wistful for the old days, when they had hundreds of recruits at their beck and call. He had tattoos to cover up all the knife scars he'd gotten from the fights he was in during his early years in the gangs. These days, recruitment numbers were down. They didn't have rickshaw boys, coolies, construction workers, and shampoo boys to draw their numbers from anymore. The old clichés of guns, drugs, and prostitution rings that fueled crime movies are falling by the wayside. The gangs were now moving into lower-risk high-reward venues like selling stolen and forged goods online, selling black market seafood and fake upmarket fish. The penalties for those were not as bad as a bullet in the back of the neck. No Triad was going to be sent to jail for twenty years for getting caught with cheap tilapia treated to look like lobster meat. Being aboveground and not in jail was the preferred state for gangsters like Brother Bull these days. You can't blame them, really.

"We danced and flirted with Brother Bull and his friends, but they all seemed to observe the 'look but don't touch' rule with us. They knew whose wives my posse of women were. Brother Bull was in a jolly mood after five cocktails and was perfectly happy to tell me about the deal he had going with the Chinese government. They still used the Triad for information, to occasionally lean on people, even duff them up None of this was a surprise to me, given what I already knew about what had been going on in the last few years. It was merely confirmation. I welcomed it.

"I had bought a new burner smartphone, and created a new ChattyMe account. Everyone got very chummy by the end of the evening and exchanged contact details. That should be useful."

TWENTY

It was dark by the time we got through the traffic jams and left the hills, arrived in North Hollywood. The brushfire smoke gave the sky a reddish tinge. The sounds of helicopters and sirens filled the air for miles. For those of you not familiar with Los Angeles, North Hollywood was not the glamorous hub of show business and movie companies, but a rather faceless residential basin full of anonymous Californian houses and shops in the San Fernando Valley. There was no sense of history here, only a kind of dystopian eternal present, a blank slate where you might have quiet dullness in the heat, or, as with tonight, a dry, cold wind blowing from the Santa Anas and roving gangs of looters enacting a minor Armageddon. We actually heard the occasional crack of gunfire in the distance.

"Santa Ana winds, man," Ariel said as she made a right turn into Cahuenga Boulevard. "Makes everyone a little crazy."

Jarrod grunted.

Reyes was listening to the police bands. Turned out he was their communications expert. He and Mikkelford communicated from the other SUV via radio.

"Sounds like we got out of the hills just in time, folks," Reyes said. "Cops, emergency services—the brush fire gettin' worse means the 405 is closed off, the 105 is closed off. We're boxed in down here in the Valley."

"Not good," Jarrod said. "Best option is we get to the safe house and hold out till the morning."

"Damn," Reyes said. "ICE is doing a sweep in the Valley tonight."

"ICE?" I asked.

"Immigration and Customs Enforcement," Reyes said, listening on his headset. "Roundin' up illegal immigrants in their houses starting around Oxnard Boulevard."

"Picked a hell of a time for that," Mikkelford said. "What with the looting going on."

"They must have been planning it for a while and decided not to let the brush fires stop 'em," Reyes said. "A lot of people are going to be holed up in their houses tonight. The ones that don't speak English or know their rights will get scared into opening their doors when they don't have to, and that's when ICE'll have 'em."

"Is that even legal?" I asked.

"A lot of gray areas here," Reyes said. "They'll say they're after unregistered immigrants who committed felonies, but they're sweeping up families, too. You don't have to let 'em in the door unless they have a court order. You don't have to say anything to 'em."

"Land of the free, home of the brave," Ariel said, full of sarcasm. Of course she could drive and be sarcastic at the same time.

"Fuckers are grabbing people when they leave church or a court-house," Reyes said, seething. "Arresting a grandmother who's getting her brain tumor treated at a hospital. All because they're here illegally. Soft targets before they go after the supposed violent criminals and gangs. Total gestapo shit!"

"Committing a criminal act makes an illegal eligible for deportation," Mikkelford said. "You know that's the law."

"Entering the country illegally is technically a criminal act," Jarrod said. "So they *are* criminals. Just saying."

"Hell, they're arresting people who are in this country legally! They arrest green card holders! How do you explain that? Huh? What the hell happened to the difference between the spirit of the law and the letter of the law? Fuck all of you!" Reyes spat. "Shit."

"If they grab this many people in a sweep," I said, "where do they take them? Surely they don't take them to the border right away."

"They take 'em to a holding center somewhere in Arizona, out of the state, then they keep 'em there till they can deport 'em, and who knows how long that can take," Reyes said.

"They sound like black sites," Julia said.

"You say 'tom-ah-to,' we say 'tom-ay-to,'" Ariel said.

"Fact is, ICE'll lie, say anything to scare people," Reyes said. "They'll kick down the door and raid a house even if they don't have a warrant."

"Worried you got an uncle who's gonna get grabbed and deported to Mexico?" Mikkelford asked with a chuckle.

"Fuck you, man," Reyes said. "My family's Puerto Rican. And they live in New York."

This only made things even worse for Julia and me. We were here without the need for visas since we had British passports, but here we were riding in a car full of guns, with a group of heavily armed mercenaries, the most conspicuous thing you could possibly imagine driving around Los Angeles during a virtual state of emergency, with riots and looting, police making arrests all over. Julia could plead ignorance, that she was a tourist who went along with her dodgy dark-skinned boyfriend, i.e. me, and what the bloody hell was I doing in possession of the most illegal-looking firearms you could possibly think of? I would be lucky if I just got deported. I could end up being interrogated under suspicion of terrorism and sent to Guantánamo and forgotten about.

Great, now I was seeing the Pandavas' army fighting against the Kauravas' army, straight out of the *Mahabharata*. I really didn't need the lamp-lit streets of North Hollywood to be livened up by this vision. The soldiers were shouting as they rushed into battle with their swords and spears, but I heard only silence. North Hollywood really could be eerily quiet after dark.

As we drove, a small crowd of kids were smashing the window of a sporting goods store and making away with sneakers.

"Look at all that," Jarrod said. "Just total godless chaos. It's like Babylon. This is why Colonel Collins is right. We need a cleansing fire to burn all this darkness away."

"You really believe that?" I said.

"Colonel Collins is the one with the vision. He believes we're working to bring the Second Kingdom to Earth. Gotta be better than this cesspool. I'll do my part."

"Do you believe that all the people you kill are going to hell?" I asked.

"That's above my paygrade, brother," Jarrod said. "Better to let God sort them out."

"So you're just following orders, then?" The hackles were rising in my voice. "Is that how you justify it to yourself?"

"I'm doing a job," Jarrod said. "And a lot of the people we killed were trying to kill us at the time."

"Including the women and children in those villages you shot up?" I asked.

"That was a bad day where nothing went right."

"How about those unarmed bankers in London?" I asked. "Were you following orders or was it self-defense? Perhaps they were threatening you with negative interest."

"None of those guys were innocent, brother," Jarrod said. "You were there."

"Let's try this," I said. "After all the things you've done, all the people you've killed, do you believe you'll get into heaven or hell?"

"Not my call, brother. Like I said, let God sort it out."

I despised Jarrod for his matter-of-fact attitude to killing. He took no pleasure in it. It was just a job. In some ways, I found that callousness worse.

I was amazed we managed to pass all the police checkpoints as we drove down from the hills and into the Valley. The trick was to stay within the speed limit. We gave them no probable cause to check the cars and see the crates in the back. The support provided by Benjamin from his hotel room in Venice certainly helped. True to his word, he accessed half a dozen prototype high-altitude drones that floated hundreds of feet over the city and provided us with intel on what streets to take all the way down from the hills, through Laurel Canyon, and down into the Valley. The route we ended up taking was so circuitous, the streets so crowded, that it took us two hours when a normal traffic day would have taken us half an hour at most.

"How did you end up in this mess anyway, brother?" Jarrod asked.

"Complete coincidence," I said.

"That's it?"

"That's it."

Julia continued to look out the window at the surreal chaos of the city, but she was listening to everything.

"You didn't pick up the assignment 'cause you wanted the cash?"

"Not worth my while. Julia and I just stumbled into this whole thing."

"And you volunteered?" Jarrod said, incredulous.

"Keith was out of his depth and freaking out. I felt sorry for him. I told him we'd take care of it," I said.

"And bear in mind Ravi and I are completely inexperienced in dealing with guns and trained killers," Julia said.

"You do realize this job is worth the upper six figures to us, right?" Ariel said.

"Actually, I didn't," I said.

Jarrod looked at me, not quite believing.

"Brother, you are either a calculating genius or one lucky son of a bitch."

"I wouldn't call stumbling onto you lot lucky," I said.

"I have met people who are too stupid to live." Jarrod shook his head in disbelief. "You are too lucky to die."

"I told you, Jarrod," Ariel said. "He is that good."

"If he really was that good, he'd be working for our shop," Jarrod said.

"He's got gods on his side," Ariel said. "You don't need lucky when you have gods on your side."

Jarrod grunted. Knowing he wasn't going to win any argument with Ariel, he went back to conferring with Mikkelford and Reyes on the radio.

"You know you totally got under my boss's skin?" Ariel said.

"I don't know how I could possibly do that," I said.

I still remembered my sister's wedding night more than six months ago when Laird Collins showed up and tried to headhunt me for his private military company. We had words. We talked about our core beliefs. I saw just how insane he was and knew I didn't want anything to do with him. He believed in the Apocalypse, Armageddon, and that everything he did with Interzone was pushing the world closer towards bringing about the Second Coming and the Rapture. He had a smooth charisma about him that made talking about all that apocalyptic bollocks sound like the most reasonable thing in the world. He was off his nut and he was a monster. His company did a lot of wetwork for the CIA and God knows how many black bag operations, of which this was just another on the list. He and his employees were all terrifying and a scourge on the world. It was bad enough that my job brought me in contact with the lot of them and made me complicit in the horrors they enacted. That was a karmic debt I was going to have to pay somewhere down the line.

"What did you say to him that night anyway?" Ariel asked.

"We said a lot of things," I said. "I don't even remember anymore. I had a lot on my mind."

I wasn't about to admit that I remembered exactly what I'd said, and that I was taking the piss.

"Well, when he got back to the States, he got obsessed with finding out what Morris dancing was. He even looked up videos on YouTube, and that only made him even more confused. He started to believe there was some hidden meaning when you brought up Morris dancing to him."

"I barely even remember what I said."

"He thought you had to have a deeper reason for mentioning it to him, like there was some kind of code embedded in it."

"Oh, come on."

"He said there is no way a village dance that looks that dumb could possibly exist except for some secret it was conveying, especially if it's as old as it is."

"It's just a vaguely Old English pagan dance ritual for the harvest and fertility and all that stuff," I said, reeling.

"Uh-huh. He said you wouldn't come clean and explain. He thinks you were cluing him in on another secret, a counter-narrative to the world. Mr. Collins is all about researching all the narratives that counter the one he believes in. You drove him nuts."

"As if he wasn't nuts enough already," I muttered. "It's bad enough he believes he's doing his part to bring about Armageddon, the Second Coming, and the Rapture. How can you go along with that?"

"It's a job," Ariel said breezily.

"Haven't you thought about the implications of what you do, Ariel? All the people you killed, all the bastards you propped up, the system you reinforced? Have you ever thought what it might be doing to the world or the cost to your soul?"

"Sure," Ariel said. "I read up on history. I read about wars and power and empires and their ends. And you know what? It's all the same. It's always been the same. Men in power doing shit using fodder like us to make their ends. And in the end, they all fail, and they all die. The world goes on. And we get a ringside seat to the show."

"That's what this is to you?" I said. "A game?"

"It's a job. With a good paycheck. Man, you're looking at me like I'm some kind of monster. That's cool. According to my psych profile, I'm wired in a certain way that makes it easy for me to do this job without the trauma or PTSD that might come with it."

"You mean you don't have a conscience?" Julia asked.

"Pretty much. And at the same time, I have the intellectual capacity for higher thinking, and a curiosity about spirituality, that maybe there's something bigger and higher than we are, but not necessarily God."

"I thought your whole bit about going to India and seeking wisdom was an act."

"Ravi, I keep telling you, it's for real. I'm into it. That's why you're so interesting to me. You're so hung up on doing the right thing and karma, it's kind of funny to me."

"I'm glad to be a source of amusement to you."

"Come on, you know it's more than that. We have a connection."

I glanced at Julia, who didn't react. The amused smile on her face didn't waver, but her eyes were cold.

"So here we are," Ariel said. "In this crazy little caper where you're shitting yourself and you need our help. That's the way things go. That's how we stay in each other's orbit. We meet the people we're supposed to meet in this life. I think that's hilarious."

Julia laughed, too.

I didn't.

TWENTY-ONE

From Olivia's recordings:

"The book Derek published was a roman à clef, names changed but the vices and habits of the Chinese elite characters were apparently all true. Tales of taking bribes, lavish dinners at top restaurants, excessive spending at designer shops in Central, spending on mistresses, visiting prostitutes—the usual salacious stuff you found in any tabloids you could buy off the street. That was what drew the attention of the authorities on the Mainland. Did Derek even know who the book was about? Were they sweating him to find out the name of the writer? I hadn't heard any news about a writer or journalist who had disappeared from the streets of Hong Kong. My guess is, Derek wrote the book himself. He would probably have confessed that to his interrogators by now. It wouldn't surprise me if his wife helped him with it, but he would probably have taken all the blame to protect her, or they threatened to arrest Marie as well to make him take the fall.

"It occurred to me that Derek's interrogators might have wanted him to give up his sources for the book. The anti-corruption drive was continuing apace in China, and poor, hapless Derek might be a pawn in this game of cat and mouse between the corrupt and the inquisition. Given that he seemed to think he was publishing a larky, snarky commentary on the spending habits of Mainland Chinese officials once they're let loose in Hong Kong, he might have been asking for trouble, but not everyone is as paranoid as I am, and in this day and age, I don't believe you can ever be paranoid enough.

"But a book that didn't name names was not good evidence in a trial. Gossip was just hearsay. Without names and actual documentation, its contents were not actionable if a prosecutor wanted to crack down on corrupt officials. I had to think of Derek's disappearance as part of a larger game being played. Derek was just a small part of it, and I had to find a way to put an end to that part so he could be sent back home.

"Time to use the wives' emails.

"I bought a cheap new laptop on which I could create entirely new accounts that weren't connected to my usual accounts. I phoned Ravi while he was in Los Angeles and asked him to upload some programs I had planted on his office laptop to a server I'd set up so I could download them to this laptop so none of it could be traced to me or Golden Sentinels. I couldn't risk having those programs on a computer I might have brought with me when I flew into town. Best to start clean. I will probably have to destroy this new laptop before I leave, to erase any traces of what I get up to here.

"It didn't take long for me to hack into the wives' emails. I got a good map of what online websites they shopped at, sussed out their favorite brands and shops. I used the programs Ravi uploaded for me to create discount coupon images from their favorite online shops, offering huge savings on their favorite brands, and embedded the coupons into emails made to look like they were from the shops. Their sense of Internet security was a bit lax, and I knew they couldn't resist clicking on a discount coupon for designer brands. That downloaded the payload into their computers, which enabled me to root around them.

"Within an hour of my sending out the emails, I could see that the wives had clicked on the coupons, which downloaded my keyloggers into their computers.

"Twenty minutes after that, I had full access to their computers. From there I had the passwords to their bank accounts and I could look at their balances and transactions. I tracked when large sums of money were transferred into their accounts, which were then spent on buying luxury and designer goods. I could see their accounts on the Chinese retail sites they used. Some of these sites were well dodgy, and I got the wives' order histories. Designer bags, shoes, watches, jewelry—all stolen goods, no imitations, *only the real thing for these ladies. All costing more than a government official could afford. Time to do some cross-referencing. I'm going to need a spreadsheet.*

"Brother Bull just texted on ChattyMe, offering me and mine a good deal on upmarket seafood like rock lobsters and shark fin from Australia, said he would make sure it was the real thing, not the cheap forgeries or rubbish. Hm."

TWENTY-TWO

We arrived at last at the safe house, an unassuming white condominium on Vineland near Hatteras. It was obviously picked for its anonymous, completely unexceptional appearance. Far be it for me to judge whether this was the best spot to have a safe house in. Jarrod mentioned that it was because this situation was an emergency, so they had to use this condo on short notice. It just happened to be a property Interzone owned. It was mainly for housing its operatives when they were in town on a job. Marcie had told me that the CIA and various agencies kept safe houses all over Los Angeles. I wondered how they could avoid a scrum where different spies, agents, and their marks would run into one another all the time, but Los Angeles was big and scattered enough for it not to be an issue, I suppose.

"We can stay in the blind spots," Ariel said. "As long as we stay in the car, the street cameras won't catch our faces."

The windows were tinted so no one could see inside. The license plate was a dummy number that would come up clean on a police computer. Ariel drove us into the garage and shut the door with the remote. We got out and went through the door into the living room.

"It's going to be a little crowded, but we're just going to spend the night, then leave when the fires die down and traffic's back to normal," Jarrod said.

It was a cheap, nondescript house that a low-income family might live in. White walls, with no effort to decorate to give it a human touch or personality. No posters or photos, no plants—nothing to indicate humans actually stayed here. This was the type of house that drug dealers might use to stash their gear. In this case, it was a private military contractor keeping weapons and communications equipment.

"Entry and exit points aren't the best," Ariel said. "At least we have access to the freeways."

The walls of the living room were lined with boxes of spare ammo and guns. A cheap IKEA dinner table was the parking spot for a radio system, laptop, and modem. Two Rakshasas—I mean, Interzone men—sat on the sofa watching the Home Shopping Channel. They wore shoulder holsters and drank canned soup as the TV was selling special teeth-whitening products.

"Williams, DuBois," Jarrod called as we entered.

"Yo, Sarge," Williams called and waved. "You get the package?"

"Secured in the garage," Jarrod said.

The two men on the sofa locked eyes with me.

"This is the guy?" DuBois said.

"The very same," Ariel said.

"Damn," Williams said. "Never thought I'd meet a bona fide shaman."

"Sorry?" I said.

Julia looked at me.

Williams and DuBois got off the sofa and shook my hand.

"The man who talked to gods," DuBois said. "My family in Haiti told me about guys like you all my life."

"Er, right," I said. "It's not all it's cracked up to be."

"The Colonel said you were part of God's plan, even if he hasn't figured out how yet," DuBois said.

"Don't bet on it," I said.

"How's your package?" Jarrod asked.

"Five by five," DuBois said.

"He's in the bedroom," Williams said. "Finally stopped talking after you guys took off."

"I get the feeling he might be in shock," DuBois said.

"He's either chatty or shut down," Williams said. "No in-between for him."

"Well, you can't blame him," Ariel said. "Most guys who are targeted for assassination for the first time go into shock."

"Who is this, anyway?" I asked.

"Name's Hamid Mahfouz. Heard of him?" Jarrod said.

"Can't say I have."

"You've heard of his late father, Abir Mahfouz."

"The dictator?"

"Daddy Abir was a US ally," Ariel said. "His country has a ton of oil. Since he was killed, the country's been in a state of civil war, so the CIA has decided that another Mahfouz needs to take power to bring the country under control."

"So what's Hamid doing here in Los Angeles?" I asked.

"He's lived here for over ten years," Ariel said. "Owns a couple of restaurants, runs a production company that makes one of the top-rated kids' variety shows on TV."

"He was third in line for the throne," Jarrod said. "But his two brothers were killed along with their dad, so Hamid is going to have to go home to take up the reins and bring stability back to the country."

"Hang on," Julia said. "If Abir Mahfouz was overthrown in a people's uprising, why would they accept his son?"

"Because the country's in chaos and terrorists are threatening to set up shop there," Jarrod said. "The people would rather have the old regime back to keep everything stable over a bunch of Jihadis who set bombs and want to wage war on the West."

Then something occurred to me.

"Does Hamid know Gossamer Rand Ross?" I asked.

"They're drinking buddies," Jarrod said. "They hang out at the same country club, the same three-star restaurants, charity events."

"So those damn guns we were carting around," I said. "Ross wasn't holding them for Hamid, was he? As a favor for both Hamid and the CIA?"

"You got it," Jarrod said.

"And there are assassins here to get Hamid, which accelerated the timetable for getting him out of the country and back home? They were part of the group that came to Ross's house earlier?" I continued. "And the guns are a gift, aren't they? For Hamid to present to the national army courtesy of the US in their fight against the Jihadists?"

"Did you just put this together without a prior briefing, man?" Reyes asked.

"I told you he was good," Ariel said.

Behind me, the gods gathered in the living room and watched for my reaction. This was where I'd ended up yet again. I thought I was avoiding chaos and weirdness on this busman's holiday in Los Angeles, only to end up where I always had since I began working for Golden Sentinels. Julia and I were off the books, yet here was another labyrinthine, fucked up case where we were in over our heads and teetering on the edge of total disaster and possibly death. A-bloody-gain. Julia and I had no other choice except to stick with these maniacs from Interzone and the guns till the end. We were trapped by a literal ring of fire with looters and Immigration cops knocking on doors. How much more apocalyptic was this going to get?

Lord Vishnu smiled, this time ruefully, as if something tragic about humanity had been confirmed to him yet again.

My smartphone rang.

Saved by the cell.

"Excuse me," I said, and stepped out into the hall to answer it.

"All right, Ravi? How's it hangin'? We have you on speaker."

"Ken? Clive? What's up?"

"Just checkin' in. You know your Mrs. Dhewan is in the middle of a gang war, yeah?"

Ken was unnervingly chipper in his tone.

"What? No."

"Well, we just wanted to let you know everything's under control," Clive said.

"Why wouldn't it be? Are my parents safe?"

"You wanted us to keep an eye on your folks, yeah?" Ken said. "Well, to do that, we inserted ourselves into Mrs. Dhewan's scenario, as it were. Then your mum played it a bit close."

"What happened?"

"She's a right firecracker, yer mum. Roped yer dad into it, too," Clive said.

"What? Roped into what?"

"Don't worry. We got it under control," Ken said.

"What? What was it that you needed to get under control?" My voice was starting to crack.

"Calm the fuck down, mate," Ken said. "It's over. Your mum and dad are safe and sound and in bed as if nothing happened. They insisted on going out on the hunt with us."

"Hunt? What do you mean, 'hunt'?" I said. "Ken, you're speaking in bloody code."

"All right, keep yer knickers on," Ken said. "Long story short, we did a bit of diggin' for Mrs. Dhewan. She wanted to know which gang was stealing from her food bank. Mark chipped in and traced them to Hammersmith. Gang of teenage small fry callin' themselves the King Street Massive."

"So what did my mum and dad have to do with that?"

"Your mum insisted on coming along to make sure things didn't get out of hand," Clive said.

I groaned. Of course she did. She was still a schoolteacher at heart, and she wasn't going to let a bunch of kids go all the way down the dark side.

"So of course your dad insisted on comin' along," Ken said.

"With his cricket bat, right?" I asked.

"Yeah. So we head down to the King Street Massive's little gaff, me and Clive with Mrs. Dhewan's nephews, and your mum and dad."

"Did it kick off?" I said.

"Of course it did," Clive said. "It was bloody glorious. Like one of those old-school skirmishes Clive and I thought didn't happen anymore."

No wonder Ken and Clive were in such a good mood. They'd had a bit of violence to feed their bloodlust at last.

"I'm glad you enjoyed yourselves," I said through gritted teeth. "Where were my mum and dad in all this?"

"We left 'em in the car to wait, of course. Once we had the little bastards on their knees, your mum came stormin' in and stopped Mrs. Dhewan's boys from breaking their knees. It was beautiful. She was givin' them a right bollocking right there. Then your dad started on the King Street Massive. He laid down a lecture about morality and second chances, and how this was their chance to start from a clean slate. Now I see where you got it all from, mate."

"So what the hell happened?"

"Your mum made these kids promise to give up on the gang shit and volunteer at the food bank," Ken said, laughing. "She negotiated with Mrs. Dhewan not to break their legs to send a message, but to turn them into part of the community outreach program. In return, they could help themselves to some of the supplies at the food bank."

"This all sounds a bit neat," I said.

"Well, Mrs. Dhewan's boys were holding machetes," Clive said. "And they were going to be there as security to make sure there was no thievin'.'"

"Machetes," Ken said.

"Ah," I said. "So it's over, then?"

"Our work here is done," Clive said. "Mrs. Dhewan was well chuffed. She said to thank you for sendin' us to her. Job well done."

"Thanks, chaps," I said. "For looking after my parents. I owe you."

"One day we'll collect on that," Ken said.

At the time, I didn't think that ominous at all. Given the situation I was already in, it didn't occur to me that Ken and Clive promising to call in a favor was going to come back and bite me on the arse later on.

We hung up.

"Is that a British accent I hear?"

The bedroom door opened and a slightly haggard man in his thirties emerged. He wore designer slacks and a rumpled but expensive golf shirt, like he'd been plucked off the golf course and spirited to this safe house. His dark features were chiseled, a hint of plastic surgery to smooth them out to a more bland handsomeness that many people in Los Angeles seemed to favor.

"Mr. Mahfouz, I presume?" I shook his hand. "We're from Golden Sentinels Investigations and Security."

"Yes, I've heard of you lot. What brings you here?"

"It's a long story, but we had to retrieve the guns Gossamer Rand Ross was holding for you before the brush fires got them."

"Oh God! Those bloody guns!" he cried. "They're going to be the death of me!"

He himself had a hint of a British accent, which meant he'd gone to school in the UK.

"I haven't spoken to anyone other than these bloody killing machines for days!" he exclaimed. "Please! Come in! Talk to me!"

"What would you like to talk about?" I asked.

"I may die in the next twenty-four hours," he said. "I need someone to hear my story! I don't want to be forgotten, and these private military nutters don't give a toss!"

"Bearing witness," Julia whispered.

"Why not?" I sighed. "It's not like we have anything better to do. And I'd rather not sit in the living room watching the Home Shopping Channel with those bastards."

"At the rate things are going, this is probably going to turn into another case," Julia said.

And it did.

THE RELUCTANT DESPOT

ONE

"Tammy was blowing me in my suite when it came on the news: my father had been overthrown," Hamid began.

"I remember the news on the telly," I said.

"I was coked to the gills at the time," Hamid said. "A martini in my hand and savoring Tammy's tongue-work so the words from the dude on CNN barely registered. I glanced up from Tammy's bobbing head at the footage of the rioting protesters marching down the capital and thought, 'Huh. That looks awfully like home.'

"When they marched the sour-faced, gray-haired man in the military uniform out of the presidential palace and proceeded to string him up from a lamppost, I remember thinking, 'Huh. That looks awfully like my dad.' Then my head cleared a bit and I realized, 'Oh. That *is* my dad.'"

"So you watched it all live on the news?" Julia asked.

Hamid nodded.

"It is a testament to the quality of my dealer Loo-Loo's cocaine that not even the spectacle of my dad's not-undeserved demise shown live on satellite television dampened my hard-on one bit. Tammy didn't notice any reaction from me other than maybe a slight twitch that hardened my hard-on even further a split-second before I came. Not once did she even bother to look at the TV as she wiped her face with a Kleenex. The rest of the evening was a bit of a haze. Tammy collected her money from the glass coffee table and bid me good night. I sank farther into the leather sofa and threw my head back. I contemplated the lights of Los Angeles as they twinkled on the horizon."

"Well," Julia said. "I'm glad you were able to keep your priorities straight and not be distracted by something so trivial as your father's execution."

I looked at her sharply. That was a rookie mistake, to judge someone you were interviewing as a prospective client. That had been drummed into me when I was starting out, but then Hamid Mahfouz wasn't really a client yet. We were just talking. However, he might decide to become a client.

"When the protesters set my father's twitching body on fire," Hamid said, "the first thought that came to my head was that I was free . . . free at last. As I sank into sleep, I didn't know how utterly, tragically wrong I would turn out to be."

"Where were you before you ended up here?" I asked.

"The Four Seasons in Beverly Hills," Hamid said. "I have a suite there. It's practically my home."

Hamid explained that he had over ten million in the bank from a trust fund his parents had set up. He owned a couple of Michelin three-star restaurants here in Hollywood that gave him some decent passive income, and was also a partner in a production company that produced four successful shows for kids and teenagers that were a nice little earner for him. He and his sister were the youngest in the family and his two older brothers had always been the ones considered next in line to rule. Hamid had thought himself lucky to be spared a life of politics, even if his life of privilege was funded by blood money.

"Our family CIA guy paid me a visit the next morning," Hamid said. "I was hungover and recovering from the last night's coke and booze, but he at least waited for my first cup of coffee to get me lucid enough for a sit-down. He didn't mind the ramshackle state of my hotel suite. I had the feeling he'd been witness to even worse and more depraved debauchery in his time and what I got up to was positively vanilla compared to what he'd seen."

"I've found that CIA people have that trait in common," I said.

"So we had an unmade bed, some empty bottles, dirty dishes on the room service cart, and I'd managed to shower and change into a clean Hugo Boss shirt and jeans before he arrived. There wasn't any blood on the walls or dead hookers for him to clean up, and I hoped he was grateful that I didn't go for that kind of thing. Moderation was always my motto, even when it came to being a decadent playboy douchebag."

"You have a remarkable self-awareness for someone in your position," Julia said.

"Thank you," Hamid said. "I should have known something was up when the Company liaison had to come see me first thing in the morning. I'd known Carl Burdecker most of my life. He was my father's CIA contact since before I was born. He was always reassuring my father that the family was protected, since Dad was a valuable ally and asset. I assumed Carl was just here to purr the usual assurances, but something was up.

" 'Terrible business,' Carl said, shaking his head. 'What they did to your father.'

" 'Uncle Carl,' I said. 'Since when has the stringing up and burning of someone ever been "pleasant" business?'

" 'Oh, off the top of my head, I could think of a few instances,' he said, a wistful look in his eyes. Then he decided it wasn't a good idea to go there and returned to the topic at hand.

" 'Hamid,' he said, fixing me with his pale eyes the way he must have been trained to do to engage someone and make them think he was the most empathetic man in the world with their best interests at heart. 'You have my personal assurance that you and what's left of your family are still under our protection, so your safety is assured.'

" 'Even my sister's?' I asked.

"With that, Carl went silent. I just couldn't resist that little dig. You could say what happened to Kareena was as much his fault—or rather, the Company's fault—as my dad's."

"What happened to your sister?" I asked.

"Not much," Hamid said. "Other than the fact that she joined the insurgents who led the overthrow of my father and brothers. Anyway, Uncle Carl told me my mother managed to fly to Switzerland a week before they overthrew my father, so she's perfectly safe now. I'm sure her first stop will be Chanel for some retail therapy. Surviving a revolution can be stressful work. Then Uncle Carl said the Swiss authorities had frozen both her and my father's accounts and assets."

"I think that might be protocol," I said.

"Poor mum," Hamid said. "Just how is she going to survive on the Krugerrands and bearer bonds that I'm sure were in her emergency suitcase?"

"I'm sure she'll manage," Julia said.

"Then Uncle Carl got a bit serious and asked me if I knew what had happened to my brothers. I didn't want to admit that earlier in the evening, my homies and I were playing *Call of Duty* on the Xbox, so CNN was not being followed. Carl told me to brace myself, then didn't even wait before he gave me the full report. Kabil had been pulled out of his Lamborghini by protesters in the capital town square and, well, they ran him over with his own car. Thirty times."

Julia and I winced.

"Well, he did love that car," Hamid said. "More than he loved anybody or his country. That was ironic. The other thing about Kabil was, well, you know that joke I made about dead hookers in hotels that needed to be cleaned up? For my older brother, it wasn't a joke, more a hobby. The sex workers of the world, especially in Las Vegas, New York, Monte Carlo, Bangkok, and Dubai, are suddenly a lot safer now. I wonder if the Lamborghini is going to be shared by the local community from now on. I really don't think people are that magnanimous when it comes to luxury goods. Would the car be claimed by the first guy who pulled my brother out of it or the first guy who got behind the wheel to drive over him? That's something the new society was going to have to decide on. I have a feeling no one is going to commemorate the spot on which Kabil had become permanently affixed as a red smear. They're probably just going to hose it clean by next week."

"What about your other brother?" I asked.

"Mirza? He was convinced he was going to lead the army and quash the insurrection and take over from my father."

"Didn't the army decide they were on the people's side when the rebellion started?" I asked.

"That's right," Hamid said. "Mirza wouldn't have had many options left other than join our dad in the panic room in the basement of the palace. I think you can guess that the protesters managed to breach the panic room."

"How did they do that?" I asked.

"It seems an insider gave them the pin number to the keypad."

"You look like you know who the insider was," Julia said.

"Uncle Carl didn't need to tell me who that might have been," Hamid said. "My sister Kareena. Dad always thought her hatred of him was just a passing phase, but then he always did underestimate his youngest, and for her being a girl. One thing he and my brothers never understood was that women were world-class champions at bearing grudges, far more than men."

"True," Julia said.

"So what did Mirza do?" I asked. "Did he try to save his own arse by throwing Dad to the dogs and declaring he would be a people's champion when he took over?"

"That's what I heard he did," Hamid said. "Again, there was Mirza's fatal mistake: assuming he would be accepted as leader when he spent his years as a virtual prince abusing, raping, and casually murdering his fellow countrymen for fun. I asked Uncle Carl what they did to him. I'd fallen asleep by then and was no longer following the news. He said the insurgents got him. They took him before the crowd could, since they were the ones with guns. As I slept, they streamed the trial they held for him on the Web."

"Is that video still online?" I asked.

"Yes," Hamid said. "I practically leaped for my MacBook Pro and did a search. Sure enough, virtually every news site was carrying the vid, with the advisory that viewers may find the footage disturbing. I clicked PLAY without hesitation. They held the makeshift trial in the town square, right under the lamppost where hung the still-smoking remains of my dad. Mirza had been forced to kneel while the leader of the Maoist Liberation

Movement read out the charges against him, nothing the whole country didn't already know: rape, murder, assault, theft. Mirza was being tried as a proxy for the whole family. The symbolism was deliberate and preplanned. The leader announced that sentence would be passed henceforth, as the country needed catharsis from the thirty-five-year nightmare of my father's reign. The Maoist soldiers were dressed in green military fatigues and berets, very Che Guevara. They began to pass out baseball bats to the people nearest to them and told them to have at it. I always had a feeling Dad's attempt to popularize baseball in our country as part of his ploy to suck up to America might come back to bite him in the arse. The members of the eager public who were lucky enough to get a bat proceeded to use Mirza as a piñata for the next ten minutes. Most of the news sites cut the video off before the first swings went down, but I found a site that played the whole thing through uninterrupted."

Again, Julia and I didn't say anything.

"Uncle Carl and I knew straight off that the speech had obviously been written by Kareena. She and I had talked about political symbolism and acts of catharsis years ago when we were in college here in the States and we were hanging out smoking a joint together, talking about Political Science 101. She was right there in the video, standing behind the leader in her own green fatigues and black beret, the power behind the man. The leader wouldn't have been able to wipe his own arse, let alone write a coherent speech, without her. She was the power behind that throne. Of all the extreme leftist movements, I never understood why she chose to be a Maoist as opposed to a Leninist, Trotskyist, or Stalinist, not that most Americans would be able to tell the difference between them, considering most of them have never met a real extreme leftist or Communist in their lives, and if they did, it would blow their minds. Kareena had succeeded in translating her daddy issues and hatred of men into epic, mythical proportions, and this looked like the culmination of her lifelong war with our dad. From sheltered princess to rebel princess. Go Sis, I guess."

TWO

I looked at Hamid Mahfouz, this rueful man, and how he and I had ended up here, together in this safe house in North Hollywood, surrounded by a literal ring of fire above us in the hills. One of the tenets of spirituality was to look for the commonalities you share with another man to achieve empathy and understanding of yourself and others, but this was well over-the-top. We seemed like distorted mirror images of each other, both here, someplace neither of us wanted to be. His family was even more dysfunctional than mine. He even had an evil sister, where mine was merely opinionated. Was I just rambling and drawing these comparisons between us because I was knackered and stressed out about my current predicament? Oh, great. Kali was in here with us, listening. Of course she was enjoying this.

"I thought I could take consolation in the fact that I was too far away for the rebels to be able to come after me," Hamid said, shaking his head. "That is, after all, a big reason I swore off politics and decamped to LA. The point was to put entire continents between my family and me."

"I asked Uncle Carl if the rebels were going to take power. He said, 'Over my dead body. Bastards are trying to take credit for the uprising when it was a spontaneous occurrence and the dominant group has been moderate.' The CIA was going to get the various factions to sit down and talk. There's the remains of my father's cabinet who might still have some sway. It was gonna be touch and go for the next few months. Wheels were in motion. Uncle Carl told me to stay put here in LA, to go about my life as usual. He assured me that my diplomatic immunity should still stand. He would put in paperwork for me to claim political asylum. Meanwhile, I wasn't to do anything to call attention to myself, to stay out of trouble—not that I ever went looking for trouble. Then he left. I didn't tell him that going about my life as normal was exactly what I was planning to do anyway. No way was I going to get involved in any of the negotiations or rites of succession or whatever bullshit Carl no doubt was going to be involved in. I have my own life here that I quite like."

Hamid seemed to be indulging in some kind of depressed reverie as he spoke. Julia and I were tired, so neither of us was inclined to stop him. It was easier to let him speak. It wasn't as if we were going anywhere, so what the hell. Hamid was probably trying to take his mind off the present by talking about his life as much as we were by listening to him tell it.

"My normal day here in Los Angeles generally goes like this," Hamid said. "Spend about two hours working out with Janos, my personal trainer, put in a couple of hours at my production office in Beverly Hills, then lunch around the corner at a three-star French bistro I have a controlling interest in. You might assume I'm another playboy douchebag loitering around Hollywood, but the production company and six restaurants I own do earn me a decent income, you know.

"Now, my morning workout done—Carl complimented me for the work I'd been doing with my abs, which are decidedly non-flabby so that I might at least maintain a decent façade of not looking like a fat bastard drunk on booze and red meat—I go down to the lobby, past Bobby the concierge, with whom I exchange a knowing wink in a gesture of bro-camaraderie (God knows I tip him more than enough every week, and that's on top of the drugs I score from him), and my Mercedes is brought to the front by Jerry, the parking attendant, which is another twenty bucks discreetly passed through our daily handshake. I don't use a chauffeur, I prefer to drive myself to work. I don't need to be too ostentatious in my displays of wealth and status here in LA. The point is to show you're not a nobody, but not to put yourself too far in the public spotlight. We have movie stars and reality show victims for that, so that those of us with real money and power can hide in the shadows should we feel the need. Celebrities are the canaries down the coal mine in the world of the rich and privileged. The most successful celebrities are the ones fully aware of this role; it's the ones who fail to grasp this duty that crash and burn. I've been in Hollywood for more than ten years and I learned this very quickly.

"My day at the production company generally consists of meetings to justify my being in the office: hustling producers and filmmakers pitching projects hoping for some investment money to help them set up their movies; I'm usually surfing the Web and doing some shopping while pretending to listen to their pitches before having my assistant Kelly usher them out the door. They'll invariably send a screenplay over. Jane will dutifully read it and write up a report telling my partner and me how awful it is and why we shouldn't put a cent in it.

"And yet I couldn't shake the sense of unease that had started with Uncle Carl's visit the day before. As much as I wanted to pretend I was going to have a normal day, my father and brothers did just get overthrown and massacred in a violent revolution back in our home country the night before. There was something Carl seemed to implying that I was missing, and I had a feeling it wasn't going to be something I would like.

"I was saved from this bout of brooding by my partner Harold Florsheim, who burst into my office in his usual the-sky-is-falling manner. 'We have a problem,' he said. I could have guessed that, since Harold only ever comes into my office when we have a problem. 'Dana Leveson is all over TMZ. She lost her shit at a club on Sunset on Saturday and tried to fight four girls at once.'"

"Sorry," I said. "But who's Dana Leveson?"

"Oh, I forget," Hamid said. "You're not from here. She's only the highly popular star of a teen show our company produces and owns that happens to be the highest-rated show on TV, more than any prime-time network show. *Hangin' Out* is a fairly innocuous teen sitcom with mostly harmless situations and mild moral lessons dressed up in the colorful glamour of how teenagers would like their lives to be. So Harold and I got on the Internet and saw the video that a clubber had taken of the fight. Dana was so drunk or stoned or high that her attempts to swing at the girls only succeeded in sending her sliding rather ungracefully across the dance floor. She was more successful beating *herself* up than the girls. Of course, there was the obligatory up-skirt shot that had to be blurred out. I bet the guy who filmed this is an aspiring filmmaker."

Hamid found the video on his smartphone and played it for us.

"This isn't so different from what we get in the tabloids back in the UK," Julia said.

"Yes," Hamid said. "But over here, the stakes are much higher. We're talking possibly tens of millions of dollars higher. The network wanted a meeting to discuss Dana. Harold was freaking out. I told him to handle it and he only panicked even more. The star of our top show, the show that justified the existence of our production company, had crashed and burned in spectacular fashion. Totally in keeping with the myths of Hollywood, I must say."

"So I've been finding the more I spend time here," I said.

"I told Harold I was sure the network was going to say they would put their support behind Dana in her time of difficulty and suggest that she take time off to deal with her personal problems, which we will attribute to exhaustion. Of course, we all know she has been a walking mental illness textbook since we first cast her on the show. It just happened that she was popular with the kids and managed to deliver ratings for the last three seasons. It was time to get her into rehab and find her replacement. She had already violated the morality clause of her contract, but we still had the show to make. The supporting cast could carry it for a few weeks while we searched for a new lead. The writers were already writing Dana out, and we were about to put out a casting call to find the next teenage ingenue to lead the show."

"That all sounds perfectly normal," I said. "But how did you end up here?"

"Well," Hamid said. "I should have paid more attention to what Uncle Carl was saying between the lines. He was really prepping me to fly back home and lead the government."

"I'd guessed that," Julia said.

"I didn't," Hamid said. "I think I was in denial. Before I knew it, Uncle

Carl came back and told me the wheels were in motion. The surviving members of my father's cabinet would accept me as the new president. Uncle Carl said we needed to give the army some new guns that would give them the edge over the rebels, and arranged for some surplus to quietly leave the facilities here. It would be a sort of dowry for my new political career. But first they had to sneak the weapons out and keep them someplace safe until they got on the plane with me."

"And that's where Gossamer Rand Ross came in, I take it?" I said.

"I'd been friendly with Gossamer since I helped finance three of his last movies. That's how I got executive producer credit. Gossamer also knew Uncle Carl, and he was eager to help the CIA in any way he could. Uncle Carl convinced him to hold the guns for me, since no one would suspect a Hollywood director."

"Then who was it that's after the guns?" I asked.

"That happened all within the last twenty-four hours," Hamid said. "Uncle Carl called and said my life was in danger. There were rebel sympathizers here in Los Angeles like a cell, and they were activated to assassinate me. They also wanted the guns for themselves to fight the army with back home. These private military chaps—"

"You mean Interzone?"

"That's them. Uncle Carl contracted them to take me from my suite over to this safe house until they got me and the weapons to the airfield and flew us back home."

"And that is how Julia and I ended up in this situation," I said.

"That was unexpected," Hamid said. "But you're professionals, right? Not private military like Interzone. You're more problem solvers and fixers, aren't you?"

"We're really private investigators," I said, as much to remind myself as anything else. This was way beyond what we usually handled at Golden Sentinels. The morality of this situation was off in orbit. I wasn't even sure there was truly a right thing to do anymore. This was only chaos. This was why Kali was here in the room with us.

"What I don't get is," Julia asked, "how did the rebels know about you and the weapons for all this to become so messy so quickly?"

"Read between the lines," I said. "Hamid here was the one who leaked to the rebels. It was you all along, wasn't it?"

"Damn right!" he said. "I knew the back channels. I got word to my sister."

"Why?" Julia asked.

"Look at him," I said. "He's terrified. He doesn't want to go back and rule the country."

"You know what happened to my father and brothers!" Hamid cried. "That is my endgame! To be a puppet of the CIA until I'm no longer useful or they can't protect me anymore! I don't want to go back! I just want my silly, placid, trivial life here in Los Angeles as a playboy and dilettante producer! I don't want to die!"

"I'm sorry you're in this situation." I said.

"Help me!" he cried. "Can you help me? You know I can pay you. Gossamer told me Golden Sentinels were experts at fixing problems."

"Well, this might be a bit bigger than we usually deal with," I said.

"This is life or death for me!" Hamid said. "If I get on that plane with the damn guns, I am a dead man! It could be a week, it could be months, but sooner or later I'm going to wind up dead! In the meantime, I'm going to be forced to do some horrible things to remain in power! Look at Assad! He was studying to be an optometrist in London! An eye doctor! Then he had to rule Syria and turned into a bloody monster! Do you see the cycle I'm going to be forced into? I didn't ask for this! My father did! It isn't fair!"

"You do realize that your sister was probably the one who put out the hit on you, right?" Julia said.

"I didn't expect the kill order," Hamid said. "I just thought they'd seize the guns and be on their way."

"You didn't exactly think this through, did you?" I said.

"The thing is," Hamid said, "I forgive her. I don't blame her at all. She's doing what she has to, as am I."

The door suddenly opened, and Ariel came in with her pistol drawn.

I knew that look in her eyes. They were sparkling with excitement.

"Be vewy, vewy quiet," she said, grinning, finger to her lips. "We're being raided by ICE."

THREE

Why are ICE raiding this house?" I asked.

"Who knows," Ariel said. "They got the wrong address? That's been happening a lot. They don't give a shit and are just knocking on every door? Someone who's fucking with us tipped them off? Take your pick. Either way, we have to play this cool. Here, put these on. Just in case."

Ariel handed us balaclavas and surgical gloves so if the ICE agents came in, they wouldn't see our faces. And we wouldn't leave fingerprints.

"Are they going to force their way in?" Julia asked.

"Looks that way. They have a whole squad outside banging on the door," Ariel said.

"But surely none of us is in this country illegally," Hamid said. "I have a diplomatic passport. You two have British passports."

"ICE are just going to raid first, and they don't even bother asking questions later," Ariel said. "Jarrod is going to try to talk them into going away."

"And if that doesn't work?" I asked.

"We're on US soil and these are cops," Ariel said. "So we can't kill them."

"Thank God," I said.

"Nonlethal takedown. Beanbag rounds."

"Oh, Christ," I said.

"Now stay quiet and don't open the door till it's over," Ariel said, and left the bedroom.

Julia switched off the lights and we sat in silence.

So this was what Hamid, Julia, and I faced: getting taken into custody by ICE and detained at their bloody detention center in Arizona for anywhere between a week and God knows how many months. Julia, having the luck and privilege of being white and British, would probably be released much earlier and be sent back to the UK. It didn't matter that we were here legally. Hamid having a diplomatic passport might cause an international incident, but what did they care? They just wanted to nick someone tonight. The best I could hope for was not to get sent to a black site as a terror suspect, and if I made it back to the UK, I could look forward to getting interviewed by the *Guardian* for the liberals to tut-tut over. Well, fuck that. We had work to do here.

We heard the ICE agents banging on the front door down the hall.

"Open up!"

"There are no Mexicans in here!" Jarrod cried. "We're all Americans in this house!"

"We have reports of guns being kept in there!"

"Bullshit!" Jarrod cried. "First you said you were ICE! Now you're hunting for weapons? Which is it?"

"Open the door! We won't say it again!"

"You got a warrant?" Jarrod called. "You're not coming in without a warrant!"

We heard the sound of a battering ram slamming against the front door, then the metallic splintering of the hinge shattering as the door fell open.

"GET YOUR HANDS UP! NOW! HANDS—"

A clattering sound hit the floor.

I recognized that sound from more than a year ago when I was on the receiving end of it with Ken and Clive: a flash-bang grenade hitting the floor.

"Cover your ears!" I whispered to Hamid and Julia.

A loud bang went off out in the hall, followed by yelps and cries of surprise.

Shotgun rounds went off in rapid succession. Screams. Then bodies hitting the floor and footsteps advancing.

"Secure their weapons," Jarrod said.

"Clear," Ariel said.

"Clear," Reyes said.

"Clear," Mikkelford said.

"Clear," DuBois and Williams declared.

More sounds: chains, the tightening of zip-ties, the ripping sound of duct tape.

Finally, Ariel opened the door to the bedroom.

"You can come out now," she said.

Six burly ICE officers were facedown on the floor, all alive, thankfully. Jarrod and the gang had used their own cuffs, chains, and zip-ties to restrain them, and covered their mouths and eyes with duct tape. Their ears were probably still ringing from the flash-bang.

"Ladies and gentlemen, this safe house is blown," Jarrod said. "We are leaving."

"To go where?" I asked.

"Anywhere but here," Jarrod said.

"We could be driving around for a while," Ariel said.

DuBois and Williams dragged the ICE officers out into the street while Jarrod and Mikkelford packed up the spare ammo and equipment and put them in the back of the second SUV in the garage.

"Reyes," I said. "Are you still pissed off about them nabbing people who may not deserve it?"

"What do you have in mind?" he asked.

We took the keys off the ICE officers and went out to the street where their van was, balaclavas on in case the street cameras picked us up. Mikkelford opened the back to find a family of four (including two children), a couple in their thirties, and three men, all Mexican or Latino. It was entirely possible, even likely, that some of the men had committed felonies, might be drug dealers or gang members, or they might have just had a parking ticket, but the children and most likely their mothers were innocents here. We cut the zip-ties that bound their wrists.

"*Eres libre de irte,*" Reyes said. "*Vamonos.*"

They thanked us and ran off into the night. Mikkelford fist-bumped me and Reyes. Did they think I was one of them now? Sod that!

The two black SUVs drove out of the garage. Reyes and I got into the one with Julia and Hamid in the backseat. Ariel was driving. I was glad Jarrod was in the other one with the rest of the Interzone gang.

"We have your friend Benjamin to thank," Jarrod said on the radio. "When we can understand what the hell he's saying, anyway. He was the one who spotted the ICE team heading our way, with his satellite drones."

"We ought to buy us some of those," Williams said.

"Damn straight," DuBois said. "We got the budget for it."

"I'll put in a request when this is over," Jarrod said.

Great. Benjamin had turned this night into a tech demo that sold some surveillance drones to a private military contractor. Just what we all needed. I'm sure he pissed himself laughing at this.

"ICE will be busy trying to figure out what the fuck happened here tonight, and trying to track down the illegals you guys freed," Ariel said. "Good thinking, Ravi. Child of Chaos for the win."

As we drove away, Ariel pushed the button on a small detonator.

An explosion erupted behind us—the safe house went up in a ball of fire.

"Was that really necessary?" I asked.

"Didn't want to leave any forensic trace we were there," Ariel said cheerfully. "They'll think it was a drug gang or cartel or something. More confusion. Fog of war is the shit."

"We fuckin' hated that house anyway," Reyes said. "Good riddance."

"Maybe we can talk the boss into buying the next one in Beverly Hills or Brentwood," Ariel said.

People came out of their houses to look at the fire. Someone called 911 and fire engine sirens filled the air. Or were those sirens for another fire in the area? It didn't matter.

I glanced out the back and saw Rakshasas dancing in front of the flames next to the onlookers.

We were gone from that neighborhood before anyone really noticed us.

FOUR

We drove for nearly an hour before settling on a motel. At least this part of town was quiet. The night manager asked no questions. He looked like he was used to dodgy people coming and going all the time. He probably only ever got dodgy people as guests here. Jarrod used his company credit card and got us three adjoining rooms. We parked the two SUVs just outside the rooms so we had them in full view, since they still had the crates with the guns.

We were still trapped in North Hollywood till the morning.

"Might as well catch some Zs," Reyes said. "Jarrod's gonna call in for where to take the package in the morning."

"I resent being called a package," Hamid said.

As he should.

"I mean the weapons, sir," Jarrod said. Good save.

Williams and DuBois took a room where they would watch over Hamid. Mikkelford and Reyes took another room with Jarrod. Ariel happily took the one Julia and I were in.

I was not enjoying witnessing how Interzone operated firsthand. The sooner Julia and I were shot of them, the better, but it looked like we were stuck with them for the rest of the night.

"Hey, there's a liquor store just across the street!" Ariel said. "And it hasn't been robbed or looted so far."

"We're still on the clock," Jarrod said, annoyed. He seemed to get annoyed with Ariel a lot, I noticed. I think that was their dynamic. This indicated to me that they often worked together.

"I mean after this is over," she said. "We'll know where to grab some sweet relief!"

The room had a faint smell of musk. The wallpaper was peeling slightly. There was hair in the bathtub drain, and we ignored the promise of premium cable stations as we kept the local news on to keep tabs on the rioting and looting in parts of the Valley. The fires in the hills gave the sky a menacing golden glow. The sheets were slightly yellow and only minimally clean. This was the type of motel where hookers took their johns while their pimps waited outside, where drug addicts came to shoot up or smoke meth. The smell of bleach was there to kill any stench of stale sex and burned drugs. This was the type of motel where any of the rooms might have been a crime scene with tape outlines of bodies on the carpet.

So now Julia and I were getting the American Sleazy Motel Experience as well. This was turning into quite the Tour of America we were having, complete with guns, threats of wrongful arrest, and people out to kill us. It really was a busman's holiday.

"So how is this supposed to go?" I asked. "What's the endgame?"

"In the morning, we ought to drive Hamid and the guns to a private airfield," Ariel said. "He and the shipment will be flown home, where he'll be greeted by his handler from the CIA and members of his father's Royal Guard and the surviving generals."

"So he's supposed to form the new government once he gets there?" Julia asked.

"That's the plan," Ariel said. She had a full-auto 9mm pistol in her shoulder holster and had brought an AR-15 into the room for good measure.

"You guys really ought to get some basic gun training," she said. "Could come in handy."

"No, thanks," I said.

"You're so British and squeamish," Ariel teased.

"Ravi, stop pacing around," Julia said. "Take the weight off your feet. Lie down on the bed."

I felt myself sink into the bed. At least the mattress was still reasonably firm. Julia climbed on the bed with me.

"I'll be glad when this is finally over," I said.

"Come on," Ariel said. "You love it. I bet you were getting bored with how normal everything you were seeing at your little LA office was. You just had to find a way to land yourself into something crazy."

"I was just helping out Keith," I said. "There was no way I could have predicted this was where we'd end up."

"You had the gods watching you," Ariel said. "Waiting for shit to happen. You had to have some expectation of chaos erupting whenever you got bored."

"I was not bored," I said.

"Yes, you were," Julia said.

"Look, this started when I was doing Darryl and Liz a favor," I said. "We're in a city and a job where things could go doolally when you walk through the wrong door."

"Uh-huh," Ariel said. "And you chose to walk through that door when you could have just gone back to the office, sat around answering emails, surfed the Internet, and then gone home. You two could be asleep in your rental right now."

"I was getting a bit bored," Julia said.

"Do you feel alive?" Ariel asked. "Like your nerves are all jangly and singing? Like you took ten hits of cocaine?"

Julia smiled. This was not good. This was her addiction getting gratified with an adrenaline rush. Kali was in here with us. She was standing behind Ariel, stroking her chin and licking her lips with that long tongue of hers, as if this was going swimmingly. And next to me, on the bed, sat Lord Vishnu, sagely observing, waiting for the punch lines.

"Technically, you don't need Julia and me around for the rest of this, do you?" I asked.

"But I like having you guys around," Ariel said. "You and I are the intercompany liaisons, remember? It's good for us to hang out and improve relations between Golden Sentinels and Interzone."

"Whose idea was it to call the company 'Interzone' anyway?" Julia asked. "I don't see Collins as a William Burroughs fan."

"That was his first partner when they formed the company together," Ariel said. "Before my time. He's dead now."

"Did Collins kill him?" I asked.

"That's what the rumors say." Ariel shrugged. "It was probably over money and the direction of the company. And it didn't happen on US soil. It might have been in Yemen or Somalia, I don't remember which, where there wouldn't have been an investigation. Either a mysterious death or friendly fire."

"Lost in the fog of war, then," Julia said.

"Somehow, that doesn't surprise me," I said. "I see where this case is going."

"You're calling this a case?" Ariel said, amused.

"What else could it be?" I said. "Interzone's job doesn't end with babysitting Hamid Mahfouz till he gets on that plane tomorrow, does it? You lot are angling to get in with him and his government, perhaps even become his personal bodyguards because it's obvious his own army can't protect him over there. That's going to be another cushy contract for Interzone worth millions of dollars. And it puts Laird Collins closer to another player on the global stage."

"Damn," Ariel said. "Even when you're tired and rambling, you're drawing connections."

"Everything's about connections," I sighed.

"Close your eyes," Julia said. "Get some rest."

I did.

"My brain's still buzzing," I said. "I'm not going to fall asleep."

I fell asleep.

FIVE

From Olivia's recordings:

"I compiled my dossier, an interactive digital file that let the reader cross-reference names, accounts, and amounts of money with designer goods bought from their respective websites. If you opened it up and looked at the whole thing, it would look like a hypertext spider's nest. I had to design the user interface to make it easy to navigate so a child could understand it.

"I avoided putting in my own theories or opinions. This dossier had to present nothing but cold, hard facts. There were still things I wasn't clear about, though, pieces that were missing. Who gave Derek the idea to publish the book? Was Marie truly the blameless worried wife in all this? Was the book part of a bigger game and Derek's disappearance the part that backfired? Or was he just collateral damage in someone's campaign? The Hong Kong Police were investigating Derek's disappearance as a missing persons case. There were demonstrations demanding Derek's release. These were good optics for the pro-democracy movement that painted the Mainland as authoritarian and overreaching, threatening Hong Kong's fragile autonomy and showing up the limits of freedom of expression. Hong Kong was supposed to have its own set of Basic Laws separate from the Mainland's, which included less censorship and more freedom of speech. The Mainland was violating that Basic Law in snatching Derek and other publishers like him. There was no comment from the Mainland, no confirmation that they were holding Derek, but everyone knew it was them.

Online videos of pro-democracy activists condemning the autocratic actions of the Mainland were going viral. As I saw it, there might be more than one game being played here on multiple levels, and more than one governmental department involved in this. The dossier I compiled, for example, would be of great interest to the Anti-Corruption Squad back in the Mainland. My job here was just to get Derek released, not play political chess. Or get arrested myself.

"It was time to toss the bait into the water to see what bit.

"I contacted Marie and her lawyer and gave them the dossier on a thumb drive. I'd uploaded multiple copies of it to the cloud as my insurance policy. I told Marie and the lawyer that the dossier was crowdsourced, that I found a bunch of hackers on a forum who put all the information together.

"Marie's lawyer contacted the Chinese authorities and proposed a trade: Derek's release for the dossier.

"A series of negotiations were about to take place. Marie and I could only wait now."

SIX

"Wake up, mate," Mark said. "You'll want to see this."

I opened my eyes. Mark was shaking me.

"Mark? What are you doing here?"

"I've always been here, Rav," he said. "David's going mental. Everything's gone pear-shaped."

I sat up on the office sofa.

"What's happened?" I asked.

"We happened. Chickens come home to roost."

"Finally pissed off the wrong people," David said, walking in and gathering up another batch of files. "I knew this would happen one day. Bloody Roger."

"Roger said this day would come," Julia said.

The office was a mess. Cheryl was busy pushing papers and files into a shredder, as fast as Ken and Clive could pass to her. David added his to the pile. Benjamin was whacking away at the computers with a fire ax, wearing a manic grin.

"Wa-hey!" he said. "Nice of you to join us, Ravi!"

"Honestly, Benjamin," Olivia said, irritated. "I told you, the best way to get rid of evidence on a computer was thermite or C4."

With that, she pushed the button on a detonator and all the computers in the office exploded in puffs of smoke.

"Let's see them try to recover the data," Olivia said, satisfied.

"What the hell did we do?" I asked.

Mark chuckled.

"More like what *didn't* we do," he said.

"Where's Roger?"

"Gone," Cheryl said. "They've taken him."

"Who's taken him?"

"Who do you think?" Ken said with a sneer.

"All his fancy friends in high places," Clive said. "They fucking sold him out, didn't they?"

I looked around.

"Where's Marcie?"

"Her masters called her home," Cheryl said. "In disgrace. Nothing left for her here. Probably her fault."

"Bloody typical," Olivia said. "She comes here, makes a bloody great mess of things, then buggers off to do the same thing somewhere else."

"So what's going on here?" I asked.

"What does it bloody look like?" Ken said. "It's the end, innit?"

"Gotta cover our arses," Clive said.

"Golden Sentinels is toast," David said. "And we have to get out of here before they show up."

"Bloody right," Ken said. "We don't want to be here when Special Branch shows up."

Benjamin helped Ken and Clive pour gasoline over the whole office. Once finished, they tossed the cans aside and joined us at the exit.

"Cheryl," Olivia said. "Will you do the honors?"

Cheryl lit a match and tossed it into the office. We didn't stay to watch as everything went up in flames.

"No forensics for them to recover," Benjamin said.

"Parting is such sweet sorrow," Mark said as he blew a kiss at the burning office.

Mark and David led us through the door out into the street.

Farringdon was in pandemonium. Black smoke was everywhere,

billowing into the sky. Sirens in the air. Burning cars. Riot police chasing protesters with placards that read "NO MORE LIES!" I heard helicopters overhead.

"Yes," Mark said. "It's gone a bit J. G. Ballard, hasn't it?"

Somewhere in the distance, clear as a bell, a boy was singing "Jerusalem."

"And did those feet in ancient time,
Walk upon England's mountains green:
And was the holy Lamb of God,
On England's pleasant pastures seen! . . ."

As I looked around for where the singer was, Julia pulled at my arm.

"Ravi, look."

"Roger?" I said. "What are you doing here?"

In the middle of the street was a metal table at the top of a twenty-foot wicker man, and there sat Roger, handcuffed to it. Gone was his expensive Savile Row suit and tie. In its place were the orange prison overalls you found in American jails. Roger was unshaven, his eyes red from lack of sleep and weeping.

"Ahh, Ravi old son, the bastards finally got me."

"I warned you everything would come a cropper one day," Cheryl said, her rage barely contained. "You just had to chance it."

"What's the point in saying sorry, eh?" Roger said.

We all stood in front of the desk like a tribunal, judging him. He looked like an exhibit, a cautionary tale in the middle of the street, an art installation by some Goldsmiths graduate who'd used found objects to capture the times.

"All your wheeling and dealing," Cheryl said. "All your favors, all the dirty laundry you had us hide and clean, and this still happens."

"Yes, yes," Roger said, all fight gone from his body. He looked shockingly frail, broken.

"You're not takin' us down with you," Ken said. "I'll tell you that."

"I'm not taking you down," Roger said. "It's all me. Just me."

"Too right," Clive said, and began to pour gasoline over the wicker man, Roger, and the table.

"Listen," Roger said, spluttering. "I can still get out on top. It all depends on you, Ravi."

"Me? What the hell can I do?"

"You know what the big picture is. You know where the bodies are buried now. I want you to use it. You'll know what to do with it all. We can still come out a win. Work with Olivia."

"Sorry, Roger," Olivia said. "I'm off to run a bank in Shanghai. This is all my past now."

"And I look forward to being your kept man, babes," Benjamin said.

"We'll see how long that lasts," Olivia said with a sniff.

"Come on," Roger said. "Just one last hurrah, eh? What have you got to lose?"

"Enough!" Cheryl said. "We've lost everything thanks to you! I followed you for over twenty years, you bastard! I loved you! You were always a disappointment! I waited for you to become the better version of you! But no, you liked the gutter too much because scraping for leftover power was all you ever went after! Once a chancer always a chancer! Now everything we built up has gone up in flames! Only one last thing left to burn!"

Ken passed Cheryl a box of matches.

"Is this absolutely necessary?" I asked.

"We have to get rid of all evidence that comes back to us," Cheryl said. "It's every man for himself after this."

Roger just nodded sadly.

We watched the wicker man burn in this final ritual. Roger disappeared in the smoke and the flames. I bet he never thought he would end up a sacrifice to the forgotten pagan gods of the British Isles. We all turned away.

"And did the Countenance Divine,
Shine forth upon our clouded hills?

And was Jerusalem builded here,
Among these dark Satanic Mills? . . ."

Where was the singing coming from?

Mark tossed the car keys to me.

"Ravi," Mark said. "You're driving."

"I've got the legal paperwork and your statements all filed," David said. "We should be in the clear. You get into any trouble, call me."

Julia and Mark joined me as we got into the black BMW and drove off. Everyone else got into the other cars. It felt like this would be the last I would see of them. I thought of Ken and Clive. What would become of them now, unleashed from the restraints of Golden Sentinels, where they were barely restrained to start with? They were going to be sink back into the fabric of the land, become murderous urban legends, hunting the truly wicked. Why was I so certain of that now?

And still the singing in the air. I heard it even through the closed windows of the car and fair hiss of the air conditioner.

"Bring me my Bow of burning gold;
Bring me my Arrows of desire:
Bring me my Spear: O clouds unfold!
Bring me my Chariot of fire! . . ."

"Where are we going?" I asked.

"Grosvenor Square," Mark said as he lit up a spliff. "We need to lie low for a bit."

He took a puff and passed it to Julia, who took a puff and passed it to me. We were past caring about the police stopping us for smoking a spliff in a car. They had bigger problems on their hands, what with London—hell, the whole country—falling apart around their ears.

I felt an overwhelming wave of sadness wash over me. Had everything we'd done, everything I'd done, come to this? I'd tried to do the right thing, tried to do right by people who needed my help. Roger never showed us his big picture, and it blew up in his face. This was all our fault. We all played a part. I hadn't thought it would fall apart this badly. I couldn't believe everything was gone, just like that.

I had to call my parents. I didn't care that I was still driving. I desperately wanted to hear their voices.

"Ravi?" my dad said on the other end of the line. "Is that you? How is London?"

"Falling apart. You and Mum picked the right time to move to Mumbai."

"We saw the writing on the wall," Mum said. "Are you and Julia all right?"

"We'll be fine, Mum."

"Good. We're off to see your grandparents for dinner."

"Um, didn't *Dadaji* and *Dadiji* pass away ten years ago?"

"They're cooking tonight. It's going to be a nice dinner. We'll send them your love."

"Thanks, Mum."

"And Ravi," Dad came on, "keep listening to the gods. You can't go wrong."

"I will, Dad."

And with that, they were gone.

Mark took my phone and Julia's phone, removed the SIM cards, and tossed them all out of the car.

"No more tracking us by GPS," he said.

"I will not cease from Mental Fight,
Nor shall my Sword sleep in my hand:
Till we have built Jerusalem,
In England's green & pleasant Land . . ."

At least the singing stopped by the time we arrived at a posh building in Grosvenor Square. It must have been worth over ten million pounds, had once been an embassy, but since then had been abandoned and taken over by a band of anarchist squatters who happened to be Mark's mates. The entrance was fortified with sandbags and police barriers. Mark introduced us to Spider, who led us to one of the many empty rooms and said, "Make yourselves at home. Stay as long as you like." Spider and his friends had turned the building into a small community. There were families who would have been otherwise homeless living here. Spider's girlfriend Ginny had organized a crèche and ran a little school for the kids. They had a full staff running the kitchen canteen, and meals were served at set times. There was a playroom with a large flat-screen TV and a PlayStation games console with loads of DVDs and video games for keeping everyone entertained. The bookshelves were well stocked with everything from Dickens to the latest crime novels and potboilers.

"This is where you've been living for the past year?" I asked Mark.

"I helped them find this place and break in," Mark said. "This is the future, mate. Government falls apart, anarchy reigns, the best collectives survive."

Mark went up to the roof to check his marijuana plants. He was the supplier to the whole of what was left of Mayfair, which brought a fair amount of money and services to the building.

"I trust you children will make yourselves at home," Mark said when he came back down. "Dinner's in the communal area in the living room at seven. I'm going to be at the orgy on the third floor. It's on at six. You're welcome to join us."

"Thanks, Mark, but we'll pass," I said.

"Well, the invitation's open if you change your mind," he said, and wandered off down the hall.

"All in all," Julia said, wrapping her arm around my elbow. "This has been a very English apocalypse."

Where were the gods in all this? They would usually show up in a mess like this. It was their jam. Not once through all this did Kali or Lord Vishnu or Ganesha or any of the pantheon show up to watch. Or did they orchestrate all this after all? They weren't here because they were up there on high, having designed all this and put us down in it. Perhaps this was the end of their long game after all, the punch line to the story I was a hapless player in.

Julia and I went to our room and lay down on our sleeping bags. I had to think about what to do with my life now. All bets were off. The whole world was in free fall and so were we.

"Ravi," Ariel said. "Come on, babe. We gotta move."

I opened my eyes.

Ariel was wearing the leather bustier and thigh-high boots Julia had worn in Gossamer Rand Ross's panic room.

"Oh, Ariel, not now," I moaned.

"I'm serious," Ariel said. "We got a situation."

The motel room came back into focus. It was morning in North Hollywood.

"Keith's been taken hostage," Julia said.

"You what?" I said.

"It's the guys who are after Hamid Mahfouz," Ariel said. "If we don't give them Hamid and the guns, they're going to kill Keith."

SEVEN

Everyone gathered in our room and looked at Julia's phone. The abductors had texted her a photo of Keith looking terrified with two guns pointing at his head. They'd called Julia. She and Keith had exchanged numbers so she could touch base with him and set his mind at ease that we'd dropped off the guns.

"They must have had to go with a new plan when their friends didn't come back from Gossamer Ross's house," Julia said. "Decided to grab Keith from his flat to use as leverage if their mates didn't get the guns."

"When did all this happen?" I asked.

"They phoned me while you were asleep," Julia said.

"Why would they do that?"

"Keith had my number on his phone, not yours. They think I'm his girlfriend, and that I'm Gossamer's other assistant."

"Why the bloody hell would they think that?"

"Because I told them."

"You what?! Why?"

"Because I needed to keep them talking and stop them from hurting Keith."

"Good thinking," Ariel said.

"No it's not!" I cried. "Why didn't you put me on the phone?"

"You needed the rest," Julia said. "And I'm an investigator, too, remember? I took the initiative just as you or Mark or any of the others would. Stop trying to protect me, Ravi."

I could only splutter.

"We have to rescue Keith," I said.

"He's not the mission," Jarrod said.

"His boss is a client of ours," I said. "That makes him our responsibility."

"Your responsibility," Jarrod said. "Not ours."

"Fuck off," I said. "You don't need Julia and me anymore anyway. We can just call the police. That means telling them what the hell we've been up to for the last twelve hours with you lot, and they'll want to question you as well."

"Do you really want to kick this hornet's nest, brother?" Jarrod said.

"Do you really want to suddenly make the headlines and become more famous than you want to be?" I said. "Or do you want to rescue Keith and keep a lid on this whole situation before it gets totally out of hand?"

Jarrod and I glared at each other. He was probably weighing up the pros and cons of just shooting me at that point.

"They don't even know where we are," Williams said. "We are free and clear. Fuck 'im. He's not our problem. We deliver Mahfouz and the package and we're home free. They got no leverage."

"And isn't this mess partly Keith's fault?" Ariel said. "He was the one who left the gate open and let those guys in. Let him stew."

"He was thrown into this by his boss and out of his depth," I said. "You only found out about this because he brought me into it, which helped you with your mission here, so we owe him."

"So give him a goddamn medal," Reyes said.

"And this adds additional risk," Mikkelford said. "Puts extra hours on us."

"They've been after us and the guns anyway," I said. "This is a chance for you to remove a whole threat vector from this scenario."

They looked at me skeptically.

"I insist that you rescue Keith!" Hamid suddenly declared. "He is in this situation because of me!"

"Sir," Jarrod said. "Our first priority is your safety. This goes against all protocol not to mention common sense. It is not our problem. They miscalculated the value of their hostage."

"What kind of ruler would I be if I let someone die in my stead?" Hamid said. "He is my friend's employee and I have a moral obligation. You may be the professionals here, but I am the boss! I say we save him! Your future contract with me is riding on this!"

"Besides," I said. "For you lot, it'll be fun. Don't you live for this shit?"

The gears shifted in their heads. Ariel licked her lips. She reminded me of Kali there, only her tongue wasn't as long.

"Keith is an employee of my friend," Hamid repeated. "Granted, Gossamer is not a close friend, but there is an ethical consideration here on top of basic human decency."

Jarrod sighed, seemed to soften a bit.

"It's still not your concern," he said. "Ravi here is right. We could just phone this in to the police and let them take care of it."

"You know the cops will fuck this up," I said. "First the cops may not get there at all because of the chaos from the brush fires, and second they don't know what they're up against. This could end up in a siege and a standoff and be a huge mess."

"Be great cover for us to get Hamid out of Dodge, though," Williams said.

"I am declaring right now that we have to save Keith!" Hamid said. "And I am going nowhere until we do!"

"Sir," Jarrod said. "That puts you and the package at unnecessary risk."

"And I am the leader of my country, and as an act of goodwill, I have to put the safety of an innocent man first! What kind of ruler am I if I just let him die? Let this be my first act as a sovereign!"

Jarrod grimaced.

"All right. We have to discuss tactics."

He took the men and Ariel to the corner, leaving us in ours.

"Well put," Julia said.

"Well, I've come to the conclusion that only a megalomaniac, a narcissist, or a sociopath could be a despot, and I want to avoid becoming any of those," Hamid said.

"That's awfully astute," I said.

"I've gone through this with my therapist. Took years."

"Ah," I said. "Of course."

I knew Hamid wasn't necessarily agreeing to rescue Keith out of the kindness of his heart. This was also another way to delay his getting on that plane to fly back to the country that would end up being the death of him.

Jarrod and the men finally decided to play ball. Ariel was just along for the crack of it. I worried Julia was, too, and what would she do if this sort of thing wasn't enough to sublimate her addictions?

I got on the blower to Benjamin, who had been on standby at his computer in his hotel room in Venice Beach.

"Wotcher, tosh!" He addressed Jarrod. He really was laying on the South London accent thick while he was here in the States. "We have a clear line to these arseholes because we have poor li'l Keith's mobile number, which means I'll be able to track them via GPS. We already own them. Wa-hey!"

Really laying the accent on thick.

EIGHT

kay, ladies and gentlemen," Jarrod said to Reyes and Mikkelford. "You know the drill. This is a hostage extraction. Breach-and-clear. In-and-out."

They locked and loaded their guns, all business now.

"And we're on domestic soil," Jarrod continued. "Homeland means no canoeing. I'm looking at you, Mikkelford."

"Wait," I said. "Canoeing?"

"Oh, it's a term that came out of Seal Team Six," Ariel said, shrugging. "It means mutilating an enemy corpse for kicks."

Julia shuddered.

Another wave of disgust washed over me. These fuckers were monsters. I saw them as Rakshasas, their burning skins and glowing eyes belying their hunger for violence as they set out for the hunt.

"It's all gone a bit J. G. Ballard," I muttered.

"Sorry?" Julia said.

"Just something Mark would say."

"I wonder how he would deal with all this if he was here instead of us," she mused.

"Probably better than I am," I said. "He'll think this was all typical of the big cosmic joke."

"Now, they don't know we have Hamid as well," Jarrod said. "So we use the guns as bait."

"So we best keep Mr. Mahfouz out of sight and the hell away from any of this," Reyes said. "Which means splitting up."

"One team takes the guns and runs the op to extract Keith," Mikkelford said. "The other keeps Mr. Mahfouz safe."

"They want Ravi and me to drive the guns over to them in exchange for Keith," Julia said. "No police or Keith is dead, of course."

"So they know about me because Keith must have told them we were taking care of the guns," I said. "Do you reckon they would let us go or kill us since we're witnesses?"

"Best not to take any chances," Ariel said. "Kill 'em all."

The meeting was set for the Starbucks on Camarillo Street. That made sense, since it was near a busy intersection that gave them access to a freeway on-ramp, which would let them get away, if the traffic had cleared up by the time we met.

"Hang on," Benjamin said on the phone. "Are these people idiots or what? It's in a strip mall with a cramped parking lot that's chockabloc all the time. If either side wants to get away, they and you would be stuck in the sodding parking lot for ages. Find someplace else."

I called Keith's phone to introduce myself.

"I need to have proof of life," I said. "Put Keith on the phone."

"I'm sorry!" Keith said. "They just grabbed me! I don't even know who the fuck they are!"

The man with the accent snatched the phone back.

"We meet in an hour," he said.

"Hold on," I said. "You do not want to meet at the Starbucks."

I told them the situation with the traffic in that area.

"Don't try to trick us," the man with the accent said.

"No tricks. We don't want to be trapped in that damned strip mall and neither do you," I said. "We need someplace else where we can both get away from each other as quickly as possible. Traffic is only starting to ease up from the brush fire."

There was a pause as they conferred amongst themselves. They were obviously not from around here, but then neither were we.

"Goddamn amateur hour," Jarrod muttered in the background. Hopefully the man on the phone didn't hear that.

"Excuse me," Hamid whispered. "Are you really hoping these bastards would be a bit more competent and have a better chance of killing us?"

"Just saying," Jarrod whispered.

"I, for one, am grateful they're not as professional as they ought to be!" Hamid hissed.

Julia hushed them.

"Tell them to meet at the parking lot of the North Hollywood Recreational Center," Benjamin said via my Bluetooth headset. "The part that's on Chandler Boulevard. Easy enough to drive away."

Of course, the point was to not let them drive away with the guns. There should be plenty of spots for Jarrod and his team to set up and lie in ambush.

The man agreed. I recommended they used Google Maps to suss out the best route to get to the park. Julia and I were to drive the guns out there in an hour. They would be in a van with Keith. Once they confirmed we were alone and had brought the guns, they would put the guns in the van and give us Keith, and we would part ways.

Benjamin told us that judging by the GPS on Keith's smartphone, they were in his apartment. Jarrod and the team debated storming the place. It was close quarters, with too many variables in the confined space of a cheap apartment building with thin walls. The risk of stray bullets hitting neighbors in a shoot-out was not worth it. There was also the strong possibility of Keith ending up dead and members of the team getting shot. At least Benjamin had used thermal imaging on his drones and determined there were four of them holding Keith in his apartment. Just like he used thermal imaging to detect the ICE agents making their way to the safe house in the middle of the night.

Not being an expert at these types of tactics, I couldn't judge whether meeting out in the open at a park would be any better than raiding an apartment building. With the apartment, there would be nearby buildings to use as vantage points. Walls to hide behind, easier ambushes to be laid. I just had to take their word for it, which didn't make me happy.

Of course, all this was to confirm where they were. We were already outside Keith's apartment building by then.

And the gods were back, watching with anticipation.

NINE

We had left Hamid back at the motel with Williams and DuBois watching over him. The meeting was at noon, but we had chosen to drive out towards Keith's place an hour earlier to catch them before they left. Benjamin monitored Keith's phone and would tell us when they went on the move. Then there were his drones, of course.

The dry Santa Ana winds were still blowing through the air. Vayu was still in the sky. Smoke clouds were still flowing from the hills.

Jarrod, Reyes, and Mikkelford went into the building while Ariel, Julia, and I sat in the SUV with the guns in the back. They wore their bulletproof vests and were armed for bear. Our backup plan was to show up at NoHo Recreation Center to make the exchange if Jarrod aborted the raid. Then the idea would be to get Keith back while Jarrod and the team tried to pick his captors off.

Ariel had her Bluetooth earphone on. Julia and I declined to listen in. They were the professionals here. We were out of our depth.

"It's going to be a standard breach-and-clear," Ariel said. "Kick down the door, flash-bang, pick them off, and take the hostage out."

I heard a guttural roar outside the SUV and saw Rudra jumping and waving his arms. This meant things were about to kick off.

"Get out of the car, my son," Kali suddenly whispered in my ear. "Now. Go into the building."

What? Kali was standing outside the window on my side of the car.

"Mark my words and act," she said. "Your lives depend on this now. Take your two lovers with you."

"We have to get out of the car," I said.

"What are you talking about?" Ariel said.

"We have to get out now," I said. "Kali just talked to me."

Julia and Ariel barely hesitated, which surprised me.

We got out of the SUV and ran inside the building. As we headed up the stairs, Jarrod, Reyes, and Mikkelford were just coming down with Keith in their arms.

"What are you doing in here?" Jarrod said.

"Something came up," Ariel said. "What about you? That was fast."

"We busted in the door and there was only Keith," Reyes said.

"He said they just up and went out the door about ten minutes before we showed up," Mikkelford said.

"They got a phone call," Keith said. "They were speaking Arabic, I think. I didn't know what they said."

We turned back and headed outside, in time for gunfire to erupt.

Ariel threw Julia and me to the ground—Jarrod dropped as bullets speckled the wall next to us—Reyes and Mikkelford fell back into the building and pulled Keith in with them.

We saw the hostage-takers firing their Uzis at us as they got into the SUV with the guns. Two of them stood next to it and laid down cover fire while the driver set about hot-wiring the engine.

I grabbed Julia and pulled her into the lobby of the apartment building with me while Ariel and Jarrod returned fire. If we had stayed in the car, they would have come across us and shot us before taking the vehicle. They would have taken the keys off Ariel and driven off.

Jarrod and Ariel managed to drop one of the gunmen. As he lay dying on the grass, the SUV revved up and the remaining gunmen got inside and sped off.

Ariel fired her pistol at the SUV, trying to hit the tires. Jarrod and Mikkelford fired their AR-15s, shattering the back window of the departing SUV. Reyes left us in the lobby and joined them in laying down fire.

Rudra's roar grew louder and filled the air. It was almost deafening, but only to me. No one else was hearing it. He was standing behind me. I didn't want to turn around and see him.

The SUV screeched off, approaching the corner that would take it out of our view.

Then a sound like the Earth cracking, at the crescendo of Rudra's roar, and the SUV literally disappeared.

"What the hell?" Jarrod said.

Rudra stopped roaring. The street was silent at last but for the faint howl of the dry, cool wind. And Rudra settled into a mischievous chuckle. A god of retribution chuckling was not a sound anyone should ever find pleasant or soothing.

We approached the spot where the SUV disappeared.

"Whoa," Ariel said.

There was a massive hole where that section of the street had been, and the SUV had been swallowed up. We could barely see the vehicle at the bottom of the pit. It was at least thirty feet deep, with broken pipes and water filling the bottom, tiny fountains blooming. There was no need to speculate on the condition of the gunmen inside the car.

"Sinkhole," Jarrod said.

"Is this type of thing common?" I asked.

"Yeah," Reyes said. "More and more these days."

"Holy shit," Keith said.

Lord Vishnu, Kali, Rudra, and Ganesha looked on and applauded. This was a good twist to the show they were watching. Was this a scenario they had written together or one they'd just been waiting to see? I didn't want to think about that question.

"I guess the package is a write-off," Mikkelford said.

Ariel was looking at me.

She knew.

She knew Kali had told me to get her and Julia out of the car before we got shot.

"Which god caused this?" she asked, mischief in her voice.

"We don't have a god of sinkholes," I said without much conviction.

Jarrod looked around. People were coming out of their houses to look at the sinkhole. Sirens were in the air. Someone must have dialed 911 when they heard the shooting.

"We gotta get out of here," Jarrod said.

Jarrod, Reyes, and Mikkelford went off to steal a car.

"Rendezvous at the motel," Jarrod said.

"Keith," I said. "Can you give us a lift?"

TEN

Keith drove Ariel, Julia, and me back to the motel in his Prius. We had the radio on to listen to the news. There was a report of a squad of ICE officers being ambushed the night before, and a house being blown up. Authorities suspected that the officers had attempted to raid an address that was controlled by a drug gang whose members were on the list of violent criminals who were in the country illegally. Now those gang members were at large, and considered armed and dangerous. A police manhunt was under way. The fire brigade, or as they called them in America, the fire department, had declared that the brush fire was slowly being brought under control, and traffic was starting to move again, but slowly. Access to the freeways should be opening up soon. Reports were coming in about a shooting near Vineland, and a sinkhole had erupted nearby. Details were still unclear as police and emergency services were still en route.

Keith was lucky on so many levels. Since his apartment hadn't become the venue for a firefight, he was spared having to make up some story about being taken hostage. There would be no connection drawn between him and the gunmen at the bottom of the sinkhole in an SUV with crates of classified military weaponry in its back. In fact, the world at large would be no wiser to his connection with the cache of military weapons or the heavily armed dead men in the sinkhole. It was going to take a day for the fire department to fish the SUV out anyway. By then we would be long gone.

Keith thanked us and drove off back to his life. He would have something to write about for his screenplay now. Williams and DuBois told us Jarrod and the others would be back shortly once they ditched the car they'd stolen.

"What a pity the guns were lost in the sinkhole," Hamid said, not regretful at all.

"Good thing we kept half of the package in the second SUV, huh?" Ariel said.

"Honestly," Hamid said. "There weren't enough weapons to supply the whole army back home. Those are really a sample to convince them to buy more. More money to the US for arms sales. They were a symbolic gesture to the generals, that I was able to deliver some state-of-the-art American weapons for the struggle to regain power from the rebels and terrorist groups trying to gain a foothold."

"Does this jeopardize your standing with the generals, then?" I asked.

"Oh God, I hope so!" Hamid said. "Perhaps they'll think me incompetent and pick someone else to take over the country! Leave me out of it!"

"Hamid," I said. "Did you make a call to the rebels when we left? To tell them we were coming? I was wondering how they could leave Keith alone in his apartment and then double back around the building to grab the car with the guns in it."

"I called my sister and she passed it on," Hamid said. "And I'm glad you didn't get shot."

"You've been playing your own double agent," Julia said. "Trying to sabotage your own campaign to go back and rule."

"Guilty," he said. "And I really should be punished, don't you think? As ruler, I declare that I should be exiled from my country, condemned to live out my days here in America."

"Don't look at us," Williams said. "We didn't have orders to stop him from making phone calls."

"Sneaky fucker," DuBois said. "Went in the bathroom and made those calls on his cellphone."

"I have spoken to Uncle Carl," Hamid said. "And I put my foot down.

I am not getting on that bloody plane back to my country. It is not safe there. I am staying in Beverly Hills."

"And he's okay with that?" I asked.

"Of course he isn't, but I didn't give him a lot of choice. I spoke to Mr. Collins and hired Interzone to be my personal bodyguards here in Los Angeles, and I'm going to form my government-in-exile here."

"So you're going to rule as a despot in Beverly Hills?" Julia asked. "How is that going to work?"

"It doesn't," Hamid said. "But until they sort things out over there in a way that guarantees I don't get assassinated within a day of my setting foot there, I'm not going. And they can't force me. Let the military gain control first. *Then* I'll think about going back."

"What about the guns?"

"I've contacted the military attaché at my embassy and told him to send someone to pick up the guns. They can try to ship them back home for the army to use."

"So what you've done is bought yourself time again," I said. "You're just putting off going back there. Sooner or later, you're going to run out of excuses."

"Let me enjoy life as a civilian a bit longer," Hamid said. "Let me be a restaurant owner and a producer who has to deal with a star who has to go to rehab."

"Fair enough," I said.

"And if, say, the weapons failed to get to my country, then there's even less incentive for me to go back."

When Jarrod and the rest of the team got back, Hamid briefed him on the situation. Jarrod called Collins to confirm that Hamid was now a client and under Interzone protection. The CIA had contracted them to protect Hamid and secure the guns in the first place, but now Hamid was directly contracting them, possibly sidestepping the CIA's original brief for them. I wondered if there was a conflict of interest there, but that wasn't my problem. Jarrod didn't have to like it. Hamid had already arranged a bank transfer of a few million dollars to Interzone to secure their services.

Frankly, none of this made much sense to me, but then neither did the last twenty-four hours. I was just a private investigator on a busman's holiday who got a lot more than he bargained for. There were so many ambiguities, uncertainties, and outright mysteries to this world that I should just stop trying to make sense of it. The best I could do was to stay in one piece and, as Julia said, bear witness. And there was the rising karmic debt, which I was sure I would be called upon to pay someday.

Ravi," Hamid turned to me, "if you represent what the Golden Sentinels agency has to offer, then I am impressed. I may call upon your services one day."

"Well, you can talk to Gossamer Ross and get the agency's number from him," I said.

"Excellent."

Roger was going to be pleased.

We would be stuck in the San Fernando Valley for one more day, waiting for the city's traffic to normalize. The next few hours were spent sitting around the motel watching daytime telly. Hamid complained about the Mexican takeout Jarrod bought from the local restaurant up the block. He regaled us with stories about how brutal the generals were in his country and checked with Jarrod on how many of them were still alive. To his disappointment, it was more than he had hoped.

"Murderous bastards all," he said. "Even if I call some of them 'uncle.'"

More palatable were his stories about the Hollywood actresses he had bedded, especially the A-listers. That got everyone's attention and passed the time better. His attention turned back to his drug-addicted teenage sitcom star and how he was going to have to hold auditions for her replacement and the nightmare of dealing with stage mothers who invested all their hopes and dreams in their hapless daughters who were going to be fucked up by show business. All this was just to hold off thinking about the inevitable: that sooner or later, Hamid was going to have to fly back to his country and face the music, to be America's puppet in ruling the place. His family wasn't Muslim but Christian, which made them much more attractive to Western allies who had an eye on the oil fields that gave him his leverage. Hamid was spoiled, privileged, lazy, and entitled in typical rich-kid fashion. He also had a massive capacity for duplicity, an ability to play all sides against one another while trying to keep his hands clean, but still possessed a modicum of self-awareness and even a core of basic decency. That might still save him, or he could still become a monster. There was a chance he could have gotten us killed today, but he depended on our professionalism and luck to stop that happening. I didn't want to think about it at the time, but this was not the last I would see of Hamid Mahfouz. He was pretty much a client by now.

For the time being, I was mainly thinking about Julia and me, and how we probably had had enough of Los Angeles by now. I was starting to miss the gray, damp dystopia of the UK. Sure, things were bad there, but it was ours. I grew up there, amidst its history and its flaws. My morals came from there, and I missed the sense of the roots I had there as much as my family had roots in India. The emptiness of Los Angeles didn't suit me at all, its perpetual erasure of history as it kept renewing itself with new architecture and trends. The gods might find it amusing as they found everything amusing, but I think even they were more at home in London with me. This was also a busman's holiday for them. They were, after all, my gods, not this city's.

And I didn't know what to think about their actions here in the last few weeks. A man saw them the same way I did, even if he was probably on drugs at the time. Kali told me to do something that saved my life. Did Rudra open a sinkhole that stopped those gunmen from escaping with a carful of military-grade weapons or was it just a coincidence? Was I channeling them as Ariel and Julia believed? Was this what being an untrained shaman in a city was going to be like? Or was I doing exactly what they expected of me? What was their endgame? Was there an end to this or was I stuck dancing for them forever?

It was night now. Julia and I were back in our motel room after that Mexican dinner. We were all set to retire when there was a knock on the door.

It was Ariel, all smiles, with a bottle of tequila she had bought from the liquor store across the street.

ELEVEN

"Marie's lawyer reached a deal with the Mainland. Derek would be released shortly after he appeared on television reading a confession that he had traveled to China to assist with anti-corruption investigations. Marie just had to keep this quiet and let it play out.

"I continued my cover of going about my days shopping and lunching. When I texted the wives on ChattyMe, I was met with silence. I phoned their houses, and the housekeepers told me they had left. Their husbands had suddenly been called back to China. I stopped by Hua's place and was told she and her husband had left in a hurry. Same with the rest.

"Interesting.

"Three days later, Derek appeared on the news. He had been held in Shenzhen. He looked exhausted and had lost weight. He sat at a table facing the camera with two uniformed Mainland policemen standing behind him. He read a statement in halting Mandarin, since it didn't come naturally to him, and he occasionally slipped into Cantonese as he 'confessed' to crossing over the border into China without the proper papers and having paid the penalty. He had spent the last few weeks in China helping the authorities with their inquiries into the publishing of morally corrupting materials in Hong Kong, and apologized for aiding and adding to the atmosphere of decadence and salacious gossip.

"They drove Derek back to the border that night. Marie and their lawyer went out to meet them, along with a small army of photographers and reporters. Derek was now the latest victim of China's autocratic overreach. Academics and activists would be citing him as an example in their push for upholding democratic rights in Hong Kong.

"I went over to visit Derek and Marie the next day, after he got in his first good night's sleep for six weeks. He was still tired and shell-shocked. There was one surprise: they'd told him to continue to publish the book, but an updated edition that named names—the husbands, the wives—with a new afterword describing how they were found out and sent back to China to face the consequences of their corruption and decadence. Contrary to killing the book and shutting down Derek's publishing company, he was allowed to carry on. The book actually suited the Mainland government's anticorruption drive after all. It sent a message they wanted out there to the officials: that corruption and bribery were not tolerated, and they were watching.

"I've thought about this for hours now, and here's my theory: the Mainland's Anti-Corruption Squad got ahold of the book and wanted to know who the officials depicted in it were, so they got in touch with Brother Bull to arrange for his men to grab Derek and deliver him to them. That way, no Mainland officers or agents would be implicated in Derek's disappearance.

"What did Brother Bull get in return for this little assignment? They would turn a blind eye to his black market fish sales to the Mainland. Hua's husband, he of the Ministry of Agriculture, might have been getting a kickback from Brother Bull for a hand in smuggling the fish in. Fay's financier husband might be the one handling the extra pocket money they were all making in Hong Kong, hiding it in dummy accounts and stock investments. Bee's husband, being in Public Morals, might have been the one who blew the whistle on Derek and demanded he get arrested as a way to draw attention away from them.

"And the Anti-Corruption Squad might have been on to the lot of them, and used Derek's arrest to flush them out. Unfortunately, Derek didn't have real evidence or names, and they had to keep sweating him in case he was lying and protecting either his sources or them. The squad must have suspected who they wanted to go after, but these officials might have been too well connected for them to risk going after without concrete evidence. That they had the privilege of being sent to Hong Kong was a sign of their high status within the party.

"So Derek's original source for the book might have been the squad themselves, the information passed to him via proxies in Hong Kong. I started to have a feeling that Marie might be one of those proxies. She might be the one who helped Derek write the book after all. After all, who else could he trust enough to do that, and for a book like this? He probably didn't think it was anything more than another gossipy book like the ones he usually published as his company's bread and butter, and wasn't expecting to get snatched and spirited across the border for it. Perhaps Marie didn't expect this either, and in desperation, she called me to help get him back. I'd known her since secondary school in London, so of course I'd come back and help my friend in her time of need. Did Marie know she was acting as their agent or was she as much of a patsy as Derek was?

"That means they might have known about me all along.

"Bugger. Piss! Shit! Buggeration!

"For all my vaunted attempts to remain anonymous, in the shadows, I may have been operating at their leisure all this time, a useful tool that they let run free. Did they know about my hacking skills? Or did they just know me as Wong Ong Meng's black sheep daughter who worked as an analyst for Golden Sentinels and therefore was a deniable third party who helped them maintain their cover?

"I'm clever, and clever enough to know that us clever people will always get tripped up by our cleverness. You're never as safe as you think you are, no matter how much precaution you take. I hate that. To be clever is to be cursed with knowing that you will never, ever be clever enough, or safe enough.

"This was the chess game being played, and we were all pawns. Did Marie know? Was she a willing asset? Was I always part of their stratagem or the unknown factor that delivered the final piece of their puzzle to them? I was never going to get any clear answers, and probably shouldn't bother trying.

"I did my duty next: briefed Golden Sentinels Hong Kong and Roger. I *went in the office and gave them the rundown, with Roger on speakerphone in London, staying late at the office to hear how this all turned out. Unsurprisingly, Cheryl was there and so was Marcie Holder. Marcie must have been chuffed to have some new information on how they played their games in China. Roger seemed pleased. He always seemed pleased with a successful result from an international case. He said he had spoken a day before to some prospective Chinese clients who were eager to have Golden Sentinels on retainer for jobs, to be paid at top rate. Apparently, what I had been up to in Hong Kong for the last few weeks impressed them enough to want to become clients. How did these people know about me unless they had ties to the government?*

"This was my cue. I've been here long enough and I don't want the Mainland taking any further looks at me. Time to head back to London. Cold, gray, messed-up Blighty, oh, how I've missed you. Even Benjamin and his sarky South London silliness. There, I've said it, Benjamin. I actually missed you. I'll see you all in a few days."

TWELVE

I woke with a splitting headache, in a tangle of sheets and limbs.

. . . Wait, there were more limbs than just Julia's.

My eyes focused and a familiar tattoo of Kali caught my attention. Then the arm the tattoo rested on. Julia sighed and shifted, and Ariel rolled over to me and curled around me.

Shit.

Shit. Shit. Shit.

The night before was a blur. We were at a bar. I remember Ariel whipping out a bottle of tequila. Then another. I'd been wound up so tight for the last few days that the booze hit me like a tsunami. Julia was laughing at something I said. Jarrod, Reyes, and Mikkelford stayed with the car and the rest of the guns, even though they said all imminent threats had been neutralized. Jarrod gave the nod for Ariel to go off to the room with Julia and me, where we continued to drink and talk. Then I didn't remember when we went beyond just talking.

I sat up and looked around for my clothes. Saw the used condoms wrapped in tissue paper and dropped in the plastic wastebasket. Oh, thank God we remembered condoms!

And of course Kali was in the room watching me. This was the payoff she'd been waiting for. I should have known. She sat in the chair, her legs crossed, licking her lips. This was the last thing I wanted to happen with Ariel. Now we'd never be rid of her. This would bind her to Julia and me even more than ever! Kali seemed to be reading my mind and shook her head in amused sympathy. Thanks a lot.

I got dressed and went outside. Jarrod and the men were gathered at the cars.

"Water?" Jarrod said, holding out a bottle of mineral water from a small cooler they had in the backseat of their SUV. I murmured something and accepted it, took several large gulps. The winds seemed to be dying down, and Reyes was sitting in the SUV, listening to the news. The fires seemed to be subsiding. Traffic on the freeways was finally easing up, so we were clear to go.

Hamid was long gone. The moment traffic opened up, he had Williams and DuBois drive him back to his hotel in Beverly Hills.

"Confirmed the rendezvous to hand over the package to Hamid's military attaché," Jarrod said, indicating his smartphone. "Final stretch, brother. We get the hell out of the Valley, up towards the hills again, near the woods, for the handover. You can call your people to pick you and the princess up before the attaché shows up for the guns."

"Isn't it a bit irresponsible for Ariel to go off and get drunk the night before an op?" I asked. "Even if this thing is almost over?"

"She dances to her own tune, brother," Jarrod said. "Besides, she never gets hungover. At least, we never saw that happening. Always on point on the job."

"She's a damn good driver and wingman," Reyes said.

"Sniping skills ain't bad either," Mikkelford said.

"She's solid backup," Reyes said. "Team player, even if she's a pain in the ass. Knows her shit. Five-by-five."

This didn't reassure me about her mental or moral state.

Eventually, Julia and Ariel showered and came out. We bought breakfast from a drive-through and headed to the rendezvous point. I still took the wheel of the car, Julia next to me while Ariel rode in the back, guns loaded.

"So Julia said you were thinking about quitting," Ariel said. "After all this fun?"

"Fun? We're running guns to a CIA-backed oppressive regime in the

Middle East. They're going to be used to kill people, and I'm party to that. I already got an entire family killed back in London," I said.

"They were a bad family," Ariel said. "Bad, bad, bad."

"Ariel, they're not a bunch of naughty dogs. They were people."

I didn't even stop to ask how the hell she knew about the Harkingdales, but of course she would know about them. Interzone kept tabs on us. Bastards.

"Dude, you are in sooo much denial," she said. "I saw your face during the shoot-out. I saw the look in your eyes when the sinkhole opened. You were so fucking alive you were ready to explode."

I glanced at Julia. She was watching us intently. When I turned back to Ariel, Lord Krishna was standing behind her looking at me, his arms crossed, a smug smile on his face. I didn't like where this was going.

"Come on, Ravi," Ariel said. "Don't you remember the *Bhagavad Gita*?"

Of course.

"I know that's a rhetorical question," I said. "Don't tell me you've read it. Which edition?"

"The classic translation, of course." She smiled. "The one the Hare Krishnas used to try to give out at airports. That one was actually shocked that I not only accepted it, but gave him money and asked about it."

"You read all of it?"

"Hey, deployments are long, boring periods of waiting broken up by moments of sheer violence. I get a lot of reading done on the job."

I sighed.

"Where is this going, Ariel?"

"Think about it. It's about Arjuna feeling doubt and questioning whether he should keep going."

"So now you're saying I'm Arjuna?"

"You're in the same place he was in the *Bhagavad Gita*. Krishna tells him he should keep doing what he's doing because of his obligation and his duty. It's pretty much his lot in life. It's his mission. It's his path. What would he do if he quit? He's a warrior, so shut the hell up and get on with it."

"Thanks for taking a key epic text in Hindu culture and making it all about me," I said. "If I were a flaming narcissist, I would have thought every single religious text I read back when I was doing religious studies was about me."

"Ravi, you're all about doing what's right," Ariel said. "You can't help it. You have the most developed superego I have ever seen. And you keep beating yourself up over it."

I saw Krishna saying all this to Arjuna in parallel to Ariel and me. This was starting to piss me off.

"So you're saying we just survived an epic battle in the last few days?" I said.

"And we came out of the other side," Ariel said, eyes ablaze. "The fire in the hills is finally dying out. We passed through a crucible."

"And the San Fernando Valley has been our field of dharma," I said.

"You're getting the picture," Ariel said, relishing the imagery.

I turned to Jarrod.

"Does she talk about this with you all the time?" I asked.

"All the time, brother," he said and shrugged.

I looked out over the hills, at the dark smoke plumes rising into the skies and swirling in the gusts of the Santa Ana winds. The gods stood at the edge of the precipice surveying the Valley and the hills as if they'd orchestrated it all.

THIRTEEN

We drove all the way back to the Hollywood Hills. Through Laurel Canyon, onto Mulholland Drive, past the well-off neighborhoods and up, up, up into the wooded area off the beaten track. This was where the contact was supposed to show up to collect the damn guns. This might also be the perfect place to disappear someone. Ariel cheerfully explained to Julia and me what a good spot these hills were for dumping bodies. Hikers may venture through these woods, but very few of them would go this deep off the beaten track. Coyotes, stray feral dogs, mountain lions, even the odd wolf lived and fed in these hills. They were also full of ravines for tossing a body down. Someone could disappear for years or forever up here.

Were they going to get rid of Julia and me here? Did we know too much? Were we too inconvenient? Would this be a message to Roger? A salvo in the war that was brewing between Roger and Laird Collins? Would Collins kill us just to fuck with Roger, to show his superior power and ruthlessness? Why was I thinking all this now? Was this going to be the gods' final joke on me? For all my efforts to do the right thing, and all the failing, was I going to end up as coyote food in a ditch here in the hills?

I looked over at Julia. Was she thinking the same thing? She was as calm as I looked.

"End of the line," Ariel said, and we got out of the car.

The gods were all here, gathered like an audience at an outdoor play.

The winds were still blowing lightly. Vayu was still gently blowing.

The sky was blue and clear again. The dry air almost stung my nostrils. I pulled the car over at the side, not far from the edge of a ravine. Jarrod, Reyes, and Mikkelford were out of the black SUV and lighting up cigarettes. They were relaxed, guns holstered.

"You call your friend?" Jarrod asked. "He coming to pick you up?"

"He's on his way," I said.

Julia came over and stood with me as I looked over the horizon. If these was going to be my last moments on Earth, I wanted to get a good view.

"Ravi." Ariel came up to us. Was she going to be the one to pull the trigger? "Boss wants a word," she said, and handed me her phone.

"Ravi." Laird Collins's voice, smooth as ever.

"Mr. Collins. What can I do for you?"

"Oh, you've done plenty. I've been talking to Roger, and once again, our people have worked together like a smooth, well-oiled machine."

"That's up for debate," I said.

"Modest as ever," he said. "I just wanted to congratulate you for a job well done. You did the Lord's work."

"I don't really see it that way."

"Everything goes according to God's Plan, Ravi. You just have to embrace it."

"God's Plan is to run guns to a violent rebel group trying to take over a government?"

"I've said this before, every action, every outcome we effect is another step towards bringing the return of the True Christ and the Kingdom of Heaven to Earth, Ravi. And you've played your part."

"I think things are a lot more chaotic than you think, Mr. Collins. And you don't always get the outcome you want."

How long before I feel a bullet slamming into my back and everything going black forever?

"That's why we must be careful how we move the pieces, Ravi," Collins said. "Ariel told me how calm you were through this whole operation. She was impressed. I want to extend my offer of employment to you again."

"I'll pass, thanks."

"Let me give you some free advice. Roger Golden only cares about money and power, without any ideals or higher purpose behind it. That means one day, he will sell you and everyone in the agency out. And he won't lose a night's sleep over that."

"Thanks, but this isn't exactly news to me."

"And the day that happens, I want you to remember that I offered you a place."

"Honestly, Mr. Collins, you can do much better than me."

"You're selling yourself short again. You have access to your gods, to signs and portents that have kept you alive and thriving. I have to know your place in God's Plan."

"I'm just muddling along. The gods are just watching me for shits and giggles. That's all there is to it. You could say I'm just mentally ill. Or some kind of holy fool."

"Holy fools and shamans speak the truth, Ravi, and have insight that no one else does."

"You're saying you want every card in the deck so you'd have a full set for your plans."

"I think more in terms of chess."

"Mr. Collins, I'm just a failed religious scholar and failed high school teacher. The things I said that you took far too seriously are just snarky jokes that any Londoner makes on a Tuesday night at the pub. We take the piss out of Morris dancing because it just looks naff."

" 'Naff'?"

"It means silly. Tacky. Excuse me. British slang. I'm just earning my salary and trying not to get killed. I don't fire guns. I don't do targeted assassinations. And I'm certainly not happy that I'm helping you deliver guns that would start a small war that is almost certainly going to kill a lot of brown-skinned people abroad. According to your beliefs, the non-Christian citizens are going to hell for not being Christian. And that goes for me, too. I don't agree with your vision of the world. It disgusts me. I will never come to work for you."

"That day may come sooner than you think, Ravi," Collins said, not a hint of emotion in his voice, still casual and courteous. "Don't be surprised if our companies end up working together again."

"Next time I'll take a rain check."

"Roger may despise me, but he's a pragmatist, and he might have to use *my* services for some of his plans for the future. Sometimes I might need his, case in point you lucking into this situation and helping us out. Roger's ambitions are small, but he needs a lot of resources, which includes you and our coworkers."

"Why are you talking in code, Mr. Collins? You seem to know something I don't and you're dying to tell me."

"All in due course, Ravi. I would love to ask you what your gods have been telling you. It has to be exquisite."

"It really isn't," I said. "What my gods do is tell stories. They reenact stories that are parables. It's about metaphors and allegories of human life experiences. It's about our aspirations, our fears and our hopes. My gods don't declare absolute power and dominion like your God does."

"And yet you've helped my people deliver those guns."

"That was self-preservation on my part."

"That's only what you think. Even though we're going around in circles, I do enjoy talking to you, Ravi. You know things you think you don't know. You are truly blessed. I have never met someone who was as touched as you are, and that makes you valuable. Until we meet again, Ravi."

He hung up.

I handed the phone back to Ariel.

"Told ya he had a hard-on for your gods and shit," she said.

"So I'm part of his God's Plan," I said.

"That's what he really believes," Ariel said.

"Do you believe that?" I said.

"I believe you're never boring. You're just bags and bags of fun."

Julia was watching me, and behind her, so were the gods. Kali and Vishnu stroked their chins, waiting for what would come next.

What didn't come next was bullets for Julia and me.

"What did your boss mean about us working together again soon?" I asked.

"Your boss has plans," Ariel said. "You ought to ask him when you get back to London. Or maybe you should stay here in LA. Start working over here. That way, you can get out of Roger's clutches and still do what you do."

"No, thanks. I'd rather go back to London. Less guns and less apocalyptic fires there."

"So you gonna quit?" Ariel asked, eyebrow raised.

"I'm following Arjuna's story, remember?" I said. "I'm going to stay in the job, because it's what I do. I have a duty to do the right thing and try to keep things from going completely pear-shaped. Julia was right. I have an obligation to bear witness."

I squeezed Julia's hand.

And I'm not part of your Plan, Collins, you fucking madman.

Benjamin arrived in a Tesla, on loan from the company he was working with that day. Thankfully, he was driving it rather than using the autopilot. He smiled tightly and greeted Ariel and Jarrod.

"Ready to go?" he asked.

"Let me get my jacket," I said.

I walked over to the SUV and opened the door. As I reached in to grab my jacket, I released the hand brake. I shut the door and put my jacket on as I walked towards Julia and Benjamin. Behind me, I could hear the SUV starting to slowly roll forward. Ariel, Jarrod, and the other men had their backs to it and hadn't noticed.

"See ya around, brother," Jarrod said curtly.

"I hope not," I said, and got into the Tesla. Julia was already in the back.

"Don't say anything," I said to Benjamin. "Just fucking drive. Step on it."

"Ravi, what did you do?" Julia said. In the rearview mirror, I saw her lips curl into a smile.

"Benjamin, just drive," I said.

He stepped on the accelerator and we started to speed away. In the widening distance behind us, Jarrod and the men were slowly turning around to see the SUV roll away from them and over the hill.

"How high do you reckon is the drop off that hill?" I asked.

Benjamin started laughing hysterically.

"At least a thousand feet," he said. "Roger's going to love this!"

Julia looked out the back window at Jarrod and the men running after the SUV, but it was too late. It was already over the edge.

She started laughing as well.

Nobody was going to be using those guns.

Ariel didn't run after the SUV. She just watched it and the guns inside it disappear. I imagine she must have smiled to herself and shrugged. Everything was a cosmic joke to her. She was that type of sociopath.

I didn't laugh. I didn't feel the urge.

When we got back to Benjamin's hotel, he started up his laptop and showed us the raw video footage that one of his satellite drones had filmed from the hills. It was a perfectly framed video of the SUV rolling right over the edge of the hill and plummeting down the ravine. The crumpling destruction of the car as it rolled down the ravine, losing pieces of itself and the gun parts getting mangled and falling out, was grimly satisfying to me. This was a fitting end to my LA adventure.

DEBRIEFING
IN BLIGHTY

I watched the city move away from me out of the car window while Julia drove. Benjamin sat in the back editing the footage of the SUV going over the hills and crumpling into the trees. He was slowing it down in glacial, graceful slow motion, and adding Strauss's *Blue Danube* over it.

"And there we go," Benjamin said. "One for Roger's private collection. Other people have porn, Roger has footage of his enemies coming a cropper. I bet he'll kick back at the end of a long day with a glass of his most expensive whiskey to replay this over and over again, reveling in his frenemy Laird Collins losing a result."

"Did Roger know this was going to be the outcome?" I asked.

"Nah, mate," Benjamin said. "Roger would have to be bloody psychic to predict all this. No, he trusted you to be you. You always give him an interesting and entertaining result."

"Him and the gods both," I muttered.

The gods, the whole lot of them, didn't need to be riding in the car with us. They were gods, after all, so they could just fly alongside us on clouds, happily commiserating with one another on the latest show they'd just seen, like a miniseries about me and Julia and our exploits in Los Angeles, one of those special event programs of a TV series. Was that what I was to the gods now? Their favorite reality TV show? Arrgh!

They're expressions of my own turmoil, but this doesn't make it less galling. My own mind was out to make fun of me.

"So, kiddies," Benjamin said. "Have we had enough of our Californian adventure? Shall we get on the first Virgin Atlantic flight back to the familiar gloom of London, where nutters don't run around with guns?"

"Good way of summing it up," Julia said happily. Her thirst for dangerous thrills was satiated for now. "I'd say yes."

"LAX, here we come," Benjamin declared. "Wa-hey!"

Cheryl had used the firm's corporate account and points to get us seats in business class, so we got to sleep in horizontal cots. Thank God for small rewards. I loaded up my system with booze so that I would be knocked straight out after takeoff. It would be days after we were safely back in London that I would find out what went down after we left.

Marcie told me. Rather than just legging it and getting out of town, Jarrod and Ariel met with the military attaché who was going to collect the guns for the militia group. No surprise that he was not well pleased. What I dreaded might happen did: a firefight ensued. With hardcases like Jarrod, Ariel, Reyes, and Mikkelford against a hot-tempered foreign military attaché and his men, there was no contest. There were plenty of places deep in the woods in the Hollywood Hills to bury bodies, and if no one knew where to look, they would never be found. I didn't want to weigh up the sheer amount of chaos we had left in our wake in Los Angeles. Ariel texted me a selfie of her winking and holding up two fingers in a peace sign. Julia and I never believed it would ever be easy to get rid of her.

"No hard feelings," Ariel's caption read. "Besides, I got all this bitchin' new leather gear that Julia wore."

Back at Golden Sentinels, Marcie didn't even seem terribly upset about that failed operation. As far as she was concerned, losing that military attaché and his men was just a bit of a setback.

"Oh, those guys were a major pain in the ass anyway," she said. "Always making demands, changing their minds, changing plans, running up their tabs. Interzone did us a favor and got rid of them, and we'll just find new liaisons, make a new deal to sell them new guns. The world keeps turning."

Roger told me that Chuck and the Los Angeles office was very impressed with Julia and me.

"Tell Ravi he'll always be welcome in LA," Chuck had told Roger. "We'll have a place for him here if he needs one."

"Good result," Roger said. "Better than I could have hoped."

"Roger laughed for days when he heard what you did with the guns at the end," Cheryl said. "The first time in ages anyone managed to queer a deal for Laird Collins."

Was that approval in her voice? I couldn't read Cheryl's expression, but she didn't say anything to contradict Roger or his general demeanor. The gods were lounging on Roger's sofa and happily applauding me. Deeper and deeper I sank into this world of gray karmic debts. Marcie beamed as if proud that her prize protégé was proving to be the right investment. Julia thought it fascinating the way I seemed to fall upwards whenever I was sinking deeper into the moral depths. None of it made me happier. I wonder if Collins suspected I had deliberately sabotaged the arms delivery deal, and if he might want payback down the line. He had, after all, killed people for less. Or was I reprieved for the time being because he still wanted to glean the secrets he was convinced I held?

"Get this," Benjamin announced to everyone when we went to the roof to smoke one of Mark's spliffs. "Ravi was all sad-face because he had a threesome. Seriously. I need to get planning permission before Olivia lets me touch her bra! Sorry, mate. No sympathy from me."

Olivia punched Benjamin in the arm. Hard.

My ritual humiliation done with, I checked in with Olivia. She had gotten back a few days before Julia and I.

"That's sweet of you, darling," she said. "Roger was tempted to let word get out that this was a Golden Sentinels Hong Kong Limited investigation. Cheryl talked him out of it. She didn't think we'd want Golden Sentinels to be known publicly for exposing Chinese government corruption. I have a feeling Roger will let it slip to prospective clients just to show off how far we can reach."

"So what happens to the husbands now they're nicked?" I asked.

"They face a humiliating trial, and might even be executed. Perhaps not, though. The government might want to present themselves to the international community as becoming more merciful in the future. Perhaps they'll just be in prison for a long time."

"Do you feel bad about that?"

"Not particularly." She shrugged.

Unlike me, Olivia did not have a problem with her karma. She was a great believer in retribution and the justice of revenge. She was also perfectly comfortable with carrying it out. She was certainly much harsher than Quan Yin, the patron goddess of mercy she prayed to.

Julia and I settled back into the usual caseloads of helping celebrities with secrets they needed hidden, hunting down stalkers, proving infidelity in expensive divorce cases, and having celebratory drinks down the local pub whenever we closed a case. Ken and Clive were a bit nicer to me. They seemed to like that I owed them one. David was relieved to have me back. He said I was his oasis from the madness that went on in the office and the types of things he had to draft legal paperwork to protect the agency from.

"And how are things at home, Mark?" I asked.

"Which home?" he asked coyly.

"You have more than one?"

"Well, I've been thinking about giving up my flat, mate," he said. "Been going around with some mates of mine, part of an anarchist collective. We're breaking into posh empty buildings all over Knightsbridge, Belgravia, Mayfair, and setting up squats there to house the homeless."

"Bloody hell. How long have you been up to this?" I asked.

"About a year. Takes ages for the owners and courts to get round to issuing summonses and court orders to kick everyone out. And when they do, we just move on to another property. Plenty to pick from all over London."

"It's a trip," Marcie said. "I've been on some of these outings with him."

"What could the CIA want with anarchist collectivist squats in London?" I asked.

"Keeping an ear to the ground," she said. "And you never know where the next assets are going to come from."

"By my reckoning," Mark said, "I'll have over six places to live in the poshest parts of Central London by next month. It's a great laugh."

"And potential safe houses," Marcie said.

"You really like having a finger in everything, don't you?" I said.

"We're only as good as our networks," she said with a smile.

I suddenly remembered the dream I had in Los Angeles. How did I know about Mark and the squats? Did the gods send me that dream?

In the corner of my eye, Lord Vishnu kicked back on the office sofa and whistled, looking coy.

Of course the gods knew. They knew everything.

EPILOGUE

Sunday dinner at my parents'. How we settled into the old routine like a comfortable coat. Los Angeles already felt like a distant dream, a past life, and a short and temporary one I was glad to see the back of. The normal routine still felt unreal to me, though, as if I was going through the motions, swimming in a new dream.

"I bet with Sanji you were going to up sticks and just move there," Vivek said.

"Yeah," Sanjita said. "Why didn't you just go the Sunny California route, leave all this behind?"

"And leave you lot behind?" I said. "What would you do without me? Mum and Dad would just drive you mad."

"That's a fine thing to say about us," Dad said, not entirely seriously.

"We were doing perfectly well without you," Mum said.

"Mum, I'm crushed."

Julia smiled. My family was in an uncharacteristically good mood. I suppose Mum and Dad bonking regularly again was helping. I suddenly felt queasy at the thought and wished it hadn't come to me.

"No, really," Mum said. "Your two colleagues, Ken and Clive, they looked after us very nicely."

"We offered to pay them for their services," Dad said.

"Christ, you didn't!" I cried.

"They put themselves above and beyond to keep us safe," Mum said. "And they turned down our money. I made them dinner instead. They seemed quite pleased with that. It was quite the adventure," Mum added, eyes twinkling.

I wasn't sure how much of this cheeriness from my parents I could take.

"Mum, Dad, what exactly happened?"

"Oh, not much." Dad was uncharacteristically coy. Was he even my father? Who replaced the grumpy old curmudgeon with this guy?

"We had our own little adventure while you were away." Mum was being equally coy. I was screaming inside.

Julia looked amused, but then she related to people who kept their little secrets, since the big secrets were the ones we needed to watch out for.

"Mum and Dad went all Batman on that gang with the help of your colleagues," Sanjita said.

"Hunted them down and everything," Vivek said with some glee.

"How can you be so cheerful about this?" I asked.

"There was no harm done," Dad said. "They won't be coming to this part of town anytime soon."

"Not with Dad and his cricket bat around," Vivek said.

"Or Mum gave them a stern talking to," Sanji said.

Yeah, Mum gave them a tongue-lashing with Ken and Clive looming over them like golems. I was sure Ken and Clive were happy to get some punching and kicking in, and getting a nice little earner from Mrs. Dhewan. They found another side gig here. Win-win for everyone.

"All right," Sanjita said. "Vivek and I have kept this quiet long enough. We have an announcement to make. Since Mum and the aunties have finally stopped nagging us, we were able to get on with it, and I can announce now that I'm pregnant."

Cue cries of joy from Mum. Dad smiled and expressed satisfaction that life was moving forward as it should. Sanji exchanged a look with me: *Can you believe this shit?* Vivek beamed. Julia hugged Sanji.

In the days that followed, things would go as I anticipated: The gang at Golden Sentinels would have a whip-round and buy Sanjita and Vivek a pushchair from Mothercare. Roger would send a check for £2,000 for

Sanji and Vivek to put towards the baby, which would shock them again. Mum would start planning for the baby shower, *Godh Bharai*, even though that wouldn't be until Sanji was seven months gone. Once again, Sanjita would have to bite her tongue and be fussed over by Mum and the older ladies bringing gifts and food. Mrs. Dhewan would stop by with a gift of silk she'd had sent in from Mumbai. Dad would even manage not to resent her presence in the house, probably because of his adventure with her and Mum that restored his masculine pride and his sex life.

Later, Dad and I had a chat in the garden.

"It's been an interesting few months," he said.

"You seem different," I said.

"Your colleagues, Ken and Clive, they're interesting men. I wouldn't say they were necessarily good men, but they think they're doing the right thing. They follow a code. They think highly of you. They seemed to feel obligated to you, which is why they came to look after your mother and me."

"Really? I was afraid they would take things too far."

"Things were already going a bit far by the time you left for the States and they knocked on our door. Your mother and I were already deep into whatever it was Mrs. Dhewan was embroiled in. If anything, Ken and Clive put things in perspective for me."

"Dad, what exactly happened while I was away?"

"Oh, this and that." His tone was unusually light and breezy.

"Dad—"

"Your mother and I had our own adventure, Ravi. Let us have that. You don't need to know everything."

"Is it over? Are you safe?"

"Oh, yes. Ken and Clive made sure of that. They bent over backwards to reassure us. And I managed on my own with my cricket bat."

"Did you feel young again?"

"That's a simplistic way of looking at it, boy," Dad said, irritated. "But yes, I suppose I did. Your mother seemed to enjoy that."

"Enjoy tangling with gangsters?"

"She needed to feel useful, and threw herself into this. I couldn't very well let her go into this alone, could I?"

"Just promise me the two of you aren't going to do this sort of thing again," I said.

"You know," Dad said, "I think I'm beginning to understand why you're in your current job. The thrill and the sense that you might be making a difference in the world."

"I wouldn't say the difference I make is exactly a good thing," I said.

"And what do the gods say about it?" Dad asked. "I imagine they had an opinion?"

"They're enjoying themselves watching me make an utter prat of myself," I said. "But something's changing. I had at least one instance where someone else saw them, too."

Dad raised an eyebrow.

"He wasn't even Indian or Hindu, and he saw Kali in the same place I did, and heard what she said the same way I did."

"Interesting," Dad said.

"And then there's another thing," I said, not sure if I should spill it all, but who else could I talk to about this than my professor father? "Kali told me to do something and I avoided a big disaster. Rudra may have rained vengeance on some people right before my eyes. A sinkhole opened and swallowed them up. There was no way I could have foreseen any of that."

Dad looked at me for a moment with utter calm.

"Remember what I said about you perhaps being a shaman?" he asked.

"I preferred not to think about that."

"These could be the first signs. You've been seeing gods since you were young, just like your uncle. He didn't even get this far because he couldn't cope and he died from it. You're still here and in one piece."

"But what does it really mean?" I asked. "Am I being groomed to be some kind of shaman? That's untenable in this day and age, and the job I'm in. I'm not doing any kind of great work. You said it yourself. It's a seedy world I'm in."

"Perhaps that's where the gods are needed most," Dad said. "Not as a means to gain more converts, but as a way to remain relevant, to become part of the fabric of people's lives, and your clients are not ordinary. The gods must be in on whatever progress you're making in the world. You are their conduit, their instrument for whatever plans they have."

"And what do you think I should do?"

"Have they started telling you to do terrible things?"

"No. They even saved my life."

"Then keep listening to them."

"This still feels outside the realm of rationality."

"We have to allow for some mystery, Ravi," Dad said. "We are often the biggest mysteries to ourselves. You have an added layer."

"I'm so glad happiness and peace of mind don't come into it," I said. "Even if that's what we really crave."

"Is it, though? Dad asked, raising an eyebrow. "We get bored when things become too peaceful. You've always been like that, and lately I've rediscovered that about myself."

"Bloody hell, Dad. Everything's different now. We could never have had this conversation a year ago."

"You and I were very different a year ago."

"If the gods start exerting their influence, things might change even more," I said, shuddering.

"Perhaps they always did and you're only now noticing," Dad said. "Onwards and upwards."

Was that a wistful smile on his face?

I'd never seen that on my father before.

Things really were changing.

"Do you feel reassured now?" Julia asked as we drove home from my parents' house.

"I suppose I should," I said. "But I see the other edge of the sword. Yes, the gods look out for me just as I look out for them. It would be easy to just go for that, I could feel loved and cared for, but we both know all that also ties me to the firm even tighter. Roger's a silver-tongued Machiavellian and we're his gang, just as Interzone is Laird Collins's gang. The two of them are after power in the long run, and they'll use the rest of us to get it. I wouldn't put it past them to sell us out if they had to."

"Are you scared, then?"

"I'm always fucking terrified," I said. "I don't know how you're not, or you're really good at putting up a brave face."

"I should be afraid," Julia said. "But I'm not. I'm not as blithe about everything as Ariel is . . ."

"That's because she's even more damaged than you are. She's empty. And she's trying to fill that void with spirituality. She can understand it intellectually, but I don't think she can feel it. It intrigues her because it's mysterious and unfathomable, which is a contrast to her job as a mercenary. That part is all strategy and violence, which are not mysterious, and she gets bored with it once she has it down. Spirituality won't get boring for her because its mystery is endless."

"And she's very good at it."

"Which makes her monstrous. She likes us because she's not bored with us."

"It's you she likes, Ravi. You represent the mysteries of spirituality, and no one can predict what kind of chaos you're going to introduce to any situation. That's why she won't kill us anytime soon. Even Laird Collins will keep you around because he wants to crack the mysteries he thinks you're privy to."

"What he wants is access to the gods."

"I think his belief in his God might not be as strong as he claims," she said.

"Let's not forget Interzone are monsters," I said. "And Collins is the biggest monster of them all, because he's genuinely mad."

"Do you really think he's going to bring about the end of the world?" Julia asked.

"He's going to make a bloody good go at it. Rumor has it he has the President's ear. At least Roger doesn't want to bring about Armageddon. He just wants to make a shitload of money and get power."

"So we stick with Roger, then."

"Until we see a way out."

"Ravi, have you thought about getting married?"

"Quite a bit, actually. But do you really want to get tied to my family, to all that dysfunctional lunacy?"

Julia laughed.

"It's a tea party compared to what Louise and I had to live through."

"But we'll have to have an Indian wedding. You were at Sanji's."

"How do you know I don't fancy some of that?" She smiled.

"Yeah, but who do you think will have to pay for it?" I said. "Dad and Mum will insist, but they don't have the twenty grand or more it'll take, which means I'll have to slip them the money to make it look like they paid for it."

"Ravi, are you using that as an excuse to avoid marriage?"

"Not at all."

"Then we leave out the big fuck-off ceremony at first, none of the pomp and circumstance," Julia suggested.

"If you want to get married, we can just sneak off to a registry one day. Maybe during lunch break from work. We can ask Benjamin or Olivia or Ken and Clive to be our witnesses."

"Oh, Ravi! Are you serious?"

"It'll be our secret. That would be typical, wouldn't it? Keeping secrets is part of both our lives and our work now. Then we'll have to decide when to tell our parents. They won't be best pleased that we basically eloped."

"Shall we do that and not tell them for a year? All right. Six months?" Julia mused, mischief in her voice.

I pulled the car over and turned to her.

"So you're saying yes?"

She laughed and kissed me, first with happy pecks, then a slow, deep kiss.

I sensed someone smiling. A third party. I didn't need to look. It was Louise. Happy for her sister at last. Her presence was fleeting, just long enough to be noticed, then gradually faded with a kind of sigh that felt like grace.

"So then we save up enough money to pay for an Indian ceremony?" I said. "Then we tell our parents?"

"You've already planned this out," Julia said. "Why aren't I surprised?"

"Hey," I said.

"What is it?"

"The gods are silent. They're not here tonight. I don't see them or sense them."

"That's because you're happy, Ravi."

"I'm happy with you."

Of course, this was a break. Even gods needed to go off and chill. They would be back, of course, the moment Roger handed me the next case, the next spot of bother, the next boiling cauldron of utter fucking mayhem.

But for tonight, I was happy to be left alone with Julia, a full moon overlooking the Thames and pretending everything was right in the world.

We got out of the car and danced and laughed and howled at the moon.

"Reader, I married him!" Julia declared to the sky. She was still a literature student, after all.

"Are we in the right type of story for that, love?" I asked.

"Hush, Ravi! Just lift me up and spin me around!"

I did.

"My beautiful monster." She laughed and kissed me.

That was good enough for us.

ACKNOWLEDGMENTS

As ever, there are friends who kept me on the right path as I wrote this second book.

Years of conversations with Michael Wilson and Minh-Hang Nguyen continue to inform the world and the background of Ravi and his colleagues.

Alan Moore's presence continues to be felt. His thoughts on magic, gods and reality, and Britain, as well as his encouragement, fueled me to treat the story as a living, breathing thing.

Richard Markstein has kept me fed with both literal food and mind food as we looked back at the UK and shook our heads in bemusement together.

Roz Kaveney for being a sounding board for the most outlandish ideas as we each wrote our novels.

Leopoldo Gout for constantly reminding me that things should be crazy.

And Avra Scher for challenging the things I took for granted and keeping me honest with my choices.

You've turned the last page.

But it doesn't have to end there . . .

If you're looking for more first-class, action-packed, nail-biting suspense, join us at **Facebook.com/MulhollandUncovered** for news, competitions, and behind-the-scenes access to Mulholland Books.

For regular updates about our books and authors as well as what's going on in the world of crime and thrillers, follow us on **Twitter@MulhollandUK**.

There are many more twists to come.

MULHOLLAND:
You never know what's coming around the curve.

HODDER